CHRISTMAS Rewired

RenoVations Inc. * 4

REGINA RUDD MERRICK

Scrivenings PRESS
Quench your thirst for story.
www.ScriveningsPress.com

Published by Scrivenings Press LLC
15 Lucky Lane
Morrilton, Arkansas 72110
https://ScriveningsPress.com

Printed in the United States of America

Paperback ISBN 978-1-64917-428-4

eBook ISBN 978-1-64917-429-1

Editors: Amy R. Anguish and Linda Fulkerson

Cover design by Linda Fulkerson - www.bookmarketinggraphics.com

This is a work of fiction. Unless otherwise indicated, all names, characters, businesses, events, and incidents are either the product of the author's imagination or used in a fictitious manner. Any resemblance to actual persons, living or dead, or actual events is purely coincidental.

All Scripture quotations, unless otherwise indicated, are taken from the Holy Bible, New International Version®, NIV®. Copyright ©1973, 1978, 1984, 2011 by Biblica, Inc.™ Used by permission of Zondervan. All rights reserved worldwide. www.zondervan.comThe "NIV" and "New International Version" are trademarks registered in the United States Patent and Trademark Office by Biblica, Inc.™

The LORD will fight for you;
you need only to be still.

Exodus 14:4 (NIV)

Chapter 1

Trace Reno exited the Plant Manager's office deep in thought. He raked his hand over his face and down his beard.

Two weeks. Two weeks until unemployment.

Thanks for seven great years with the company. Here's your severance package and letters of recommendation ...

Downsizing had been a threat for a while since the rumor mill reported the company started a new line in Mexico.

For only the second time in his life, Trace needed to find a job, and selling himself was beyond his comfort zone. He preferred to work hard and competently. That should be enough to let people form their own opinions. But that wouldn't work this time.

I could always move to Mexico.

He paused for a second. *With my red hair and freckled complexion? Not.*

"So much for the Caribbean vacation, huh?"

"What?"

Trace was in his own head, a situation he found himself in

frequently. It wasn't that he didn't like people, he just preferred them on his terms.

"Yeah."

A deep breath and a sigh later, Trace turned to his friend and pod-mate, Zach Weatherly. Zach had just enough seniority over Trace to keep his current position. "I knew the cruise deal was too good to be true, for me. Good thing I sprang for the travel insurance."

"Hey, it might eat into the severance, but it could be worth it." Zach grinned. "Who knows? Ms. Right might just be on the same tour, trolling for her Mr. Right."

"That is so not the reason I planned this trip."

Ever since Zach got married last summer, he'd hounded Trace with attempted fix-ups and suggestions.

"Watch out, or you'll be sliding into confirmed bachelor mode."

Trace chuckled. "I'll be okay. I don't expect Ms. Right to appear out of nowhere."

"No 'love at first sight,' huh?" Zach grinned.

"You know the answer to that."

His friend shook his head. "You're missing out, man. I didn't expect to meet Abigail, but look at us now."

A chuckle broke through. "Not everyone finds the love of their life in a bicycle crash."

Zach winked. "Who says our crash wasn't fore-ordained?"

Trace brushed off the subject. "Anyway. We've got two weeks to get this last project put together and sent to the big-wigs." Trace handed him a large binder.

Groaning, Zach accepted the tome. "And then, the holidays. Does this mean a trip to Indiana for Thanksgiving?"

"Not this time. My folks moved back to Kentucky, remember?"

"Oh, yeah. What about Eli and Sam?"

Trace's twin brother and little sister were just as confused about their parents' move to their dad's hometown of Clementville, Kentucky—a hop-skip-and-a-jump from absolutely nowhere.

"Eli's 'in love,' so he claims he's not budging from southern Indiana. Sam's still on the fence. I don't know. Sometimes I think it might be nice to live in the middle of nowhere. No traffic, no crime—well, not as much crime—and solitude."

"Sounds idyllic."

"Yeah, well, now that I don't have an excuse *not* to go, I guess I'll RSVP yes for my cousin's wedding Thanksgiving weekend." The dread of attending a wedding almost overshadowed the anxiety of unemployment.

"Great place to meet chicks." Zach ducked when Trace threw the pencil in his hand.

Trace scoffed. "Yeah, and Clementville is so small, all the women in town will be there ... and I'm related to most of them."

"I THINK MAYBE God wants me to be single." Hannah Buckner tilted her head as she stirred her glass of sweet iced tea with a straw.

Mandy Reno's laugh burst forth, hand over her mouth to barely contain the spit-take sending droplets of liquid flying everywhere. "Girl, at twenty-five, I don't think you can climb up on that shelf just yet." A few more chuckles escaped. "Sometimes the right guy comes along when you least expect it."

Hannah huffed. "Easy for you to say. You with your hunky sheriff who thinks you're all that and a bag of chips." Hannah loved teasing her friend, Mandy, but there was some truth to her statement.

She continued, brushing droplets of tea off her "RenoVations Inc." T-shirt. "I'm just sayin'. I'm surrounded by guys every day of my life. If I can't find somebody in those circumstances ..."

"You know what the problem is?"

Hannah snorted. "What, O learned one?"

"You're too nice."

Here we go. "You say that like it's a bad thing." Hannah knew where this was going.

Mandy tilted her head and glared at her from beneath her furrowed brow. "You treat everybody the same. Girl-next-door. Approachable. Down-to-earth. Keep everybody happy except Hannah."

"You make me sound like Mary Richards on the *Mary Tyler Moore Show.*"

"Girl, you've got to quit watching retro-TV and Hallmark movies exclusively."

"I identify with Mary. She made it ... after all." Hannah had to laugh at her friend's face at the addition of a phrase from the lyrics of the show's theme song. "I know. Lame."

"Very." Mandy stared Hannah down. "My point is, you either need to show you're interested or play hard-to-get. Surprisingly, not everyone is as nice as you."

"There's that word again. For one thing, I haven't met anyone I would lower myself for to 'show interest,' and most of the guys I'm around wouldn't recognize hard-to-get if it smacked them upside the head." Hannah shook her head. "All I know is I may as well be happy with my life as it is. I've got a great job that pays well and is in high demand, and I've bought a house I can't wait to get my hands on." A quiet squeal and little dance in her chair served to change the subject.

"That's so cool. I can't believe you actually bought a house. What's the move-in date?"

"Probably the week after Christmas. Maybe even before, if the cabinets are ready in time."

Mandy had a small crease between her brows. "Are you sure you want to live out in the boonies?"

Hannah stared at her friend. "Most people consider the entire community of Clementville 'the boonies.' Honestly, the little lane that the Durbin place—I mean, my house—is on isn't any farther out of town than Nick and Lisa's house."

"I know. It just seems ..."

"Scary? Remote? Like a chainsaw murderer is hiding in the garage just waiting to get me alone?" Hannah shook her head. She'd heard it all before. "It's a house with a little land around it. I'll be fine."

Inside, Hannah felt a little chill at the idea of just how dark it would be out there at night, but for every negative, she had a solution—mostly.

I'm an electrician. I can light up the place like a Christmas tree if I want.

She wouldn't think about that now. Her goal was to prove to herself and everyone else who saw her as "sweet little Hannah" that she could be tough. "Sweet little things" long for adventure too.

"Whatever. I'm not saying anything Mama Buckner's not thinking."

"Oh, I know. They think I've gone rogue."

Chapter 2

"Supper's ready."

Hannah paused, anticipating the change that would come when she moved out. Soon—very soon—she would have her own kitchen.

"Coming, Mom." Hannah pulled the towel off her head and shook out her straight, dark blonde hair. Wet, it appeared positively brown. "Mousy," she muttered, with a wrinkle of her nose. Putting it in a messy bun meant it would probably look worse when it dried.

So, what? It's not like Prince Charming is going to show up at the dinner table on spaghetti night.

The smell of cheesy garlic bread drew her, though. In less than two months, she'd be on her own, finally, and responsible for her own cooking.

Hmm ...

Existing on what she knew about cooking troubled her more than the lonely locale of the house.

Mom bustled around, getting the food on the table. "Want to fix the drinks? We've got sweet tea and water."

"Sounds good." Hannah dropped ice cubes in the three glasses—two normal-sized and one a little bigger—on the counter. "Dad, tea or water?"

"What do you think?"

Hannah chuckled. "One extra-large sweet tea, coming right up."

As they came together at the table, Dad held out his hands and they both took his instinctively as he said the blessing over the food.

Taking a deep breath, she whispered a little prayer of thanks for her family. She'd been blessed.

As soon as their heads were up and the dishes were being passed, Mom started talking. "How was Mandy? Has she got an engagement ring yet?"

Here we go.

"No engagement ring—yet. And she's fine. I think she likes working for the county attorney."

"I'm glad. I was sure we'd lose her to the big city before Clay came along and declared himself." Mom picked up the plate of bread and handed it to Dad. "Here, have an extra piece."

"What happened to me needing to watch my waistline?" Dad winked at his bride as she waved him off.

"I'll be glad to watch it for you." She blushed slightly.

Oh, my.

Hannah choked a little on the laugh at the amorous glances passing between her two parents.

Time for me to empty this nest.

"I can't believe that girl is a full-fledged lawyer. How's her mama and daddy?"

"Good, I assume. We didn't talk about them."

"I don't know how you know anything about anybody. Any time I ask about something connected to a friend, you don't know. What do young people these days talk about, anyway?"

Hannah grinned. "We talk about things we like, about what our friends are doing. You know—stuff." She took a bite of the pasta with Mom's homemade marinara. "This is so good, Mom."

Maybe she'll stop asking so many questions.

"Have you decided about Del and Darcy's wedding?"

"I hate going to weddings by myself."

"Don't be silly. You wouldn't be alone. Dad and I will be there."

Hannah leveled a frown at her mother

"What?"

"Mom, Dad, I love you dearly, but most girls my age— make that *women* my age—are married or at least dating. They don't go to functions with their parents."

Dad shook his head. "Sweetheart, your dream man will come along when you least expect it." Winking, he glanced over at Mom. "That's how I found your mom."

Hannah hoped her inward sigh didn't show on her face as she braced for the story she'd heard umpteen times.

"I know. When you plowed into the back of Grandpa's Buick after the homecoming parade in ... what year was it?"

"1984."

"Ah yes, the '80s." Hannah giggled a little. "How big was your car again?"

"As big as a boat." Mom laughed. "But I never worried about getting hurt in it."

"Nineteen seventy-five Buick Electra. Now, *that* was a car." Dad sighed, staring off in the distance, then grinned, winking at Hannah. "I didn't win her over immediately, but I sure got her attention.

"YOU'RE SERIOUSLY THINKING about moving to Clementville?"

Trace's twin brother Eli's stare, and just about everything else about this conversation, irritated him.

"What's wrong with Clementville? Dad grew up there, and he turned out all right."

Eli sat across from him at Culver's, shaking his head. The cheese curds, usually amazing, tasted like sawdust to Trace.

"You couldn't pay me to live there. Summers at Grandma and Grandpa's and the occasional Christmas are enough." Eli took a long drag of his Pumpkin Pie Milkshake and considered Trace. "Of course, I like people."

"So do I. In limited doses."

"You move to Clementville, there will be expectations."

"Of?"

"Family."

"They're the only people I tend to like." Trace's ire was growing. Wasn't it enough that Eli—friendly, outgoing, life-of-the-party Eli—had it all? A great job, amazing apartment, girlfriend, buddies to hang out with. He had a life.

"Listen," Eli started, leaning toward him. "You've got to do you. If moving to the sticks is appealing, go for it. I'll be behind you—I might give you down the road in front of everybody, but deep down, I've got your back."

How was he supposed to stay gruff in the presence of that? Trace stared down at his food, then up at his brother. "Thanks."

"Just know, with Mom and Dad down there, and Samantha waffling back and forth between staying and going, I'll miss you."

"Don't worry. I won't tell anybody." Usually preferring to

hide behind his full beard, Trace felt his whiskers twitch into a smile.

"Better not. I'll deny it." Eli—clean-shaven, always-in-a-good-mood Eli—winked and sent Trace his mega-watt smile. His phone buzzed and distracted him. "Sam. She wants me to put in her order." He stuffed his phone back in his pocket and got up. "I'm going to get another shake. Want one?"

"Yeah. Thanks."

Trace went over and over the situation in his mind. Besides his brother, what held him here? He liked the church he grew up in, but once his contemporaries paired off or moved on, he didn't feel the same connection—with his friends or with God.

Where had he felt the most at home?

Grandpa's workshop.

Maybe that was why the idea of moving down there had a modicum of appeal.

"Sorry I'm late, guys." Sam arrived just in time for Trace to claim shake number two. "Where's mine?"

"Don't worry, it's on its way, along with the usual burger and cheese curds."

She sighed. "I love my big brothers."

Trace regarded Samantha, suppressing a smile when he noticed a smudge of paint just above her eyebrow.

She scooted into the booth next to Eli. That's how it often was—Sam and Eli on one side and Trace on the opposite. It wasn't that they were against him. It wasn't their fault that they seemed to lead charmed lives.

"No biggie. Just telling Eli that I'm thinking about moving down to Clementville."

"What? You're going to move in with Mom and Dad?" Her mouth settled into a distinct *O*.

Trace's laugh came out as a snort. "No way. I'll be applying for jobs and finding a place of my own." He rubbed the back of his neck. "I'm going to stay with Grandma and Grandpa until I land somewhere to live."

Eli laughed. "And whose idea was that?"

"Grandma's." He felt the heat creep up his cheeks. People with freckles should try not to ever get embarrassed. "I guess Dad said something to her about me coming down, and she called me. Said she knew I didn't want to move in with my parents at twenty-eight."

"And moving in with your grandparents is so much better?" Samantha chuckled, then shook her head and sent him a loving look. "It'll be great. We've not had much opportunity to spend time with Grandma and Grandpa on our own."

Trace gave her a half-smile. "I'm kind of hoping there'll be time for Grandpa to teach me more about woodworking. Summers were never long enough to do more than be his assistant." He quirked a brow at his twin. "Somebody was always rushing to get in front of me whenever we went out there."

"Sorry. At least I stuck with it and became a carpenter." Eli grinned.

They all had memories of time spent with their Grandparents Reno.

"I might come down a few days before Christmas, when the break starts." She took in a breath. "I'm so ready to have a few weeks without students. Maybe Grandma will share her sugar cookie recipe with me. I understand Mandy snagged it last year."

"Hey, if there's a bake-off, I'll be glad to judge." Trace smiled, and Eli muttered an "Amen."

"What about Del's wedding?" Sam leaned her chin on her hand and munched on cheese curds and French fries from her brothers' trays. "Mom said RSVPs are due this week."

"Did it last night. What about you two?"

Eli shifted in his seat. "I think I'm going to pass. Carrie wants me to go to her parents' house for Thanksgiving."

"Sounds serious."

"Maybe." Eli's slow grin gave him away. Yeah, the guy had found his girl. Why couldn't Trace?

"Isn't she from around Indy?"

"Yeah. She mentioned wanting me to meet her grandparents."

"Oooo, meet the parents *and* the grandparents?" Samantha leaned back and considered Eli. "Got that ring ready?"

Eli held his hands up in front of him. "Not yet. You guys are going to jinx it."

"Oh, brother, I figure you don't need my help for that." It was a good day when his brother and sister laughed at *his* jokes for a change. In other groups, he could never think of a comeback quick enough for it to not be awkward.

"Very funny." Eli turned toward his sister. "Sam? Are you going to the wedding of the year?"

"Planning on it. I wanted to go down for Thanksgiving, anyway." She clasped her hands on the blue Formica table in front of her. "Is it totally weird that Mom and Dad aren't just down the road? I feel like a baby bird that's been shoved out of the nest."

"You haven't lived with them since college." Trace arched a brow at her.

Sam twisted her lips and frowned at her brother. "Yeah, but it was nice to know they were here if I needed them."

Pulling up to the Reno homestead, Trace stopped the truck and stared. This was the house his dad grew up in with his brothers. Three guys who couldn't be more different. Steve, the oldest, a contractor. Uncle Ed, retired Ag teacher and short-term missionary. And Tom. Dad to Trace, Eli, and Samantha. When asked what he did for a living, Tom always said, "I'm just a farmer, like my dad."

Each Reno brother had things in common, and things that were theirs, exclusively. Same as Eli, Sam, and him.

It was interesting being the oldest child. He identified with Uncle Steve, somewhat. Of course, Trace was only three minutes older than Eli, but for some reason, he felt older.

Years older, sometimes. He never wanted to disappoint. He felt it was the least he could do.

Does that mean I have to be perfect?

It sounded dumb, he knew. Somebody had to be, didn't they?

Deep-down, he knew the answer to that. *Unattainable.*

Was it? In his black-and-white, rule-oriented engineer

brain, it should work. If he worked hard and did things just right, things should go his way. Shouldn't they?

Even I know you don't necessarily succeed by following all the instructions.

Trace shook his head and grabbed his bag as he got out of the truck. He'd packed light, leaving his furniture and household goods in the apartment for the sub-letter and storing the rest of his stuff in a locked storage unit in Marion until he figured out his next steps.

The front porch light came on, and the door opened.

"There's the boy!" Grandpa stood on the porch, waiting for him, hand in his pocket. "Grandma was about to send me out to look for you, but I talked her down."

"Usually she calls me about the time I turn down Cotton Patch Road, convinced I'm late or lying on the side of the road somewhere." He hugged Grandpa, relaxing a little when he got an extra squeeze. "Hi, Grandpa."

"Good trip?" Grandpa ushered him in the front door where he dropped his bag.

"Yeah, a little construction on Forty-one going through Evansville, and then I hit the Ohio River bridge—down to one lane—in Henderson at rush hour."

"Forgot to warn you about that one."

"It wasn't so bad."

"Good."

Trace heard the oven door slam in the kitchen and breathed in the smell of Grandma's meatloaf. "She made my favorite, didn't she?"

"Of course she did." Grandpa shook his head.

"She didn't need to go to so much trouble."

"That's what I said, and she told me to get out of the kitchen and leave her alone. She had it under control."

Grandpa stepped closer and whispered, "She's been like a kid in a candy store ever since she found out you were coming."

"I heard that." Grandma rushed into the room, wiping her hands on her apron, and headed straight to her grandson. Her hugs were magical. "I'm so glad we'll be able to monopolize you for once."

Trace smiled. If anyone had asked what a genuine, honest Trace Reno smile resembled, he couldn't have described it, but he knew this was the real thing because he didn't even have to think about it, didn't have to tell himself to smile.

"It's good to be here."

"Stay as long as you want." Grandma winked. "I think your mama might be a little jealous."

"I figured, but I knew they'd be crowded when Eli and Sam come in for Christmas."

"And you weren't ready to move back in with the parents, eh?" Grandpa chuckled.

"Exactly." He picked up his bag. "Where do you want me?"

"I've changed the sheets and cleared out the dresser in the room Tom and Ed shared."

He winked. "I'll put on my blue plaid flannel shirt and blend into the decor."

Grandma swatted his arm. "Oh, you. I keep thinking I'll change the wallpaper when it starts peeling off, and it never has."

"Hey, no need to mess with a classic ..."

Her smirk was one of her more endearing expressions. She was a boy-mom through and through, so it was well-practiced. "Go put your stuff up. Supper will be ready in about twenty minutes."

"Anybody else coming?" *Please say no.*

"Just us, tonight. Tomorrow Lisa and Mandy are coming over to help me get a start on Thanksgiving. I can't believe Del and Darcy are getting married this Friday." She shook her head. "Let's cram as much into a holiday weekend as possible."

Trace put his arm around his grandma. "I'm here to help."

"I'll take you up on that unless your grandpa steals you away from me."

"Now, sweetheart, we men are only here to serve when it comes time for Thanksgiving dinner." Grandpa dodged when she swatted at him on the way back to the kitchen.

"You two are incorrigible. Make sure to wash up before you come to the table."

"Yes, ma'am." Trace and Grandpa shared a smile as they spoke at the same time.

HANNAH WOKE to the smells of Thanksgiving. The turkey was in the oven and cornbread was cooling on a rack to be crumbled into dressing, along with a few biscuits and some toasted bread.

Christmas was great, especially since baby Vi came. Last year's Christmas morning with a two-year-old? Heaven.

But Thanksgiving was her favorite. Always had been. No gifts, no parties, no over-the-top commercialization of what should be a sacred holy day. Just family and a time to stop and remember the blessings all around them.

And Del and Darcy had to go and ruin it by planning a wedding, of all things, on the same weekend.

The sounds of Dad putting wood in the stove reminded her it was probably still a little chilly, except in the kitchen. She grabbed her fuzzy robe and slippers before she left her room. The heavenly aroma of coffee with a side of wood smoke pulled her down the hall.

"Good morning, Mom."

"Hey, sweetie. Sleep good?" Mom already had flour on her apron and her graying hair was pulled back with a clip. She'd been busy.

"Like a log." She pulled out a box of cereal and poured herself a bowl. "When are the rest of the gang getting here?"

Mom glanced at the clock, which read 8:15. "Probably a little before noon." She grinned and peered over her readers at her daughter. "There's plenty of time to child-proof the house before Vi gets here."

Hannah laughed. "She's getting to be something, isn't she?"

"Grandbabies are the best." Mom sighed. "When you were born, both sides of the family were enthralled."

"Well ..." Hannah winked at her mom. "It was pretty cool being the first grandchild on both sides. I guess my kids won't have that to look forward to." She shrugged and poured herself a cup of coffee and sat at the island across from where Mom was working. "But then I'd have to have prospects of marriage to make that happen, wouldn't I?"

When did I get so cranky about it?

Mom twisted her lips in a wry grin. "It's fine to be picky. Never think we want anything but the best God has for you."

"What if He doesn't have anybody for me?" Chin in hand, Hannah slumped a little on the stool.

"I don't think you need to worry just yet."

She munched on her cereal, gazing off into space. "I don't know, Mom. I've prayed. I've tried to keep an open mind. Think about it. I work with mostly men, and nobody—and I mean *nobody*—has indicated the slightest bit of interest in me."

"Have you been interested in anyone?"

Hannah thought for a minute and chuckled. "Come to think of it, no. Not really."

"Then there's the answer. You just haven't met him yet."

"I don't know. Maybe it would be just as well if I didn't find anyone. I can be happy by myself. Being single isn't like having a disease or something."

Mom shook her head. "Of course it's not, dear. You're overthinking."

Overthinking? Maybe. She tended to do that. In her line of work, she had to think things out. Had to make sure things were done in a certain way and a certain order. Without order, houses could catch on fire, appliances would burn out, and many other issues that bad electrical work caused.

Mom broke into her thoughts. "Oh, Hannah, what about your RSVP to the wedding?"

Ugh.

"I did last night."

"Good. It'll be fun. Mandy and Caryn will be there …"

"With Clay and Ben. I know. I love being a fifth wheel."

"Oh, don't be silly. They're your friends."

If they really loved me, really were my friends, they'd … What? They'd what? Ditch their boyfriends in an act of solidarity in the realm of singleness?

"I know." Hannah leaned her chin back on her hand and studied her mom. "How did you know Dad was the one?"

"We've told this story a thousand times," Mom said, shaking her head as she continued tearing bits of dry bread into a bowl." She laughed out loud. "It took a while."

Dad walked in about then. "What's so funny?"

"Hannah wanted to know how I knew you were 'the one.'"

Dad wiped his hand down his face. "Here we go."

"I thought your dad was an arrogant, self-absorbed—"

Dad stopped her. "We get the picture."

Mom went to him and slid an arm around his waist. "Hey, at least I don't think so now." She kissed his cheek, then turned back to Hannah. "I wasn't crazy about him, but I had a little crush on his car, once I got over being mad at him running into mine at the parade."

"It was a great car, wasn't it?"

"Nineteen seventy-eight Mustang Mach One. Much nicer than my hand-me-down seventy-five Buick."

Dad leaned down and kissed Mom on the lips.

"Do I need to leave?" Hannah huffed. This made twice in two days she'd had to witness their dove-eyes.

Mom waved her hand in dismissal and returned to crumbling the dressing ingredients.

"Your mom was the prettiest girl I'd ever seen. She was working at the café, way before Roxy owned it. I finally figured out her schedule and kept showing up until she gave in and went out with me."

"He just happened to be there the night I needed a ride."

"I was Johnny-on-the-spot." He grinned. "After that, I don't think a week went by that we didn't see one another."

Mom grinned, a slight blush on her cheeks. "Once I had him all to myself, I realized he wasn't as self-centered as I thought from seeing him with his friends."

Dad winked at Hannah. "She had this idea they were a bad influence." He laughed. "Those Reno boys might have an opinion about that."

Chapter 4

Grandma Reno had outdone herself, as had his aunts and cousins. One of the perks of not being married was that Trace could hang on to the irresponsibility of youth a little longer. He might be at their beck and call to get chairs and tables set up, but he didn't have to worry about food or kid-wrangling.

Renos knew how to celebrate with a meal. Even his cousin, Lisa—expecting her first child and turning green at half of the divine smells coming out of the kitchen and dining room—had managed to make Grandma's homemade rolls. That, and canned cranberry sauce.

Del came up behind Trace and clapped his hand on his shoulder. "Glad you're coming to the wedding."

The wedding. Yay.

"Yeah, man, looking forward to it." Trace cut a glance at his cousin, thankful he couldn't read his mind.

Del laughed out loud. "I remember being twenty-eight and single, with everybody in town trying to pair me off with somebody—anybody."

Nothing fazed Del. Trace envied his relaxed, "no worries" attitude. Always had. Eli had a little bit of that, but himself? Nope. To him, there was a downside to everything.

"Dad tells me you're applying for jobs around here."

"I thought I might give the old homeplace a try."

Trace could have said many things. Things like, "I'm ready for a change." Or "If I can't find somebody in a town with a population a hundred times bigger than the entirety of Crittenden County, I may as well give up."

"I get it." Del turned, nodding in the direction of Grandma Reno. "We won't always have the opportunity to be with them."

Trace nodded. "I put in a couple of applications in Calvert City, and at GE in Madisonville."

"Sounds good. Everybody keeps talking about hiring. Hope that parlays into a good job."

Nick Woodward, Lisa's husband, joined them after setting up the last of the folding chairs on the sun porch. "GE? I hear that's a good place to work, especially with your credentials."

"Fingers crossed. It's the one I want."

"What's up in the meantime?" Nick grinned. "Eating up that severance?"

Trace lifted his shoulders. "I guess hanging out with Grandma and Grandpa. Nobody's hiring right before Christmas."

Del and Nick regarded one another, and then Del spoke. "We're hiring grunt work for RenoVations. I'll be away on my honeymoon until Christmas, and we've got a couple of projects going where we could use some extra help."

"And I've got a very pregnant Lisa on my hands." Nick spoke softly, making sure she wasn't within earshot.

"I know nothing about construction," Trace said, hesitant to commit to something where he had no proficiency.

"Doesn't matter. Del doesn't, either." Nick feinted as Del threw a punch at his arm.

"Speak for yourself."

Nick rubbed his arm where Del hit him. "We need general laborers. Maybe an assist with electrical?"

He'd always wondered about residential electrician work. Maybe this would be an opportunity to try something different.

"We've got a great electrician." Nick winked at Del, who raised an eyebrow as Lisa walked up, the jiggly cranberry sauce from the can neatly sliced and placed on a platter.

"Set this on the buffet, please." She handed the plate to Nick.

"Yes, dear."

"Man, you're getting good at 'yes, dear.'" Del laughed at his sister as she gave him the stink-eye. Holding up his hands to defend himself. "And it's totally right that he should be."

"Much better." She turned to her cousin. "We tried homemade cranberry sauce one year. The fancy kind." She shook her head. "There was a hue and cry, and Grandma made the promise we would never go without canned cranberry sauce again. And it has to be the kind with the shape of the can intact."

"I'm getting flashbacks to the Christmas we didn't have mashed potatoes." Del's expression of disbelief resonated.

"What is Christmas dinner without mashed potatoes?" Trace was with him there.

Lisa shook her head. "It's not like we didn't have potatoes. If I remember correctly, we had hash-brown casserole, twice-baked potatoes, and roasted potatoes."

"We had to make them promise never to do that again." Del was serious.

Trace took a deep breath. "I'm glad I missed that year."

"Yeah, it was a tragedy for us all." Del glanced behind Trace as his fiancée, Darcy, joined them, slipping her arm through his and scrutinizing him.

"Wasn't that the year you threatened to make the mashed potatoes if they wouldn't?" Del's petite future wife had to look up at all the Renos in the group. "The female portion of the family knew he was serious and vowed to never let it happen again." She grinned. "At least that's what I've heard."

"Before your time, Darce."

"Oh, I've been getting indoctrinated into the ways of the Renos for a while, now. They want to make sure I'm ready for the responsibility of taking on one of the more challenging subjects."

"Makes it sound like we're a cult." Del narrowed his eyes.

"Oh, sweetie," Darcy said, patting his arm, "You Renos are a special group, but it's a good thing there are some outsiders like Nick and me in the mix to keep things sane."

"I think we've just been insulted." Lisa's laugh tinkled across the room.

BY EVENING, the noisy Reno gathering had dulled to a manageable roar due to the wedding rehearsal taking more than half of the crowd, including Grandma and Grandpa.

Those not involved were given instructions to stay put, if possible, for the "second sitting" of leftovers.

Trace was on family overload. They'd always lived away, since he could remember, anyway, and the short stints in the summer and occasional holiday hadn't prepared him for an ongoing stream of familial responsibility.

Trace's dad sat by him where he lounged on the sofa,

scrolling through his phone. Dad put a hand on his son's knee. "Things going okay, Trace?"

"I'm good. You?"

Dad snorted. "Wondering how long until you decide this is too much togetherness for anybody."

Grinning, he turned to Dad and shrugged. "It hasn't been too bad, so far. Grandma and Grandpa give me plenty of space."

"When we stayed a few weeks until we got the house put together, your mom did fine. Loved it. Me? I grew up in this house, and I thought we'd never get away."

"Is that why you didn't stay around here?" Trace had wondered why they were the only ones who broke away from Crittenden County.

Dad took a long swig of coffee. "Partly. I wanted to farm, and Grandpa was still young enough that he didn't need my help, no more acreage than we had. At the time, your other grandparents needed us more."

Trace understood. Mom was an only child, and her parents were older. Last year she lost her dad after losing her mom a few years earlier.

"Now, Grandpa needs me, and I'm glad to be here. It helps that your mom loves my family, and she can talk to a stump. Making friends has never been a problem for her."

Trace chuckled. Dad was right. Mom was the talker in the family. If nobody would talk to her, she'd talk to herself until someone gave in and joined her conversation. Eli took after her.

"Y'all talking about me?" Trace's mom, Ginger, plopped down next to her husband, tucking her sock-feet under her and laying her head, covered in her namesake's color except for a few streaks of gray, on his shoulder.

"You have radar, woman." Dad pulled his arm out from under her and wrapped it around her shoulders.

"Nice things, I'm sure."

Trace's squelched laugh came out as a snort. "What else would there be, Mom?"

"Can't help what's true."

"Is it frustrating, not being in charge of Del's wedding?" Trace did inherit one thing from his mom—the desire for everything to be perfect.

"Maybe a little?" She held her finger and thumb an inch apart. "It's just as well, though. Their plans were in place before we decided to move down here. I'm not sure I could have done a wedding, move, and build a house all at the same time." She gave them a little smile that turned grimace, and then added, "But you know, I'm looking forward to being a wedding guest for a change. It might be the last one I can."

"Mandy'll be next. I'd almost bet money on it." Dad lifted his feet onto the coffee table and relaxed.

Mom nodded. "Good eye. Clay is very attentive."

"Did you hear what he did last Christmas?" Trace still couldn't believe it.

Mom laughed. "Mandy told me all about it. He did a good job translating 'The Twelve Days of Christmas' into twelve days of presents for Mandy. If that doesn't get a girl's attention, I don't know what would."

Trace pondered a moment. "That's a lot to live up to."

"That's because you haven't found a girl you like enough to put in the effort." Dad kissed Mom on the cheek. "When you know, you know. Worth every minute and every penny."

"I like the sound of that. Should I add a few items to my Christmas list?"

"Go right ahead, honey. You've been a good girl this year."

"I have more than enough, thank you, but it's nice to hear."

Mom patted Dad on the knee and got up, holding her phone. "Just got a text from Christine. Everybody's headed back. Better get the food back out."

"I'll give you a hand."

Trace watched his parents making their way to Grandma's kitchen. When he broached the idea of moving down to Clementville, Mom immediately invited him to move in with them, and Dad sighed in resignation.

They were enjoying being empty-nesters.

Fortunately, Grandma called dibs on him immediately. She'd enjoyed having Mandy last Christmas, and now she'd have Trace.

It was a win-win.

Chapter 5

S lap a smile on your face and sit down.

Hannah was giving herself the pep-talk she needed. Or maybe it was tough love?

Glancing around the crowded church—so much for a small, intimate gathering—Hannah could tell exactly who wanted to be here and who would rather be anywhere but at a wedding.

The Reno clan filled the right side of the sanctuary, so Hannah and her parents veered to the left, to the bride's side. Sliding into the pew ahead of her mom, Hannah sat and studied the program carefully. If anyone asked her what was in it, she'd be clueless. At least having the piece of stationary in her hand gave her something to do.

Lisa Reno Woodward played the piano softly, a collection of love songs, along with some praise and worship. It was a good mix. At least the music was good.

A laugh coming from the Reno side of the wedding drew her attention. Was that "the other" Reno brother? Younger than Steve and Ed. Two kids? She saw a beautiful young woman, about her age, she thought, and a bearded young man next to her. Probably her husband/fiancé/boyfriend.

He seems nice. As per usual, he's taken. And why should I care?

Mom leaned over to whisper in Hannah's ear. "That's a lot of Renos in one place, isn't it?" She chuckled.

Hannah snorted a breath. "I hadn't noticed."

Her mom's eyebrow rose. She started to say something, but the music changed, and everyone's eyes turned toward the aisle. Mr. And Mrs. Reno, Del's grandparents, were escorted in by head-usher Ben Livingston, then Roxy Reno, mother-of-the-bride and also stepmother of the groom via her marriage to Steve Reno, pulled double-duty and was escorted to her seat by the groom, Del Reno.

She hadn't thought about the family dynamic at work here. When Steve and Roxy Reno got together after both losing their spouses, who knew his son, Del, and her daughter, Darcy, would fall in love?

The men took the platform and steps, all turned toward the main event. Pastor Mike first, then Del, Best Man Nick Woodward, and groomsmen Sheriff Clay Lacey, and Del's cousin, Robert. Darcy's friend from her late husband's military days, Ellie Rogers, entered, her russet gown skimming the floor as she walked, then Mandy Reno in a dress a shade lighter. The maid of honor was a woman Hannah didn't know.

Hannah studied at the program. There it was. Rebecca Durbin. Whoa. Hannah was buying her family home but hadn't met her yet.

When the adults were in place, the party started. Darcy's four-year-old twins, Ali and Benji, were flower girl and ring bearer.

Mom leaned toward her. "Those kids should be good at it by now."

The smile she'd tried to summon up early came out

naturally at the sight of the twins, in bright autumn yellow, coming up the aisle.

At one point, Ali stopped her precise flower distribution because her brother was fiddling with the ribbon holding the rings in place. Her whisper could be heard across the Ohio River. "Benji! Stop that!"

When a chuckle rose from the audience, Benji took notice, realizing he'd been caught. The boy spun, searching for his mom. A look of panic crossed Benji's face when he discovered the doors of the sanctuary closing. He slowly turned his head, looking up the aisle at Del, who winked and nodded for him to come on down. His sigh of relief was audible.

Hannah whispered in her mother's ear, "Didn't Benji get caught picking his nose at Lisa and Nick's wedding?"

Mom didn't make a sound but nodded and shook with laughter next to her.

Once everyone was in place, the music changed again, the melody of "When I Fall in Love" almost breaking down Hannah's defenses. Was it her imagination, or was there a collective sigh when Roxy stood, the doors opened, and Steve Reno escorted his stepdaughter down the aisle to marry his son?

HANNAH OBSERVED the crowd assembling in the café, admiring the autumnal decor.

Lights were dimmed, showcasing the pumpkins, books, and candles nestled in the center of each table with a bouquet. Large round tables replaced the normal small ones to create enough room for everyone. Informal, since there was no "head table" for the wedding party, things were organized by name and table number.

That's a relief.

Who'd have thought that a wedding on a holiday weekend would be so well-attended?

Her parents were seated with friends, and Mandy had promised to pull some strings to make sure Hannah was at her table.

At least I'm not seated with my parents.

"Hey, Hannah!" Caryn Stafford waved from the door, then made her way to her, Ben Lockhart in tow.

"I was afraid I'd be stuck here by myself until the wedding party was introduced." Hannah grinned.

"Who else is at our table?" Ben surveyed the cloth-covered surface, but there were no place cards. Just a number on a pumpkin.

Caryn busied herself scanning the room, waving at different people, ignoring his question.

Ben looked across the table at Hannah and shrugged. "Guess we'll have to wait and see."

Was Caryn's face a little pinker than usual? Hannah was growing suspicious. Get Mandy and Caryn together, and they were a force to be reckoned with.

"Anybody sitting here?" The young woman from the Reno side that Hannah noticed at the wedding stood, smiling at the three already seated.

Caryn grinned at her and averted her gaze behind her. If possible, her smile became wider.

Hannah hadn't paid any attention to who was with her.

"I'm Samantha Reno, Del's cousin."

Hannah smiled. "Nice to meet you. I'm Hannah. I work for RenoVations."

The young man she'd seen earlier sat in the empty seat next to her and gave the occupants of the table a curt nod of acknowledgment but didn't say a word.

Samantha rolled her eyes at him, then said, "This lump here is my brother, Trace."

Finally, he glanced up. "Hi." When his gaze settled on Hannah, he tilted his head a little.

Music revved up, and Del's friend, Jay Carrino, spoke into the microphone. "If I might direct your attention to the kitchen doors, it's my pleasure to introduce the wedding party!"

When Mandy and Clay finished taking their bows, they joined them at the table, applauding the rest of the attendants. All eyes were anxiously anticipating the main attraction—Darcy and Del.

"And now ..." Jay paused for effect, then continued, his voice lowered conversationally. "You know, ladies and gentlemen, I've known Del Reno for a long time ..."

A shout came from behind the kitchen door. Del. "Jay, someday you're gonna want to get married."

"As I was saying, and now, the bride and groom, the cook and the contractor, 'short-and-sweet' meets 'needs-a-haircut' ... Mr. And Mrs. Del Reno! Give Darcy and Del a big hand!"

The applause, hoots, and whistles went on as they came out, Del twirling his bride to show off her flowing skirt.

Mandy sighed as she watched. "Isn't she beautiful?"

Caryn sat, chin in hand, looking dreamy herself. "She is."

"Hey, Trace, good to see you." Clay stood and shook his hand.

"You too. Long time, no see." Trace's glimmer of a smile was quick. If she hadn't glanced his way just then, she'd have missed it.

The strains of the song, "At Last," began playing, and the bride and groom's first dance was underway. Now Hannah wanted to sigh.

But I won't.

"What a perfect song." Mandy couldn't take her eyes off the couple, and Clay couldn't take his eyes off of Mandy.

"And easy to dance to." Ben poked Caryn, who shook her head.

"Men are hopeless."

"Aw, tell me you didn't think the same thing."

Caryn pointed her finger in his face and then dissolved in laughter. "It's true. Del and dancing don't usually fit in the same sentence."

"It's so romantic." Mandy was still watching them, enthralled.

The dimmed lights and the shimmering spotlight made the couple look like characters in an old movie musical.

Maybe other twenty-something young women would think of something modern, but Hannah's thoughts went to the dance number in *White Christmas*, where the characters discovered that "The Best Things Happen When You're Dancing."

To her, that was romance.

The dance ended with a swoony kiss between the bride and groom. As the introduction to "What a Wonderful World" started, Steve and Roxy Reno took the floor. Roxy went to Del, as his stepmother, for the mother-son dance, and Steve went to Darcy, as her stepfather, for the father-daughter dance.

As the two couples danced, the music segued into "Somewhere Over the Rainbow," and the couples hugged, then drew apart and finished the dance with their spouses.

"Wow." Hannah didn't realize she had spoken until Trace turned toward her.

"Did you say something?" His deep green eyes held hers for a moment before she could say anything.

"Um ... wow?"

Just then, his smile came back, full-force, directed at her alone.

SITTING THERE, next to Hannah, Trace's tongue felt like it was tied in one of those knots that ends up having to be cut out instead of carefully disentangled.

"Wow."

Wow, indeed. When she spoke, he realized he was staring at her, and he wasn't sure what she said, so he asked her if she said something.

When her delicate blue eyes met his, he didn't want to blink. He was afraid she'd disappear if he did.

Wait a minute. What's going on here? She's a girl. Pretty, sure, but a person doesn't just look at a girl and go all ... gooey inside. Do they? I don't even know her last name. Is it hot in here?

He tugged at his collar, pulling his focus away, finally.

Nobody makes an impression that fast. Do they?

Glancing back at the subject of his thoughts over the last few seconds—was it seconds, or minutes? He'd lost track of time. Anyway, glancing back at her, he noticed a pink tinge on her face. Maybe it was warm in here.

"When do you move into the new house?" Clay was speaking to Hannah. She'd bought a house?

"I take possession in the next few days, so hopefully between Christmas and the New Year." Hannah smiled broadly. "I can't wait to have a place of my own."

"Are you sure about living out there?"

Out where?

"I'll be fine." Hannah waved the sheriff and his deputy off. "There's a cabin on the property too. I haven't decided what to use it for. Maybe I'll convert it into a studio."

"I'd recommend a security system and a big dog for protection." Clay still had a frown on his face.

Mandy shoved her shoulder into his. "Hannah's a big girl, Clay."

"I know. I also know a lot of stuff went down out there at the Durbin place."

"I heard my name." A tall, beautiful woman stopped by the table on the way to the buffet. "Are you trying to talk her out of buying my house?" She smiled to take the sting out of the words. "It's nice to put a name with a face before the closing, Hannah." Smiling at Hannah's surprise, Rebecca said, as an aside, "Darcy pointed you out to me."

"Hi, Rebecca." Clay's face reddened. "No, just wanting to make sure Hannah knows what she's getting into."

"The old farm has been through a lot." The gentleman behind Rebecca put his left hand on the small of her back, and she leaned into it. Holding out his right hand, he introduced himself to Hannah, Trace, and Samantha. "I'm Clyde Alexander."

"Trace Reno, and this is my sister, Samantha."

"Glad to meet you." Clyde looked from Trace to Samantha. "You're from the youngest Reno set?"

Samantha chuckled. "Guilty as charged."

Rebecca laughed. "Don't say that. Between Clyde and Clay, you could find yourself in custody." She waited until everyone but Trace and Samantha stopped laughing. "Clyde is FBI, and Clay is the sheriff." She laughed up at the gentleman next to her. "A little law-enforcement humor."

"I think we're holding up the line, sweetheart." Clyde shook his head and spoke to Clay. "For what it's worth, I don't think there'll be any more trouble. The property has been swept for evidence, and where we could check it, ground-penetrating radar showed no indication the tunnel system came out as far as the house." He paused, regarding Rebecca with a sad smile. "Of course, we'd know more about the property if we'd had these conversations before Trip's stroke."

"How's your dad doing?" Clay voice lowered in concern.

Rebecca shrugged. "The doctor says his memory will get better over time, if he doesn't have other things happen—like another stroke." There was a sheen of tears in her eyes even as she smiled. "Thanks for asking, Clay."

They turned to step away, then Clyde turned back, frowning a little. "That being said, if it were Rebecca planning to move out there by herself, I'd be installing electrified fencing and finding a couple of Rottweilers."

Rebecca arched a brow. "Hannah, don't listen to him. This is the guy who keeps trying to move up our wedding date so he won't have to leave me alone at night."

Clyde twisted his lips as he turned his ardent stare toward Rebecca, taking her hand and squeezing it. She was tall, but in heels, they were at eye level. "That's not the only reason."

A blush rushed up her face as she smiled at him. "Now we *are* holding up the line. Good to meet you all."

Was there literal heat coming off of those two, or was it his imagination?

"Isn't she the one Del dated in college?" Samantha leaned forward, speaking softly.

Mandy nodded, also leaning forward. "It's a long story. I'll tell you sometime. Let's just say, we've had our fair share of criminal activity around here."

"I thought Clyde was his undercover name?" Ben asked Clay.

Clay shrugged. "I guess after ten years when the love of your life only knows you as Clyde, you get used to it and change your name to Clyde."

"Noted."

These people sure did bandy that "love" word around a lot. *A lot more than I'm comfortable with.*

HANNAH WAS OVERTLY TRYING to ignore the gentleman by her side. Fortunately, with their table mates, it wasn't difficult to blend into the background and let them take over. It would seem Trace felt the same way, judging from his limited interaction.

I mean, his sister did introduce him as a "lump."

She glanced at him from time to time, always when he was focused in the other direction.

Not bad-looking. She'd never really considered beards. Most of the guys she knew were clean-shaven or only sported a scruff. In the movies, scruff was available all hours of the day and night.

Wouldn't that be harder to maintain than a full-on beard?
But it's ginger.
Interesting.

Her crush on Ron Weasley of Harry Potter fame threatened to rear up. Trace had green eyes. Not just any green. Dark green. Almost like they were supposed to be brown, but green. And was that a little bit of gold glitter that snuck in and took the lead?

"What do you do at RenoVations?"

Trace's voice startled her, making her self-conscious about her thoughts of him. Why was she even thinking about him?

"I'm a licensed electrician."

"Really?" He grinned, obviously slightly doubtful.

"Really." That was usually how this conversation went. When guys found out she was an electrician, which very few people had a clue about except when something was wrong with it, it was like she was set apart. Weird. Afraid they'd get shocked if they touched her.

She swallowed a laugh at her own joke.

"Something funny?"

"Sorry. Thinking about something else." She cleared her throat and wiped her hands on her napkin. Why in the world were her palms sweaty? "What about you? I figure if you're a Reno, you're in the building trades, somehow."

Mandy waved from across the table. "Except for me." She stopped to think. "Hmm ... and Rob and Cassie."

Hannah shrugged. "So much for that theory."

"Trace's twin brother's a carpenter," Samantha interjected.

"You have another brother?"

In other words, there are two of him?

"We do." Trace glanced at his sister like he resented her interruption. "I'm an electrical engineer."

"Wow." Hannah smiled. "Pretty specialized, huh?"

"I guess."

"Where do you work?"

He paused. "Right now, nowhere. The plant where I worked downsized a week ago, so I'm looking for a job."

"Ouch. Sorry." She took a sip of her sparkling cider.

"Yeah. I've got my resume out at some of the area plants."

She choked a little. "Here?" She squeaked it out.

The ghost of a smile softened his demeanor. "Here."

"Good luck." She took a deep breath and turned to Samantha. "Your parents have moved here, haven't they?"

Samantha nodded. "Dad's going to help Grandpa on the farm, and Mom was ready to slow down on the wedding planning business. So far, Trace is the only sibling thinking about moving down here. Right, bro?"

He shook his head and growled out, "I think Eli would starve for a social life down here."

Hannah laughed. Trace might be a grouch, but he was funny. Sometimes.

"What about you, Samantha?"

"Undecided." She scanned the people in the restaurant. Was she searching for someone in particular? "The jury's still out. I mean, I'm an elementary school art teacher, but I'd love to paint full-time." She sighed. "If I did, I could work anywhere."

"I've done a little drawing and painting. Nothing like Lisa." Hannah smiled gently.

Samantha shrugged. "She's a good designer. Way too practical for me."

"Can't have that, now, can we?" Trace grinned at his sister.

It was nice to see a grown man treating his sister well. Hannah could tell they were close.

"At one time, I wanted to be an interior designer."

There, I said it. Out loud. Where people could hear me. But did they?

Mandy narrowed her eyes at Hannah, sitting across the table from her. "Don't let Hannah fool you. She's a painter too. A good one. And I loved it when we'd spend all night moving the furniture around in my room."

She sees me.

Hannah pressed her lips together. "It just didn't make sense to pursue it."

"Lisa did."

Turning to Trace, she was surprised at his words, and wondered at the serious expression on his face.

"I mean, if it's what you really want. It's never too late."

"I don't know." She stared down at her fingers, pleating the napkin she'd placed back on the table after the wedding cake was served. "I decided to be practical."

"Sometimes I think practical is overrated."

Somewhere, deep down, a thought kept niggling away: *He sees me too.*

Chapter 6

Did I seriously say that?

Up until now, this was going well as far as Trace was concerned. Conversation flowed all around him. All he had to do was nod and smile and answer a question now and then.

Until he decided to ask actual questions, which was totally unlike him.

Something triggered inside him when Hannah wistfully mentioned design. He couldn't imagine his sister bowing to pressure from inside or outside forces and going the practical route.

That was his job, as the oldest. He was expected to be practical.

He would fight to protect his creative sister from bowing to common sense and functionality.

But Hannah wasn't Samantha. He'd taken the time tonight to observe Hannah.

Who, from what he'd observed, was perfect.

Nobody's perfect.

Maybe.

Hair? Blondish, but not too blonde. Natural. No highlights or lowlights or whatever it was women did to their hair. Makeup, but not excessive. Nice smile. Gentle, but with a good sense of humor. She seemed to be making herself brave about moving into the house out in the country and was determined to follow through on the path she'd chosen for a career.

In his opinion, a house in town—even a town the size of Clementville—would be more prudent.

But she didn't ask his opinion and probably wouldn't.

And that bothered him.

What was going on with him? This girl—young woman—sitting next to him gave him no indication she was interested in any way.

Any way.

He wasn't someone who became interested in someone immediately, and yet, here he was, trying, in his awkward way, to get her attention.

"So, you've bought a house?"

She turned back toward him when the two couples at the table left to dance the "couples dance." No way would he ask her to dance that one.

Who was he kidding? Him? Dance?

"I have. It'll give me a chance to stretch those creative muscles for myself." She smiled, warming up to the subject of her new home. "Plus, I can save a bundle on electrical work."

"Have you thought about a security system, like Clay was mentioning?"

Hannah shifted in her seat, her back stiffening. "I appreciate the concern everyone seems to have for me, but I've got this."

Trace held his hands up as if to ward off an attack. "I'm sure you do. I would say the same to Samantha."

"Who is your sister and would probably tell you ..."

Samantha had left the table for a drink refill and came back to hear part of the conversation. "I'd probably tell you to mind your own business." She chuckled when Trace glared back at her with irritation. "When I see that line forming between Trace's eyebrows, I know he's annoyed."

"Not at all." He sent a quiet glare to his sister as he turned back to Hannah. "I apologize. I overstepped." He paused. "But I would be remiss ..."

"No, you wouldn't." Hannah rose, picking up her purse. "It was nice to meet you both," she said, focusing on Samantha and politely ignoring Trace as she left the table.

Her slender form wound through the crowded reception tables, back stiff with what he assumed was irritation. She stopped, her face lighting up with a smile as she spoke to this person and that. She leaned over and whispered to a middle-aged woman who had to be Hannah's mother. No question. Same blonde hair—a little gray mixed in, so it was lighter— and the same bone structure.

Since when did he notice things like "bone structure?"

Since I saw the ideal, maybe?

This was insane.

Honestly, if I could whack myself on the head without calling attention to myself, I'd be doing it right now.

Unemployment was doing a number on his every way of thinking. He was saying things out loud that "employed Trace" wouldn't say in a million years because, as Samantha so aptly put it, it was "none of his business."

And Hannah Buckner called him on it. She didn't know him from Adam, except what she'd heard from his cousins.

What had they told her?

Didn't matter. He sat, alone at the table, as the couples danced. Even Samantha had accepted an invitation to dance by one of the locals—was it the emcee? He looked familiar, but it wasn't in the forefront of Trace's mind. Being alone had always been his go-to. Comfortable.

Why should it be any different now?

He could have easily skipped this wedding. Del would have understood—he'd as much as told him so the day before at Grandma Reno's Thanksgiving dinner.

His cousin, Mandy, came back to the table, and then Samantha.

Mandy started on him immediately. "All right, Trace. What's the deal?"

"What do you mean, what's my deal?"

Samantha leaned in, elbows on the table, joining the inquisition. "Mama taught you better than that."

His head whipped toward her in astonishment. "Than what? Than to let someone who could be putting herself in danger run headlong into the unknown without a few warnings?" There, that should put them in their places. "Some people would thank me for having good sense."

"Trace, Hannah gets enough unsolicited advice from the current men in her life—her dad, her brother-in-law, Clay, Ben." Mandy ticked them off, one by one. "She doesn't need it from a perfect stranger."

Her scowl tempted Trace to laugh, but he cleared his throat instead. They were so serious, and for some strange reason, giddy laughter bubbled up inside him.

Giddy? Good grief.

"At least you admit I'm perfect."

Mandy sat back, arms crossed. "Not what I meant, and you know it."

Trace scoffed. "Why would she care what I think?" Whenever he didn't want to take someone's advice, he simply let it go and moved on. Most of the time.

"She's never lived on her own before." Mandy shook her

head in despair, turning to Samantha and then Caryn when she arrived back at the table with a cup of punch. "Tell him, Caryn, how hard we worked to even get her to this wedding."

Caryn nodded. "Oh, yes, we had to convince her—well, part way, at least—that God did *not* call her to singleness."

A girl that beautiful?

"Too much information, Caryn." Mandy shifted her eyes to her friend. "And you, Trace Reno, just about undid all our work." Mandy sighed, shaking her head again. "I love you, cousin, but right now, if we weren't around a lot of people, I'd throttle you."

Sheriff Clay and Deputy Ben walked up as Mandy issued the threat. They exchanged glances.

Trace held his hands up as if to ward them off, surrender, whatever they wanted to think, if they'd just leave him alone. "Okay, okay, I get it. I was out of line."

The three women sat there, staring. What more did they want from him?

He heaved a deep sigh, raising his eyes to the ceiling. "And I will apologize the very next time I see her."

Samantha snorted. "Wouldn't I like to be a fly on the wall for *that* back-handed apology?"

There was no pleasing some people.

His gaze trailed back to where Hannah had been before he spaced out. She was gone.

He had a glimpse into what Cinderella's prince went through at the ball. The clock had struck the proverbial midnight, and he was left alone holding a shoe, wondering what had just happened.

HANNAH WAS FUMING by the time she got to her car. *How dare he?* Good thing she'd opted to drive separately from her parents. They seemed to be in it for the long haul. The idea of sitting there at the same table as—not to mention next to—Trace Reno was more than she could stomach.

Forget him.

Taking a deep breath, she re-directed her thoughts. She had to admit, the wedding was beautiful. Darcy's pale yellow wedding gown, just one shade lighter than her Maid of Honor's, which was a shade lighter than the next bridesmaid, and so on.

Her mind wandered for a few seconds as she drove the familiar route to what she had called "home" for the first twenty-five years of her life.

Back to the wedding ... Mums and pumpkins rounded out the décor. Her artistic soul warmed at the care that went into the planning. Lisa's touch was all over it.

Would Lisa look at some of my designs?

Maybe she was putting the cart before the horse. The deal wasn't complete until the closing. It could still fall through.

Stopping in the driveway of her parents' house—she was trying to stop calling it "home"—she sat there a minute, thinking.

Was she crazy to move out there? Sure, it was remote, but it was difficult to find a place in Crittenden County that *wasn't* remote, and it was for sure she couldn't afford a place that didn't need renovations.

Getting out of the car, she made a decision.

She was going out there. Nobody was here to stop her. Couldn't she handle a little undiluted dark?

Go for it, Hannah. Remember, you're an electrician. You can add lights anywhere you want.

Pulling on jeans and a sweatshirt, and trading her high-heeled dress shoes for her work boots, she felt like herself again and repeated her pep talk.

I can do this.

Grabbing the car keys she'd tossed on her bed next to her purse, she headed out the door before she talked herself out of going. The house her parents had built and lived in since the early 1980s was on land developed by Steve Reno. Nice, wide suburbia-style streets, buried power, security lights, and county water had kept lots selling for the past forty years. A mixture of '80s ranch-style houses and more modern "McMansions" lined the streets on oversized properties. Nobody was within feet of their neighbor like they would be in a more populated area.

One thing about Clementville—it wasn't exactly bursting at the seams.

Since some of the industry in the county had dried up in the late '90s, it had become a bedroom community with people commuting in all directions within a sixty-mile radius. Evansville, Henderson, Paducah, and all points in between.

The few street lights illuminated her way until she made it back out to the highway, where a wide-eyed doe stared at her from the middle of the road.

The deer just stood there, brown eyes fixed on her as if to say, "Oh, did you want to go this way? Let me think about it for a few minutes. You weren't in a hurry, were you?"

Hunting season. They're all a little crazy this time of year.

It finally scampered in front of her, its white tail all she could see as it bounded into the fence row alongside the rural road.

If I lived in town, I wouldn't see this. Well, in Marion, maybe ...
A light chuckle erupted as she gained back speed.

When even the largest city in the county—the county seat,

no less—was designated "rural," seeing deer in the middle of town wasn't a stretch.

She pulled into the drive—she'd have to get a "hidden drive" sign—and noticed how narrow the lane was. It seemed wider in daylight. Limbs on the trees were too low and needed to be trimmed. Branches scraped the sides of the truck, but then, nobody had lived there in at least fifteen years.

When Rebecca Durbin, who grew up here, was at Murray State University, her mother had been murdered in the house.

Okay, so it was a little creepy. Trip Durbin, Rebecca's dad, had been exonerated of the crime. Until then, he'd kept quiet to ensure his daughter's safety, and now he was a free man after testifying against the mobster behind the decades of crime discovered in and around Clementville and even into Chicago.

When she pulled up to the house, a security light on the garage lit up the area, as well as her heart.

One obstacle overcome. It wasn't completely dark. Except for the area around the corner, anyway.

As an electrician, she could fix that. This time of year was the absolute worst, the hideously short days making her want to crawl onto a sofa with a quilt and a cup of hot something and hunker down in front of the fireplace in the living room.

A year ago, Hannah wouldn't have given home ownership any thought. What twenty-four-year-old did? But when Rebecca and her fiancée, Clyde, decided to build a new house on the river instead of moving into a place full of bad memories, the idea grew in her mind. It wasn't long until she set both her computer and phone to automatically "ding" notifications for real estate listings.

She'd saved quite a bit of money in the last few years. Living with her parents had enabled her to do more than just make a down payment on the property. She'd have room in her budget for some pretty significant renovations.

Fortunately, she knew just the experts for the job. RenoVations Inc.

She didn't need any green-eyed, ginger-bearded unconventionally handsome man telling her what to do. The Bible verse in Proverbs 25 came to her: *It is better to live in a corner of the housetop than in a house shared with a quarrelsome wife.*

Hannah figured that translated to males too. She'd rather do without than get involved with a bossy know-it-all.

Even if he is handsome.

She'd been leaning against her truck, taking in the quiet, studying the twinkling stars. As remote as Clementville was, there was still enough light to dim the heavens above. Not out here.

A rustling in the woods next to the house froze her for a moment. Wild animal? Bad person? Wind?

She licked her finger and held it up. Not wind.

I think I'll go with wild animal.

She yanked open the door of her truck and shut herself inside. With a smile, she shook her head. First, an unfortunate encounter with a nosey outsider, and now creatures of the night.

Still, resolve filled her to make this place her home.

And who knows? Maybe those wild animals and birds will help me around the house, like Cinderella.

Chapter 7

Trace went around to the side of the Clementville Café, where the service entrance was. Easy access to the basement stairs.

Nick met him at the door, a little more harried than usual. "You're here. Good."

"Everything okay?"

Raking his hand through his unruly dark hair, Nick snorted. "I'll be fine when the baby gets here, hopefully." When Trace winced, Nick shrugged. "I know, I know. If I'm not getting a lot of sleep now, how am I going to with an infant in the house?"

"Something like that." Trace laughed. "Lisa giving you a run for your money?"

The smile on Nick's face belied his complaints. "She's fine. The doctor told her she needed to rest more and threatened her with bed rest if she didn't. I keep telling her it'll be worth it. At least she's not feeling sick all the time now."

"That's an improvement, I'll bet."

"You have no idea." Nick's dimple showed in his half-smile.

"So, what's up for today?"

"This security system and safe room project in the café is starting to run behind, and Charlie and Nate need backup. Nothing technical, just do whatever they need you to do."

"I'm no carpenter, you know." If they needed those skills, they had the wrong twin.

"I know, and I've told the guys. Anything you can't handle, they can show you how to do it."

"I do have an advanced degree in searching YouTube instructional videos."

"Hey, don't knock it. I look stuff up all the time." Nick clapped Trace on the shoulder. "I've got to run to the other job site in Burna. Okay?"

"It'll be fine."

"Hannah's putting in some preliminary wiring, so she'll be here about a half-day, then she'll come out to the site in Burna after her appointment at the bank."

Closing on her house? It was none of his business, so he didn't ask.

"Gotcha."

"Hey, man, I appreciate the help with Del out of pocket."

"If I were you, I'd withhold the thanks until you see how bad a job I'll do."

Nick pitched him a key. "Here's the key to the basement door. Lock it up tight when you leave this afternoon, and then you'll have it for in the morning. Be sure and let Roxy know when everybody leaves."

"I'm surprised Del and Darcy didn't move into Del's house."

Nick nodded. "Me, too, but the loft is a lot bigger than Del's house, and Riverside Park is a block away. I figure one of these days, if they start adding to their family, they may want to consider moving into a house—that's a topic for another time." Nick lifted the corner of his mouth. "Size isn't the only reason they're moving into the apartment. The kitchen, as Lisa describes it, is 'to die for,' and Darcy doesn't want to leave it yet."

HANNAH BIT her tongue yet again. *Did I draw the short straw?*

Working in the same vicinity as Charlie and Nate, with their constant jabbering and less-than-heartfelt work ethic, annoyed her. And then there was Trace. He'd been on the job site with Nick for a few days last week. The basement was a lot smaller, and he wasn't an observer anymore.

"I hear the boyfriend is coming out to help us today." Nate was constantly trying to get a rise out of her.

She said nothing, but glowered at him from her position on the ladder, then turned back to her work. The wire she was trying to pull in the ceiling for the security camera was not cooperating. Maybe she should give in and tell Nick she needed an assistant. "I don't have a boyfriend, and you know it."

"What about young Trace Reno? The guy you were sitting next to at the boss's wedding?"

Now Charlie was just meddling.

"I didn't pick the seat."

"Hey."

Hannah's eyes flew to the owner of the quiet voice. Trace. What was he doing here? And why did she have a weird feeling in the pit of her stomach? More importantly, did he hear what the guys said?

"Hey."

Great comeback, Hannah.

He peered up at her, an odd expression on his face. Intense. Had she left off an article of clothing? Was she doing something wrong? She checked. There were her tools on her belt, wire strippers, plastic connectors, and pliers. When she glanced back at him, he'd moved over to where Charlie and Nate were patching the drywall, where she'd cut holes for various outlets and equipment.

I guess he's just strange. Yeah. I'll go with that.

She went about her business, half of her attention on what she was doing—which she could do in her sleep—and half on what the guys were talking about.

"Nick sent me over to lend a hand."

"Yeah, boss-man said they were sending us a flunky."

Hannah's gaze flew to Trace at Charlie's smart remark. What she could see of his face had flushed redder than his beard. Charlie and Nate didn't know when to keep their mouths shut.

"Put me to work. I'm here to help."

He was playing it cool. Good for him. Her respect grew.

Did he hear their question about her "boyfriend"? She hoped against hope he didn't. Even the hint of her thinking of him as "boyfriend material" made her heart beat faster and her palms sweat.

Probably not the usual response to trying to squelch a rumor, but ...

"Nice wedding, huh, Trace?"

Nate was going to do it. He would, by any means necessary, bring the conversation back around to her and Trace sitting together at the reception.

"I guess. Seen one wedding, you've seen 'em all."

My sentiments exactly. Good answer, Trace.

He glanced up at her. Was that a wink? If so, it was so slight and so fast that she could have imagined it. From her perch on the ladder, Hannah watched Trace pick up the broom and dustpan and begin to clean up the worksite, saying nothing.

"SAFETY FIRST." Grandpa strapped on his safety glasses. "Nothing like flying bits of debris to turn a relaxing, satisfying time of working with wood into a trip to the emergency room because of a splinter in the eye."

"Noted." Trace did as he was told, glad to have some one-on-one time with Grandpa. This shop, with Grandpa, was home. Here, even among all the equipment, he could relax.

"How was the first day of work?" Grandpa examined the end of a thick post before finding the dead center of both ends.

"It was fine. Mainly job-site cleanup."

"Yeah, must be hard to start on the bottom rung of the ladder after the kind of job you've had." Grandpa peered at him through the scratched lenses of the protective gear.

It wasn't fun.

"I made it okay."

"Charlie and Nate?"

When Trace nodded, Grandpa snorted. "Those guys will try to get a rise out of this piece of wood, here."

"I gathered they'd been picking on Hannah before I got there."

"Del and Nick need to have a word with those two. Can't afford to lose the best electrician they've ever had." Grandpa shook his head.

Hannah certainly had a good name among his family members. She wasn't just a tradesperson. She was a family friend.

"Is she that good? I figured electricians were electricians." Trace didn't look at Grandpa but was curious about the older gentleman's take on Mandy's classmate.

"She's that good."

Trace hazarded a glance up to see Grandpa's eyes on him, one eyebrow cocked.

"I don't know why some young man hasn't snatched her up yet. A sweeter girl you'll never meet."

"I guess I haven't seen the sweet side of her." *I'd like to ...*

Grandpa centered the wooden post onto the lathe, spinning it to make sure it was level. "She's pretty particular. Don't know if she's dated much, but whoever gets her attention will be a blessed man."

Trace didn't say anything, just frowned.

"Ah, she's not giving you the time of day, is she? I wouldn't have thought you expected all the women to be lined up to get your attention."

Am I that transparent? Gotta work on my poker face.

"I don't." Trace's mouth hung open at the accusation, his prickly nature rising and then tamping down. "Just seems like every time I'm around her, she gets aggravated at me for some reason."

"Hmm." Grandpa locked the wood into place and once again spun the piece of hardwood. "See this, here?" He pointed to the post.

"Yes." Trace probably should have been paying closer attention, but he got the gist of it.

"If I don't find dead center on both ends, it'll wobble you to death before you get rid of the excess. Gotta get it lined up right."

It took a few tries before Trace got the hang of holding the roughing gouge to turn the square post into a round one.

"Not bad." Grandpa held the gouge to check for residual rough spots.

"You make it look easy, but it's not." Trace chuckled.

"It takes a while to get the hang of it—same way it takes a while to figure out what to do with yourself in life." Grandpa turned off the machinery and pulled up a bucket to sit on. "Have a seat. If I were out here alone, your grandma would already be out here making sure I haven't keeled over or got something cut off."

His grandparents had slowed down, which was why Mom and Dad moved back down here, to help them with the farm. He didn't like to think about it, but one day his parents would be old.

Nobody prepares you for that.

"Did I do the right thing, coming down here?" He wanted to know, and Grandpa would be straight with him.

"What do you think?"

Ah, answer a question with a question.

"There wasn't any reason for me to stay around Louisville." He slumped. "Eli's got his girlfriend. And Samantha—well, I don't think Sam knows what she wants. Me? I have an empty apartment and a few friends who won't notice if I'm not there."

"I'm sure they'd notice."

"I doubt it. Making close friends has never been my forte." He shrugged. "I'd even planned to go on a Caribbean cruise for Thanksgiving instead of coming down here."

Grandpa chuckled. "Somehow, I can't see you on a cruise. You'd be sunburnt before you left port." Considering Trace for a moment, Grandpa continued, "Maybe that's why God saw fit to send you down here for a spell."

Trace snorted. "To learn how to make friends? What am I? Six?"

"Not hardly." Grandpa squinted a little. "It may be that it's more about people than a job." Grandpa shrugged. "Maybe introduce you to a different kind of woman."

"I'll be sure and tell the bank that when my truck payment is due."

Grandpa dragged himself up stiffly. "No need to borrow trouble. Just remember you're not the one in charge."

Trace didn't say anything, just followed him out of the shop and to the house. "Thanks, Grandpa."

"What for?"

"Bein' my grandpa, I guess."

"Can't argue with good logic." He winked and pulled the door open to the brightly lit kitchen, where sweet smells of cinnamon and nutmeg were beginning to be commonplace.

Chapter 8

Staying at Grandma and Grandpa's house was almost as good as living on a cruise ship. Clean laundry appeared on his bed as if by magic, there was always food—food Trace didn't have to prepare for himself—and always somebody to talk to. That part he could do with less of, but the other outweighed his need for solitude.

He liked knowing someone would be there waiting when he came back from work.

It was interesting living in the house where his dad and uncles grew up, and he tried to imagine life in their household when they were all home. Three brothers. All with strong personalities.

Who did he and Eli take after?

He loved his brother, yet when it came to the world of women and dating, their personalities were as different as their features, even if they were twins. Dark-haired Eli, easy-going, fun, gregarious, had girls calling him by the time he was fourteen. Then there was Trace. Quiet and a little on the grumpy side, he would rather play video games, read, or watch

TV than hang out with friends. He'd lost more than one girl *he* was interested in to his more engaging brother. Trace's mind jumped to his job. Or the lack thereof, in his case.

The month between Thanksgiving and Christmas was notoriously slow as far as hiring went. He knew, going in, which was why he'd agreed to sign on with RenoVations Inc. as a general laborer for a few weeks.

At least that was the plan. For now, he was assigned the jobs of broom guy and gofer. He'd been on the job site with electrician Hannah the last few days, and she was doing everything in her power to avoid him.

1. Trace walks into a room. Hannah walks out of it.

2. Trace asks her a question to get the ball rolling. Hannah gives the briefest answer and then refers him to someone else on the crew.

3. Trace smiles at her. Hannah pretends she doesn't see him.

A lesser man could take this the wrong way.

Or maybe the right way?

And then there was number four: Trace apologizes.

Except I haven't. I'll get to it …

From all accounts, Hannah was this sweet, friendly girl who bent over backward to ensure everyone was happy and the work was done to perfection.

He kept hearing about it, but he had not seen that side of her.

Why did it bother him so much? Usually he was glad when people left him to his own devices. Was he obsessed with her? Did he have an unhealthy attraction to someone who could care less about him?

More importantly, did he believe in love at first sight?

Of course not.

People who did were saps, plain and simple. People who

went around with their heads in the clouds singing, "Kum-By-Ya."

Relationships took work, and anything requiring that much work couldn't be the magical, life-altering experience portrayed in books and movies.

Because those aren't real life.

Pulling up to the Clementville Café, Trace let out a deep breath when he saw Hannah's truck. Another day of being ignored.

IF HANNAH HAD to spend one more day working with Trace Reno, she'd explode.

Surely—surely, he'll find a job soon, or at least go back to where he came from.

On the other hand, today had been an amazing day. She was now a homeowner.

After the closing, keys in hand, she and her parents drove to the house immediately. She and her dad were already making plans to gut the kitchen and bath. He'd promised her his services for the weekend.

Her phone chirped with a text message.

Mandy:

Hey, girlfriend. Want to go Christmas shopping with me?

Not really.

What's up?

Busy day.

Trace work with you today? LOL

What's so funny about that?

I sensed a little tension at the reception
the other night.

How to answer ...

That would mean I cared.

Change the subject quickly, Hannah ...

Closed on the house today!

Yay!! When can I see it?

Whenever we want ... I have the
keys now!

AWESOME!!

Maybe if she agreed to go shopping with her, Mandy would drop the subject of a certain Trace Reno.

When did you want to go to town?

Tomorrow night? I've got some stuff to
pick up. We could always treat ourselves
to Italian.

If Italian is involved, I could be
persuaded. And HomeGoods.

For the new homeowner, obviously. Rest
up. The stores are open late starting this
week. ;)

Hannah groaned. Was she becoming an old lady when it came to going out after dark in the middle of the week?

Are you there?

About to nod off. How about we meet
after work? I'll need a shower.

I'll pick you up.

Gotcha. See ya.

Night-night

"Who were you talking to?" Mom meant well, but her question just added another layer to the already-irritable mood Hannah was in.

When I get my own place ...

"Mandy." She put her phone down. "We're going shopping tomorrow night."

"Cold front's coming in." Dad's face was buried in the newspaper.

"We're big girls, Dad."

Yes, she was turning into a middle-aged woman. She'd started thinking about the weather and how much sleep she needed when anyone suggested an outing after dark. What was wrong with her?

"Think you could pick up a few things for me, sweetie?" Mom perked up.

Anything to avoid Walmart this time of year.

"Sure. Give me a list." She grinned, remembering last Christmas. "Last year, while Mandy was at her grandparents' house, she had a list every time we left Crittenden County."

"Sylvia Reno is a smart woman."

"She is."

Mom's in a talkative mood.

"You've been awfully quiet since last week."

"Not much to say, lots to think about. I'll be glad when I can move into my house."

Mom sighed. "I'm not sure I'm ready for you to fly the nest."

"Mom, I'm twenty-five years old. Old enough to buy a house. I think I'm ready."

"I didn't say you weren't ready. I'm the one not wanting to let go."

"Heather left home at twenty-one."

"To get married." Mom folded up the afghan she was crocheting and peering up at Hannah over her reading glasses. "That was different."

Ire bubbled up in Hannah at the unfairness of Mom's statement. She knew it was coming from a place of love, but she was *so* ready to get on with her life that she could ... spit.

Mom hardly took a breath. "Trace Reno is a good-looking boy."

And ... we're there.

"Alrighty, then. Speaking of good-looking boys, I'm on the search for gift ideas for the men in my life—namely Dad and Clark." She pulled out her laptop, hoping to hide behind it until bedtime. "I'll check out some online sales, make my list, and check it twice."

Mom smirked. She knew when she was being outmaneuvered. "I have a few ideas." She turned her attention to her husband. "Not that we couldn't carry on a complete conversation and he not remember a thing."

"Better be careful. Santa's watching." His eyes never left the paper, but his half-grin said it all. He heard a lot more than he let on.

Hannah laughed, feeling a little lighter, not being the subject of her parents' bickering. She bent to kiss her dad on the cheek and grabbed her laptop. If she could get out of the room before their attention turned to her again ...

Her phone buzzed with another text. Mandy again?

Nope

This time it was Lisa, the boss lady.

> Hey, Hannah, change of venue
> tomorrow. We've picked up another
> project in Eddyville.

> Where do you need me?

> Eddyville, for tomorrow. Putting together
> a lighting plan for a kitchen and master
> bath remodel.

Hannah's smile grew. Not only did she love helping Lisa create lighting plans, but maybe she'd have time to pick Lisa's designer brain and get her opinion of her ideas for her own house.

> Sounds good. 8 am?

> Let's make it nine-ish. Curvy roads, early
> mornings, and pregnancy do not play
> well together.

She laughed. Everyone—especially Lisa and Nick—was excited about their first child. Darcy's twins would finally have cousins.

> 10-4. I'll be there.

> Oh, could you carpool with Trace? He
> and Nick want to check out a new meat
> processor after. He doesn't know the
> area like you do.

Seriously? Carpool with Trace? She closed her eyes and counted to ten.

> Sure. 'Tis the season.

Yep. It's weird. Nick never expressed an
interest in hunting until last year when he
and Del got their first deer. Now it's all
they talk about. Men.

Men was right. She could suck it up and tolerate him for the half-hour drive.

Gotcha.

Maybe we can ride back together, and
they can go to the sporting goods store
together.

I'm meeting Mandy to go to Paducah
after. Could Trace drive? Can you drive
your vehicle home, or even better, want
to join us to shop?

I'll be good. It sounds like fun, but by 4
pm, I'm ready to put on my jammies.

lol

I sent him your number.

And now he has my number. Great.

TRACE SAT IN HIS GRANDPARENTS' living room, reading the text he'd just received from Lisa.

Carpool? With Hannah?

While it sounded like a great idea to him, his expectations instantly went to awkward silence the whole thirty-minute trip from Clementville to Eddyville.

"What's wrong, Trace? Quite a frown you're sporting there." Grandma spoke into his thoughts from her easy chair, looking over a snoring Grandpa.

"Sorry."

"No apologies necessary for a frown."

"Lisa and Nick want me to meet them in Eddyville at a new job site." He quirked an eyebrow at Grandma.

She tilted her head. "And?"

"And she wants me to carpool with Hannah so I can go with Nick afterward."

Trace saw her lips twitch in an attempt to squelch a grin. She studied her crochet project, which, being an expert needleworker, she never had to do.

"That's nice."

"She'll be thrilled, I'm sure." He looked down when his phone vibrated again. "And here's her phone number. I'm supposed to coordinate with her."

"How fortuitous."

"Big word for a little Grandma."

"Well, I couldn't keep saying, 'That's nice,' now, could I?" Her laugh tinkled across the room, and Grandpa awoke.

"Is it bedtime yet?"

"Sweetheart, it's seven-thirty."

"Hate this time change. What'd I miss?"

He'd fallen asleep an hour ago, about twenty minutes into the movie they'd picked.

"Too much to explain." Grandma shook her head at her husband.

"You didn't miss much, Grandpa. Small-town guy in danger of losing the family peach orchard. Big-city girl comes to town to buy them out and realizes she's always wanted to live in the boonies and work an orchard with the man of her dreams." Trace held out a hand and nodded toward the television. "And, finally, there's the kiss."

"Sounds like you've watched your share of these." Grandpa laughed.

Trace growled in disgust. "Guilty. Have you met my sister?"

"Now and again."

"Eddie Clarence Reno, you know good and well the only reason you agreed to this one is because it lasted exactly eighty-four minutes." Grandma blustered with good humor.

"I'll admit, the length of those movies is a draw, plus the lack of objectionable activity—"

"And bad language," Grandma interrupted.

"I know. But would it hurt them to blow up something every once in a while?" Grandpa winked at Trace when Grandma shook her head.

"Since I have almost no social life, Sis and I came up with an informal breakdown according to the television rating."

"Did you, now?" Grandma was getting tickled.

"Yep. Rated G, you're lucky to get one very chaste kiss at the very end. Same with 'seven plus.' PG and 'thirteen plus,' maybe two or three, and they'll be a little steamy, but not too much."

"What about 'PG-13' movies?"

Trace shook his head solemnly. "Grandma, you watch those, you're in danger for your soul."

Grandma laughed out loud. "Trace, honey, I'm glad you're here." She raised an eyebrow at Grandpa. "Gives me somebody to talk to and watch movies with."

"Sam says I ruin these movies for her." Trace grinned.

Grandpa put the footrest of his recliner down and pushed himself out of the chair. "Young man, now I have a reason to watch"

"What? To pick them apart?"

"If it keeps him awake, I can accept it, as long as I don't have to explain the plot twenty times per movie." Grandma laid down her crochet project. "Now. Who wants some pie?"

"You read my mind." Grandpa put his hand out to take Grandma's, pulling her close when she popped up.

"Gracious."

"Better watch out. Those movies might give this old man some ideas."

She leaned in and kissed him quickly. "I don't think you need any movie for that."

Grandpa smiled. "I'll follow you to the kitchen and get me a cup of coffee. Trace?"

"I'm good."

"None for me," Grandma sighed. "Wish I could, but I like sleep too much." She turned to Trace, shaking her head. "Grandpa, on the other hand, can drink it till bedtime and still fall asleep in five minutes."

"Clean living, clear mind. Nothin' to keep me awake." He made his way to the kitchen, a little hitch in his gait and a spring in his step.

"Find us another movie to watch, Trace. These are starting to make me feel Christmas-y." Grandma followed her husband into the kitchen.

Trace picked up the remote and clicked through the list of movies they hadn't seen yet. When he stopped, he felt a smile on his face.

"*Baking Merry*." Amused, he read the blurb out loud. "How does this one sound?

"Big city executive is stuck in her hometown at Christmas and gets talked into organizing the local Gingerbread House bake-off. When the main contender turns out to be the guy she had an adolescent crush on, she's intrigued, and more than a little interested in what brought the guy voted 'most likely to succeed' back home running the down-on-its-heels bakery he's inherited from his grandparents."

Maybe this guy can give me a few pointers.

WHY IS *it that the movies advertised as "comedy" make me cry, and the ones labeled "drama" are funny?*

Hannah blew her nose. Mom and Dad had retired an hour ago, and she'd decided to finish the movie they'd started.

The explosion of made-for-TV movies this time of year weren't Oscar-worthy, but they made her feel good.

And sometimes they make me cry.

She'd been anticipating watching *Baking Merry* ever since she saw it advertised as a "new this year" release, and it lived up to the hype. It was predictable, but it met expectations, which was why people kept coming back for more. Hannah's favorite actors from a certain studio stable were all there, and her all-time favorite male lead, Cliff Dawson, played the baker.

Now that guy is swoony.

Tough, sensitive, just clueless enough to make him believable as a male. She'd watch him read the phone book—if there still was such a thing. He definitely reinforced her childhood crush on Ron Weasley with his ginger hair and amazingly perfect five-o'clock shadow. Everywhere she turned, there was another man with red hair.

Her phone dinged with a text, and she caught it up and opened the app.

An unfamiliar number. It didn't take long for her to figure it out.

Unknown:

Hannah, Trace here. Lisa said we need to carpool in the morning.

Hannah sighed and saved the number in her contacts. She typed in "Trace Reno," then backed up, erasing the name, and put "Grumpy" in its place. Now *that* made her smile.

Correct. Do you mind driving? Mandy's picking me up there.

Grumpy:

Glad to. Navigate me there?

No problem.

8:30 work?

Sure. Do you need my address?

I've got it.

She was slightly taken aback. How did he know where she lived? Mandy. It wasn't like he had no ties to the area. She was overreacting.

I'll be ready.

Have a good night.

She paused, biting her lip.

You too.

The clock above the mantle caught her eye. 10:30. No wonder she was getting bleary-eyed. Tomorrow would be interesting. Not an early day, but with Mandy, potentially a late evening. The movie poster remained on the screen. She stared at it, lacking the energy to get up and wishing bed would come to her. Pulling the Christmas throw pillow and hugging it, she tilted her head and squinted, a wave of sleepiness washing over her. In the place of the buff, ginger lead was another face. One with a perpetual slight frown and a nice beard—though not as perfect as the other guy.

Cliff Dawson had morphed into the man she'd listed as "Grumpy" in her phone.

Her eyes flew open at the thought.

I should probably change the name back to "Trace" ...

Fatigue and procrastination fought the twinge of responsibility—and won.

But not tonight.

Hannah grabbed the remote, pointing it emphatically at the television and clicking "off."

If she weren't so sleepy, she'd watch something totally different as a palate cleanser.

Chapter 9

Trace had never considered himself a morning person—or any other time of day, for that matter—but today, he caught himself whistling as he entered the kitchen.

"You're chipper this morning." Grandma's bright and rested smile indicated she'd been up for hours, just like when he was a kid. Before anyone else was up, she was dressed, hair fixed, and breakfast ready. She held up the coffee pot, and he grabbed a mug and held it out to her.

"It's a beautiful morning." He shrugged and took a tentative sip of the piping-hot coffee.

Ouch.

"Wouldn't have anything to do with the fact that you're carpooling with a certain young lady today, would it?

He hid behind the cup, too hot or not, his lips tipped in a smile as he regarded the loving eyes of Grandma Reno.

"I thought so." She had a look of "told you so" written all over her face.

Trace leaned back on the counter, staring into his coffee as if it were the most interesting thing in the world. It was out of character for him, but he wanted to talk about it. If he were to confide in anybody, it would be Grandma. She was one of the only adults from his childhood who hadn't lumped him in with Eli as a twin. She saw him for himself.

"Grandma …"

She put a plate of muffins and a butter dish on the table, pulled out a chair, and sat. Gesturing to the chair across from her, she waited until he was seated, then passed him the plate.

"What's going on in that ginger head?"

"I know you and Grandpa started dating pretty young."

"Well, I was. Your grandpa has always been older, you know." She chuckled. "If you're thinking I can't possibly understand dating …"

Trace sat up straight, his eyes bulging as he interrupted. "Not dating."

"All right." She paused, narrowing her eyes. "Being attracted to—"

"I never said …"

The person who could give the most loving looks in the world could also send a withering one. "—being attracted to and wanting to date someone they just met. Hon, you forget how many grandchildren I have."

Trace nodded, twisting his lips. He leaned forward, talking quietly. "You've been around Hannah."

"Yes, I've been blessed to know Hannah and her family." She arched a brow. "I don't think you're looking for a recommendation."

Rubbing the back of his neck, he considered his words.

"She seems … nice." He paused, looking down at his hand, fiddling with his napkin. Anything to avoid her gaze. The woman saw entirely too much for his taste.

"I think her niceness has been established. She's very nice." Grandma grinned. "And?"

How could he say what he was thinking without sounding like a petulant child? His brother and sister would laugh out loud at him, but then he was an easy target—they could get a rise out of him. "It's just that ..." He swallowed. "Well, every time I come around, she seems irritated at me for some reason."

"I see." Grandma was quiet. Just sat there. Eyes on him. Saying nothing.

"I mean ... I don't expect girls to fall all over themselves around me, but Hannah is in a perpetual foul mood when I'm around." He shook his head, trying to sling the topic out of his mind. "Never mind. I'm not going to try to impress a girl who's made it clear she doesn't like me."

Grandma's gaze softened. "Trace, honey, I think Hannah has impressed *you* for some reason."

How do I tell my grandma that I think I fell in love the first time I saw her?

He could feel the heat coming from the region of his collar and knew the flush would be burning his cheeks soon. There were times, this being one, when he wished his beard covered more of his face.

"I'm not the kind of guy who attracts girls."

His grandmother frowned. "Trace Aaron Reno!"

Trace tilted his head and scrunched his nose. "You're my grandma, remember? I'm not saying I'm the Beast to her Beauty. I know I'm not as handsome or as outgoing as Eli."

She shook her head and leaned in, taking his hand. "Sweetheart, do you know who you are the most like, more than anybody in the family?"

His brows went down. Now what were they talking about? "Uh, no." He narrowed his eyes, wondering where the conversation was going.

"Your grandpa." Her laugh trilled out.

Wow.

"Grandpa? Really?" Quite a compliment. There's no one in the world he held in higher esteem than his grandpa. His dad was amazing, but Grandpa? He'd always been in a class all by himself.

"Yes. You look like him, walk a little like him, frown like him, and keep things to yourself until you know what to say." She arched a brow at him. "He was never the boy who had all the girls swooning, because he thought that was stuff and nonsense. All of it. Once I realized he was just brutally honest, I knew I had a catch."

"I look like him?"

"You've seen pictures. He turned gray before we started making color pictures, but his hair was almost the same shade of ginger as yours."

He didn't know what to say. Pondering, he considered Grandma's words.

"Trace, I never knew your grandpa to go out with any other girls before me. He was friends with them, and the way girls confided in him amazed me—made me a little jealous at first, but you know what? He's always said he fell in love with me the first time he saw me." She grinned. "And since he's never told a whopper in his life, I believe him."

HANNAH INSPECTED herself in the mirror, her usual get-up not doing it for her today. Maybe a little lip gloss.

Lips shiny, she tilted her head. Maybe it was the extra time that made her more critical. Her gray sweatshirt did nothing to improve her thoughts. Carefully pulling it off to avoid getting lip gloss on it, she dug around until she found a light blue turtleneck sweater, a gift from Mom last Christmas. She'd tried to improve Hannah's wardrobe, and Hannah would never admit it, but she absolutely loved it. So soft, and fit perfectly. It was ribbed, so it hugged her in all the right places without being beguiling.

A chuckle escaped her lips.

Beguiling. Now that's a word I'd get teased about.

Her love of reading the classics, what her friends called "outdated," colored her vocabulary, sometimes at inopportune times.

Brushing out her dark-blonde hair, she swung it around, hesitating before pulling it into her customary ponytail and then pulling it out. She put the hairband on her wrist, instead. If she needed it pulled back, she'd be prepared. She was going out afterward, and didn't want to look like a contractor while shopping with Mandy.

Speaking of Mandy ...

Hey, a slight change in plans.

Mandy:

You are NOT canceling on me, are you?

No, just a logistics change. I'm going to a job site in Eddyville with Lisa. Can you pick me up there instead of home?

Yay! Can we get an earlier start?

Yep. We'll be done by 3:30 or so.

Awesome. Send me the address, and I'll be there.

The bubbling dots indicated she was still typing away on her phone.

What are you wearing?

Work boots and coveralls.

That should get a rise out of her. Hannah chuckled to herself. Was it her, or did those dots seem a little more frantic now?

Hannah

What? JK. I wouldn't do that to you.

The mirror reflected her freshly brushed hair and a little eye makeup. Not bad. She snapped a pic and sent it to Mandy.

See? I'll try not to be an embarrassment.
Will this work? Lol

Give me a heart attack next time.

You're crazy, you know that?

Yes, but I also don't own coveralls and
work boots.

Could be a new fashion craze.

Right. Gotta go.

Me too. Trace just drove up.

Hannah winced. She did not mean to give up that information. She'd never hear the end of it, now.

Oh-ho?

It's work. Carpooling so I can meet YOU
to go shopping.

I see.

Hannah??

Oops.

Hannah realized she'd stopped to check her face one more time and didn't answer Mandy's text.

> Sorry. And no comments from the peanut gallery. I'll see you this afternoon.

Hannah closed the app before Mandy could get another word in. She turned off her ringer. The last thing she wanted was for Trace to wonder if she and Mandy were talking about him.

I mean, why would we be talking about him?

She checked herself in the mirror one more time. She'd pass.

MAYBE SHE DIDN'T HEAR him drive up.

Trace sat in the truck for a few minutes—probably seconds, actually—and then decided to go to the door. As soon as the first "ding" of the doorbell sounded, the door opened, and a smiling face greeted him.

"You must be Trace?"

He nodded, and before he could get a word out, he was ushered into the foyer of the large 1980s post-modern-style ranch with a few hints of Art Deco still visible in the pastel wall colors and the archways leading to various parts of the house.

"I'll see if Hannah is ready." She turned away, then back, shaking her head. "I am so sorry. I'm Hannah's mother, Kristi."

"Glad to meet you, Mrs. Buckner."

She waved a hand at him. "Oh, call me Kristi. We don't stand on ceremony around here."

"Ma'am, I was taught to always greet a lady with her title on the first meeting."

Her smile broadened. "Now that, young man, is manners."

Hannah came to a halt, almost running into her mother.

"Oh, there you are, sweetie!"

Was it him, or did Hannah have a slight deer-in-the-headlights expression on her face?

"I'm ready." She spoke in a rush as she gathered her jacket and purse. Kissing her mom on the cheek, she said, "I'll be late tonight," then glanced at Trace when her mother's eyebrow raised. "Shopping with Mandy, remember?"

"Oh." If disappointment had a facial expression, Kristi Buckner's current one would be the classic illustration.

"Bye." She widened her eyes at Trace. Was she trying to give him the signal she wanted to leave, and soon?

"Oh. Right." He opened the door and gestured for her to precede him. "Nice to meet you, Mrs. Buckner."

"Likewise. Come again." Mrs. Buckner's smile was megawatt, the opposite of the embarrassed scowl on Hannah's face.

He opened the passenger door for her, despite the slight glare she sent his way.

"I am capable of opening a car door."

Stepping up into the driver's seat of the pickup, he chuckled. "I know, but I thought your mom would get a kick out of it." He glanced at the front picture window, noticing the lace curtain dropping quickly.

Hannah covered her face with her hands, shaking her head. He sensed her frustration. "I am so sorry."

"For what?" No way was he going to give her this one.

"My mother." She sighed, then relaxed and clasped her hands together in her lap. "It's been a while since a person of the male persuasion came to the door asking for me. I told her we were carpooling ..."

A laugh burst from him and his cheeks heated. "I have parents and grandparents, too, you know. They're the same way. Convinced I'll miss an opportunity to find my soulmate."

Hannah turned quickly toward him, hands flung out in frustration. "Why can't they leave us to find our own person? I mean, if it's meant to be, won't it be evident to us without their interference?"

Glancing over at her, he grinned. She was beautiful with her eyes snapping and her face flushed. What would she think if he told her he was pretty sure he'd found his "person," and that it wasn't evident to her?

He didn't say anything, and it was quiet for a few miles as they drove through Marion and out 641 toward the even tinier hamlet of Fredonia.

Letting his mind drift, he imagined the scenario: *They're riding along in the truck, talking about nothing in particular. She puts her hand on the console between the two captain's chairs, thinking nothing of it. He notices and places his hand on hers, then gazes into her eyes.*

He sees tenderness there, and surprise. A quick intake of breath. His gaze lands on her lips, and he leans toward her ...

"Trace!"

The deer on the side of the road decided he'd waited long enough and that he should jump out into the first truck he saw —Trace's truck. He swerved and missed. The deer's white tail was the only visible sign of its presence as he pranced into the thicket.

"Thanks for the heads up."

"I'd rather not get killed today, if at all possible. The deer are crazy this time of year. You haven't been here long enough to know that during deer hunting season, they're nuts. You have to watch out for them every minute."

The way Trace saw it, he had a few choices. He could give

her his usual response, which would be to snap at her that *he* was the one driving. He could say he grew up on a farm not unlike this area and that the deer population was just as crazy there during deer season. If he were truly willing to alienate her immediately, he could say he would have seen it if she hadn't been distracting him.

Hmm. Maybe he'd leave off the last part.

Or, he could take the high road and apologize. Totally out of character for him, but it was a calculated risk.

"I'm sorry. I'll remember to keep my eyes sharp."

She glared at him with a shaking head and crossed arms.

Revisiting his daydream, he revised the end. *Rather than an adoring look, she yanks her hand away and gives him a scowl that would incinerate a lesser man.*

Who was he kidding? He *was* a lesser man.

WHEN THEY ARRIVED at the job site in Trace's F-150, Lisa and Nick were in the driveway, his arm around her, checking out a dent on the fender of Lisa's Explorer. Had they been plagued by a menace of the buck or doe variety?

As soon as they stopped, Hannah was out of the truck. No way was she going to wait around and let Trace open the door for her.

"Hey." Hannah got to the couple ahead of Trace. "What happened?"

She expected Lisa to be upset, which she was, but didn't expect her to be downright angry. Spitting-nails-angry if Hannah was any judge.

"What is it about deer this time of year that turns them into Kamikazes? You can go all year without hitting one, and the weeks in the year when people get their guns and bows out, they decide that if they can't find a mate, they'd rather sacrifice themselves on the grill of a truck than succumb to the indignity of a hunter shooting them for food or sport." She growled and pointed to the road. "I mean, it happened right before I turned in the drive."

Trace, serious, from all accounts, laughed out loud, causing his cousin Lisa to glare at him even harder than Hannah had earlier. She had to steel herself when she felt her lips twitch, both she and Trace sobering in light of Lisa's ire and Nick's slashing motion across his neck indicating they were treading on shaky ground.

Trace raised a hand. "I'm sorry. We narrowly missed one too."

Nick tightened his hold on his wife. "It was bound to happen. When was the last time you hit a deer?"

She rounded on him. "I didn't hit it. It hit *me*." Lisa was still steamed. "I know I said I kinda wanted to get a new vehicle, but this wasn't what I had in mind." She stuck out her bottom lip, her eyes teary, and stroked the fender of her white SUV. "I love my Explorer."

"I know." Nick bent down, noting the damage. "I don't think it'll be totaled. I'll call Farm Bureau and see if I can get a loaner until we get this one fixed."

Hannah spoke up. "In the meantime, let's get your mind off the car and into the job."

Nick nodded, seeming relieved at the subject change. Turning to Trace, she couldn't read his expression, but she took it as agreement. When she glanced back a second time, she was even more confused. He still studied her as he had earlier.

She'd just said something, hadn't she? What was it ... Oh yeah, the job.

"Hannah?" Trace's voice broke through her thoughts. Lisa and Nick were already walking away. The last thing she wanted was for any of these people to know that she'd blanked out for a bit.

"Yeah." She hesitated, anxiously searching the room for an excuse for falling behind the conversation. "Just checking where the service comes in." She walked toward the house, looking up briefly as Trace held the door for her. "Thank you."

"You're welcome."

Was it her, or was it hot in there? And for a guy who was usually pretty pessimistic from what she'd seen, he had an inordinately happy expression on his face.

Chapter 10

Riding to the shopping excursion in Paducah, Hannah was quiet. Mandy had talked almost non-stop since they left the house in Eddyville. Suddenly, the quiet was louder than the background noise of her friend's voice.

"Earth to Hannah." Mandy laughed when Hannah looked over at her, startled.

"Sorry," Hannah said, as disoriented as if she'd been thrown into a canoe in a rushing river without a paddle.

"Are you okay?" Mandy's mirth turned to concern, her brows lowering.

"Yeah. Just thinking about the house." She was so not thinking about the house.

"Really?" Mandy narrowed her eyes at her as they stopped at the stoplight before entering the ramp to I-24.

"Um-hmm." *Liar, liar pants on fire.*

"Is it just me, or was Trace actually pleasant just now?"

Hannah drew her brows together, her mind racing around, trying to make sense of her thoughts. "He was."

"I keep telling him you catch more flies with honey than

vinegar." Mandy was quiet for a moment. "But then I always wondered why on earth we'd be trying to catch flies."

"I've wondered that too." Hannah agreed, then focused on the fast-moving scenery outside the window.

"Anyway, have you noticed anything?"

"Hmm?" Hannah turned toward her friend, determined to pay attention. "Sorry. My mind wandered again. Remodeling the kitchen in my head. What did you say?"

So not thinking about that. But I can't tell Mandy I'm totally confused about my latest commitment to singleness and that I feel all weird inside when Trace is nice to me.

"Sure, you are." Mandy sighed. "Girl, I'm not even going to say what I think is going on, because I don't want to jinx it."

"Mandy. I have definite ideas about what kind of guy I can fall in love with, and Trace is not that guy."

Even if I've decided he's more Michael Fassbender or Prince Harry than Ron Weasley. Danny Kaye? Hmmm ... not exactly a heartthrob ... or a grump ... he came through in the romance department on White Christmas, at least.

Mandy's lawyer brows inched up, and a smug smile twisted her lips. "Who said anything about Trace?"

Busted. Hannah had to get her mind somewhere besides handsome ginger men. Her stomach dropped. "Nobody. Just wanted to nip any ideas in the bud."

"So, you have ideas—or would that be *ideals*?" Mandy threw the question out there.

Hannah thought for a minute. "I guess it would be ideals. When I consider all the love stories in literature ..."

"Here we go, back down the Regency rabbit hole." Mandy scoffed, swerving to change lanes.

"Not just Regency, although Mr. Darcy *is* a prime example of *not* being Elizabeth's ideal."

"Is that the one with Colin Firth where they're coming

along in the carriage and catch him coming out of the pond with his shirt plastered to him, all wet and more handsome than Mr. Darcy has a right to be?"

Hannah closed her eyes and shook her head. "I knew it was a mistake to think making you watch the PBS mini-series would be a great introduction to Jane Austen novels."

"Hey, who needs to read? I have eyes, and if that's Jane Austen material, I vote yes." Mandy chuckled. "Okay, I'll try to get on your level. Romeo and Juliet were an ideal couple."

"Ugh. If murder-suicide is your idea of romance."

"Scarlett and Rhett?"

Hannah tapped her chin. "Getting closer, although I know you're just mentioning *Gone with the Wind* because it's an old book and a movie you've seen multiple times."

"And you've read the book multiple times, I'd wager."

"You would win that bet." Hannah nodded, trying to pull up a couple in modern pop culture that would appeal to them both. "Okay, what about Jim and Pam?"

"On *The Office*?" Mandy glanced over at her, brows raised happily. "Now that is a pairing I can get behind. It was a slow burn, but in the end, good won out over evil."

"Not that there was much evil at Dunder Mifflin." Hannah grinned.

Mandy tilted her head as she drove, apparently thinking. "Know what I'm *not* seeing in all these couples?"

"What?"

"An itemized list from the heroine indicating her ideal."

Hannah thought a moment. "True. If she has an ideal, he usually turns out to be the wrong man. It always seems to be a surprise when she realizes she loves the hero."

Oh, no ...

"ARE YOU SERIOUS?"

Trace enjoyed the hands-free electronics in his new truck —the truck he was making payments on without a job. He just hoped he got to keep it. One thing for sure, Clcmentville was remote enough that, with a decent cell signal, he could carry on a conversation in the length of time it took to get anywhere.

Eli's voice came over the speaker. "'Fraid so, brother. I thought things went pretty well over Thanksgiving, but ..."

"She just dumped you? No reason?" Trace was bewildered. Eli was the good-looking twin. The fun one. Girls started calling him in ninth grade. Trace? He was the serious one. Kind of a grouch. Who would pay attention to him while Eli was around?

"It may have been somewhat mutual." Eli paused on the other end of the conversation. Trace wished he could see his face. They might be different, but they were twins, after all.

"She wasn't the one, was she?"

The brothers had had this conversation before. While Trace didn't exactly have women clamoring over him, Eli had never really trusted the ones who came on to him.

"Apparently not." Eli let out a harsh laugh. "Maybe I should move to Clementville too."

Trace had mixed feelings. On the one hand, he missed his brother. When Eli wasn't caught up in a dating relationship, they did pretty much everything together. It never failed, though, that if Trace was into a woman, once she met Eli, her loyalties changed quickly.

"Plenty of room around Clementville."

"Yeah, well, I'll come down for Christmas. I thought I'd be at Carrie's, but maybe it's time for a big Reno Christmas instead."

Trace pulled into the parking space in front of the Clementville Café. The usual breakfast crowd was there.

Grandma and Grandpa had taken off for Paducah early to get some Christmas shopping in during daylight hours and had plans to stop for breakfast on the way. He told her not to worry about him for breakfast and instead called his dad to meet him. They hadn't talked since he came down for Thanksgiving.

"You'll make Grandma's year if she has all of us under her roof for Christmas. Mom's too," he told his brother.

His dad pulled up in his vintage 1987 Chevy square-body pickup. He'd had collectors bug him about his truck for years, even in the rough state it was in.

"Hey, I gotta go. Just getting to work," Eli said.

"Me too. Meeting Dad for breakfast." Trace paused. "Hang in there, brother."

"Will do. Maybe I need to swear off women for a while."

"Maybe so."

They ended the conversation, and Trace got out of his Ford about the time his dad reached him.

"Hungry?" Dad smiled. "How'd you get away from Grandma?"

"Who said I did?" Trace grinned. "They went Christmas shopping while they had nice weather, and when I told them I had breakfast plans, they decided to stop somewhere for breakfast."

Dad nodded, chuckling. "I'd put good money on Cracker Barrel."

Roxy waved from the counter and pointed to an empty table close to the counter. "Good morning."

"Hey, Roxy. You doin' okay?" Dad grinned at his sister-in-law.

If Uncle Steve could land a catch like Roxy, Trace had hope. It seemed there was a grump in every generation. His generation had two: Dad and Uncle Steve.

Roxy was all smiles, but she seemed a little harried. "Fine,

fine. Just busy with Darcy out of pocket. What can I get you boys this morning?"

She placed the ticket on the order wheel, and the two Reno men sipped their coffee.

Once he felt the desired caffeine infusion take place, Trace spoke. "Just got off the phone with Eli."

"Yeah, we talked to him last night. Shame about Carrie." Dad didn't usually have any opinion one way or another about the love lives of his offspring. "You know Eli."

"He'll bounce back and have a date by the weekend." Trace snorted, his dad making a similar sound. "You and Mom settling in?"

"Pretty much. Sam's coming as soon as her school lets out for Christmas."

Trace nodded. "Did Eli say anything about Christmas?"

"Just that he was coming home. Said if we didn't have room for him, he'd be glad to bunk at Grandma's with you." Dad brightened at the full plates Roxy placed in front of them.

"Everything look okay?"

"Roxy, I don't know if I've mentioned it, but my brother does not deserve you." He took a bite of the hashbrown casserole and sighed. "This puts my mama's hashbrowns to shame."

"I did *not* hear that. I've got a good thing going on with my mother-in-law." Roxy laughed. "Thank you, Tom. I was afraid I was getting rusty when I offered to take on the café back for Darcy while she's gone. I have a feeling I'll be ready for my own vacation after Christmas." She surveyed the table. "Can I get you anything else?"

Dad scoffed good-naturedly. "Wheelbarrow to roll us out in when we get through?"

HANNAH HAD a feeling of dread in the pit of her stomach the entire twenty-five miles from Clementville to Eddyville. She usually eagerly anticipated starting a new job. After assessing it a few days earlier, this one promised to be one of the easier ones since it was an addition to a fairly new house right on Lake Barkley. A week should get it.

Maybe if she just concentrated on the job—and not the assistant she'd been assigned. She just *had* to mention needing help.

Trace Reno.

He was an electrical engineer and had very little clue as to how a house was wired. Part of her looked forward to his "comeuppance."

Wow. Mean, much?

It would be fine. So far, he was nothing like Mandy always described him. Shy, grumpy, know-it-all. And he was nothing like his twin, Eli.

But then, that was a cousin's description. With her, he'd been talkative when she didn't want to be, agreeable to a fault, and deferred to her just about every time there had to be a side taken.

She pulled her aging utility truck into the steep driveway of the job site house just as Trace was getting out of his new pickup. Jealous didn't begin to describe her feelings. Someday the old Dodge she'd been driving since high school was going to give up the ghost. It was a hand-me-down truck from her dad when he got his new one. She'd outfitted it with toolboxes and ways to contain any and all the tools she'd need for jobs.

Now she needed to give Trace some orientation if he was going to be her assistant. The idea still irked her.

"Morning." Trace walked up to her, hands in his pockets, well-worn brown Carhartt-brand jacket zipped up against the cold. "Thought maybe we'd get a break in the weather."

Hannah nodded. "No such luck. Ready to get the day started?" No pleasantries, just business. That's all she wanted.

"I'm all yours today."

She jerked her head up, about to bite into him at the very idea of him being "hers" today. Then, when her eyes met his, the grin on his face only showed good humor, not flirtation.

There was something ...

Distraction. Nothing more.

Heat rose to her cheeks, and she was thankful she could blame it on the cold weather.

"You may regret those words. I'm told I can be quite the taskmaster."

He fell into step beside her after taking the bags of power tools from her hands, leaving her with the lighter load.

How dare he be nice.

"I think I can handle it."

Hazarding a glance his way, she looked down to get away from his clear gaze. "How much electrical work have you done?"

"Not much. I helped Uncle Steve's crew a couple of summers while I was in college. I was pretty much a gofer until they needed me to crawl into the attic or under the house to pull wires." He chuckled. "I guess that was when I decided electricity was interesting, but not enough to make a career out of exploring attics and crawlspaces."

"There are downsides, for sure. Hope you don't mind if I ask you to do exactly those things."

"I figured." Trace chuckled, and Hannah began to relax.

As they neared the door, the sound of power tools reached them.

"I guess Nick and his crew are already at work."

Trace nodded. "He wanted to get an early start so he could

leave early. I think Lisa's got a doctor's appointment this afternoon in Paducah."

"Gotcha." What would it be like to be married and expecting a baby? Stressful? Painful? Magical? She'd stick with magical.

"You okay?"

Hannah realized she'd expelled the dreamy sigh she thought was in her head. Great.

Chapter 11

So far, so good.

Trace had decided that if Hannah wasn't interested, he wouldn't be either. As far as she would know, anyway.

He'd be as agreeable—per Grandma—as possible. A Bible verse he'd almost forgotten about "heaping coals of fire on her head" ran through his mind.

If she said a black truck was not black, but midnight, he'd agree. If she said two-plus-two equals five? He'd give it to her.

Kill her with kindness.

So far, he'd escaped being ripped into when he told her he was "hers for the day." It hadn't occurred to him how it sounded until it came out of his mouth, and when she turned on him, it struck him funny. Good thing he wasn't a guy who laughed out loud easily.

He was fine until a dreamy sigh came out of her mouth while they were talking about Nick and Lisa and their baby. At that point, he wanted to drop those bags of tools and take her hand, at the very least. Fortunately, Nick met them at the door before the conversation could go anywhere. Trace wasn't ready to touch that with a ten-foot pole.

"Hey, guys, how are you this morning?" Nick was all smiles at seven-thirty in the morning.

Hannah grinned, and for some reason, it irritated him. *Why doesn't she ever smile at me?*

"Good. Where do you want us to start this morning?"

"Come on back. We've gotten some more done since y'all were here the other day." Nick led them through to the new family room/kitchen addition. The new wall facing the lake was all glass. The doors stacked together and opened all the way from one end of the room to the other, leading out to a screened porch. The opening had been covered in plywood when they were there earlier.

"This is amazing." Trace could have stood there, the view of the water before him, all day.

"I could stare at this all day." Hannah had walked up beside him, and her words, echoing his thoughts, startled him.

He gave her a half-smile and snorted a little. "Exactly what I was thinking."

"There might be hope for you, yet." She twisted her lips in a smirk that had him smiling until he caught himself and cleared his throat, shifting his gaze to his feet. There was still no reason to change strategies.

Brows furrowed, he decided the best tactic would be to show her just how hard he could work.

"Mornin', boss."

Trace wanted to groan when he saw who else he'd be working with today—Charlie and Nate.

Nick turned to them, pleasant, but not smiling. "Glad you two got here early. I need to go over a few things."

Sounded like a trip to the principal's office. Trace was relieved to know it wasn't aimed at him.

Walking over to the enlarged opening between the great room and the kitchen, Nick pointed to the hardwood they'd laced in to patch the area where there had been a wall and now was open floor. "This will have to be reinstalled." Squatting, Nick frowned up at the two men. "The pieces you laced in are too short, and it shows."

"I figured it wouldn't be noticed when it was sanded and stained."

"Not the point. This is a million-dollar house. It has to be perfect. Besides that, I told you exactly what I wanted done, and you didn't do it."

Nate looked everywhere but at Nick. Charlie, older and—he'd have thought—wiser, puffed up.

"I've been putting in floors for thirty years. Nobody's complained yet."

Nick stood, hands on his hips, staring icily at the older man. He paused, took a deep breath, and then, low and intense, said, "I guess there's a first time for everything. I want it done today. I'll check on it this afternoon." Without another word, Nick walked toward Trace and Hannah.

Charlie's gaze faltered, and Trace stifled a laugh. Probably should have walked out of the room when the altercation started, but it did him good to see the guy who had ribbed him unmercifully about the wedding get his comeuppance. Glancing at Hannah, he met her eyes, and the twitch in her lips revealed her humor matched his.

"Let me show you where we've got to in the master bath."

They made their way almost through the house to a bedroom overlooking the water that could fit his apartment. The room had direct access to a deck, complete with a hot tub. Entering the primary bath, Trace snorted in amazement.

"When did bathrooms start needing so much electrical

work?" Hannah shook her head. Her eyes were wide with wonder. Trace figured his were too.

HANNAH WAS USED to working primarily by herself, but this was a big job. If she had to stop every time a wire had to be pulled from the attic, with access across the house in the laundry room, she'd never get done. Fortunately, working alongside Trace was becoming less distracting as they found a rhythm to the tasks.

Covered in sawdust, insulation, and grime, Trace came back to the bath where she was installing light fixtures.

"If I didn't know better, I'd think you'd aged twenty years this morning." Hannah grinned.

Trace looked down at his arms and clothing, every inch of him covered in grayish dirt. He laughed as he picked lint out of his beard. "I hope nobody mistakes me for a dust bunny and decides to throw me out."

"I think you'll be okay." She checked her phone for the time. "This would be a good place to stop for lunch. Did you bring something?"

Trace nodded. "Grandma outfitted me with enough to feed three."

"Well, growing boy and all that." She was relaxing around him. He'd been kind, professional, and agreeable, which troubled her a little but not enough to staunch the feeling of normalcy and good humor filling her as the day wore on.

He excused himself to wash up at the one working sink in the house and came back quickly, interrupting her train of thought before she could talk herself out of her good mood.

"If we're not careful, I'll start growing the wrong way," Trace said as he pulled out a Thermos, a Tupperware container, and a plastic bag of cookies. He opened the Thermos and sniffed. The aroma and the steam rising from the contents triggered her stomach growling.

"Vegetable beef is my favorite."

"Mine too." He peeked into the plastic container. "As I suspected. Cornbread."

"Wow." Hannah took out her sandwich and chips. "Could your grandma talk to my mom?"

Trace chuckled, and she sent a small smile his way. "Of course, it's pretty sad that my mom still fixes my lunches."

"I have a feeling she'll be the one missing the opportunity once you move out." Trace tucked in, devouring his lunch and finishing it in what had to be record time. His face reddened when he scraped the bottom of the container. "Sorry, I could have shared. Next time Grandma sends soup, I'll get her to send extra. Nobody should miss this."

She grinned, nibbling on her ham-and-cheese sandwich. "You need more calories than me, so don't apologize." She held up her baggie that still held half her sandwich. "I don't think Mom has let it truly sink in that I've bought a house."

He wanted to say something else. She sensed it, sure it went something like this:

1. A single woman, such as herself, shouldn't be living down a lonely country lane in a house surrounded by woods and farmland.

2. She needed protection.

3. She might get scared.

Well, of course, she'd get scared. Everybody got scared at some point. It was scary just thinking about paying for a house. Her shoulders and head began to ache, and she realized she was stiffening up.

And Trace hadn't said a word to cause it.

Not this time.

Taking a deep breath, Hannah wadded up her paper napkin and stuffed it into the insulated bag she'd brought.

"Cookie?" He surprised her when he held out the bag of cookies toward her.

"Yes, please."

She bit into the tender, bakery-worthy-or-better chocolate chip cookie. "Mmm. These are the best."

He nodded, studying the cookie in his hands as if he were trying to dissect it into its smallest particles. "Still feel good about it?"

"The cookie?"

"The house."

Did she regret it? No. Not at all.

Maybe she'd rushed into it, but she didn't exactly see God standing there with a sign of the print variety saying, "Beware of purchase."

The mental image of the Sunday School picture of Jesus— robe, sandals, and all—holding one of those twirly signs on the street for the rental TV places made her laugh.

Trace smiled at her with an odd expression. Probably just as well he know she's crazy because nothing was going to happen here, folks.

"Sorry. Just had a mental image pop up that tickled me."

His arched brow and grin made her almost want to share, but that would be getting personal, and personal was the last thing she wanted to deal with right now.

Gathering her lunch things, she finished her bottle of water with one long gulp and walked out the door to the truck. She didn't want to see a tender smile on his face.

What was she thinking? It was all in her head, anyway.

EXCEPT FOR THE hour or so he helped Charlie and Nate tear out and reinstall the offending portion of the hardwoods in the great room, Trace was at Hannah's side, fetching, carrying, climbing, and anything else she, as lead electrician, asked him to do.

He was tired, and he was glad nobody suggested carpooling from Clementville to Eddyville. Introverted as he was, he needed the alone time. It didn't stop him from glancing in the rear-view mirror occasionally to note Hannah still on the road behind him.

After Nick's correction, the two carpenters weren't as loquacious as the last time he worked with them. He didn't mind so much for himself. He could ignore people who talked incessantly, but when they gave Hannah a hard time? He wouldn't ignore that.

It was difficult enough for a woman as young as her to keep her bearings in what some would call "a man's world." It didn't help that she could pass for eighteen.

Between his mama, his sister, and his grandma, he'd been schooled early on that there was no such thing as a "man's world" or a "woman's world."

Skirting around Marion, he found himself on Highway 91 before he realized it. He was getting comfortable with his surroundings.

The text he'd found when he got to the truck kept running back and forth in his mind. Eli was coming. Next week.

Trace might be the oldest, but Eli was the one in charge, pretty much anywhere he was. Trace had only had one dust-up with Eli serious enough that they didn't talk about it. Ever.

Did Eli even know the effect he'd had on Trace that day?

Probably not.

Sometimes, for such a smart guy, Eli was clueless when it came to empathy.

Taking in the bare trees of the forest on either side of the highway, he smiled when he noticed there were still bits of green in the underbrush. It would take a hard, long freeze to kill out everything. Between the winter wheat cover crops and the random green that never quite died out, he'd forgotten how alive it was here.

Alive. It made him think about the important things. Family. Nature. Mankind. But mostly? It made him think about God.

Be still.

That's how it felt when he was alone. He was being still, and God, directly and indirectly through His Word and Trace's grandparents, had tugged him closer than he'd been in a long time.

Was he getting soft?

No. Maybe he was growing up. He'd always been the "old man" of the family, an easy target. Now Trace realized he had to stop thinking he was in control and let God take the lead.

Lifting his eyes to the mirror again, he was pulled out of his thoughts when he saw Hannah turn into a lane he hadn't even noticed. Was her house down there?

The feeling in the pit of his stomach wasn't something he could put his finger on. Something didn't sit right with him, her going down a lonely drive to an empty house.

But what choice did he have? He hadn't been invited, so to show up unannounced would irritate her. He knew it to his core. And yet, would he be able to rest, not knowing if she'd made it back to her parents' house that afternoon?

He could think about it all the way to Clementville. Instead, he found a wide spot in the road and did a U-turn, heading back to the spot where he'd last seen Hannah.

Chapter 12

Hannah proceeded up the drive to her house.

Her. House.

Just thinking it sent a little shiver up her spine and made her want to bounce in her seat like a five-year-old waiting in line for Santa. She was waiting in line, but not for Santa. She was waiting in line for the rest of her life to begin.

It wasn't dark yet. They'd knocked off work about three, so it was a great time to stop by and start making plans.

Should she call Mom? Let her know she would be there around five?

No, Hannah. She wasn't expecting you until then, anyway.

She shook her head emphatically, making a decision then and there that she would not act like she was a kid moving out on her own for the first time.

Hmm. But I am.

Grabbing her purse and carefully selecting the key, she went to her front door. The one on her house.

The house that belongs to me.

Satisfaction filled her being as she stepped up on the porch.

Granted, there had been a lot of sadness take place in this house, which was why Becca decided to sell it. To get away from the sadness and start over.

It was a house, not a living thing.

Setting her purse on the floor next to the front door, she surveyed her new domicile with fresh eyes. It was the first time she'd come in alone. She was surprised when a laugh burst from herself and clapped a hand over her mouth as if someone might hear her.

Hannah stood in the middle of the living room, held out her arms with her face lifted to the ceiling, and twirled in a happy dance. She was a little girl again, twirling around the room in her Sunday-best dress with the fluffy skirt. She'd never forget that dress. PIt was pink gingham with a white eyelet pinafore apron that was useless for anything but adding to the ruffled layers that stood at attention when she spun in circles.

Only three words came to her, and they almost made her cry, but not with sadness.

Thank you, God.

She said the words several times, only stopping mid-twirl when she heard a knock on the door.

Wiping the tears from her face, she turned to see through the sidelight the man she'd been with all day. She opened the door and stood there, staring. "What are you doing here?" She didn't want to be mean, but she hadn't asked him to come, after all.

Trace stuffed his hands in his pockets and shrugged. "I saw you go off the road and wanted to make sure you hadn't had car trouble."

She grabbed the cell phone out of her back pocket and held it up. "There's this thing called a cell phone." She wasn't angry, exactly. More like highly perturbed.

He shrugged again, this time with eyebrows raised in the

"What was I thinking" expression. For a guy who didn't talk much, his face gave him away almost constantly.

"I didn't mean to intrude."

Had she hurt his feelings? Her people-pleasing perfectionist tendencies on high alert, she took a deep breath. As much as he irritated her, there was no need to be mean. "You're not intruding."

Well, kinda, but ...

His lips twisted in a smile beneath his twitching mustache. "Oh, I am."

How is it he knows what I'm thinking? Here we go. Now is when he's going to remind me how "dangerous" it is for a single woman to live out in the boonies ...

Pausing, his eyes bored into hers. "I have no intention of questioning your decision to move out here."

He got it. He did. Hannah felt her shoulders relax—mostly.

"I appreciate that."

Trace glanced appreciatively around the living room. "This is a nice place."

Smiling back, she let her excitement loose. "Thanks. I can't wait to get in it."

"Give me a tour?"

Nodding, she beckoned him to follow her. "As you can see, this is the living room and beyond that, the dining room. The bedrooms and bathroom are through the doorway, there."

He peeked around the corner at the bathroom.

It was a total gut, and she knew it. "I want to use an old dresser and refurbish it for a vanity. I just don't have any idea how long a project like that will take."

"Depends on the piece of furniture you use."

"Oh, I've got a small dresser in my parents' storage building I'd love to use if it's viable."

They crossed the threshold into the large, family-sized dining room.

"A big table will fit in here."

The thrill of ownership fizzed in her veins. "I know. I've got my eye on one that was my grandmother's. Mom didn't think it was stylish enough for her house." She shook her head and raised her eyes to the ceiling.

"You like antiques?"

"Mainly if they have memories attached to them. That dining table was where I spent the first twenty major holidays. I've still got the six-inch-thick dictionary I used to sit on before I was tall enough to reach the table."

"That's cool." He nodded. Was he envisioning the room? "There are a few pieces in the barn at Grandma and Grandpa's I would love to get my hands on. Some of them need repairs, but I figure that's good practice."

"Do you do woodworking?"

"A little. I'm picking Grandpa Reno's brain every chance I get."

So, he wasn't just a brain.

She nodded. "I'd like to learn more about woodworking. For now, I'm pretty good at staining and refinishing, but I haven't tried to refurbish a serious piece of furniture."

His lips went up in a half-smile. "I'm sure Grandpa would be glad to show you around the shop."

Her eyes met his and held. Maybe there was more to him than she thought.

"That would be nice. Dad's done some woodworking too. He's making my niece a doll bed for Christmas. Right now, I don't have time for a project. I'm too busy trying to figure out where everything goes."

He nodded, then pointed to a doorway. "Kitchen?"

She chuckled. "'Fraid so. That will be my biggest project.." She stood next to the doorway and then walked in behind him.

The whistle that came from his lips made hers tilt up.

"Exactly how I reacted the first time I saw it."

"It's got possibilities."

"Yeah, for a gut job." She laughed. "First thing will be to widen this doorway."

"Maybe take the wall out completely."

"Maybe. I'm in the floor plan stage now. I need to get Nick or Del up in the attic to see where the load-bearing walls are."

He turned back to her after studying the layout. "What do you see?"

Not "What do you want to do?" or "How much is that gonna cost?" He asked what she saw, which tickled her, for some reason. He wanted to know her vision for her home.

She hesitated, staring into the room, trying to see it with new eyes. "The first thing I'd do is take out the little window over the sink and replace it with three."

"Three windows?" He nodded, thoughtful.

"Um-hum. Three. I want as much light as possible in the kitchen. It's on the South side, and will get the most daylight." Was he going to mention how much storage she would lose?

"I like it." His grin surprised her. "Hey, I'd rather have sun than storage, personally. If I don't get enough sunlight, I'm even grumpier than usual."

So, he knew his reputation. She laughed. "Me too."

"I thought you were Miss Sunshine and Roses? At least that's what I hear." His sidelong glance had heat creeping through her cheeks.

"Winter is hard. Usually, I am, but lately ..."

"Say no more. I get it."

He really does.

Hannah chewed her lip a little, then gathered her thoughts.

"Beyond that, I'm still working on the floor plan and gathering samples."

"Do you plan to live here during the renovation?"

"Since I plan to do a lot of it myself, yes."

"Wow."

Was that a negative "wow," or a positive "wow?"

"You don't think it's a good idea?" Her ire was beginning to rise—which irritated her even more.

"I think you will decide what's best for you."

Tension reduced, she pulled her shoulders down from the region of her ears.

"I figure since the rest of the house doesn't need much, I'll be okay. The bathroom is usable, and I can always fix up a temporary range hookup on the back porch."

"Good idea."

They walked toward the door leading out on the enclosed back porch. The backyard was her favorite spot. The cabin across the way wasn't useful for much, but it was picturesque. She'd enjoy landscaping around it.

"What's the structure back there?"

Hannah grinned at his line of thought—the same as hers. "It's a cabin. I don't know how old it is, but there's electricity to it. It would make a great workshop."

"What about renting it out? It might be a nice extra income for you."

She hadn't considered it. It wasn't a bad idea, but did she want someone in her backyard all the time? On the other hand, if she rented it out to pay for the renovations ...

"That's something to think about." She checked the darkening skies outside, realizing it was getting late. "It'll be dark soon, and then Mom *will* worry."

"Right. I'll follow you out."

Does he think I need him to protect me? He can just get that thought right out of his red-headed brain.

IT HAD BEEN a quiet week working with Hannah.

Things had been going well on Monday until he made the mistake of offering to follow her out of her remote driveway. Trace could tell the suggestion stuck in her craw. He had to remember not to make inane suggestions, even if he thought they were good ones.

Starting Tuesday morning, she was back in her shell, giving him orders, and he was keeping his mouth shut unless he needed to ask her something. He could do this as long as she could, as he was well-versed in blocking people out, anyway.

It was strange. Usually, he would be glad to give someone the cold shoulder, but with Hannah? It was hard. For the first time in his life, he found it difficult to stay out of her way.

Trace pulled up to Grandma and Grandpa Reno's house on Friday afternoon, eagerly anticipating a couple of days off. This manual labor thing was more of a strain than he'd ever realized. He'd worked on the farm with his dad and Eli when he was a teenager, but all through college he'd had internships with various plants in the Louisville area, working under an Electrical Engineer.

He'd grown soft. And then there was Hannah. Maybe if he wasn't so tense ...

Aaaand Eli's here.

He put the truck in gear and sat there for a few seconds. Was there any way he could keep Hannah from meeting Eli? If she did ...

The front screen door slapped shut, and Eli came out on the porch and leaned on the post. A brief flash from the show,

Everybody Loves Raymond came to mind. Trace knew he didn't have a starring role.

Getting out of the truck, he put a smile on his face and gathered his lunch bag and phone. "Hey, brother. Good trip?"

Eli smiled. *Why'd he have to have such a great smile?*

"Yeah. Coming through Evansville, I missed all the road work on I-65."

"That's my preferred route too. Seen Mom and Dad?"

"Stopped by there first. Mom was in the middle of painting the second guest room, so I got the hint and came on over here before she put me to work." He snorted. "Grandma was glad to see me, anyway."

"Aw, Mom was too. She's just a little overwhelmed. New house, new location, trying to get her business going in about as small a market as there is."

"I know. I just like to give her a hard time. My boss shut down the construction site until after New Year's, with the snow predicted to keep coming."

"So, at loose ends?" Trace could read Eli like a book.

"Yeah. I talked to Uncle Steve, and he suggested Nick hire me on till Christmas." He shrugged. "I need some time to figure out what I want to do."

No. No. No. No. You can't move here.

Not nice. This was his brother, after all. He'd lost his girlfriend.

Trace got to the porch and hugged his sibling. "Good to see you, Eli."

"You too." Eli looked a little choked up. "What's the latest?"

"Worked all week for RenoVations, laborer. I've got my application in at nearly every plant in the area. I'm kind of hoping for the GE plant in Madisonville."

Eli nodded. "That would be great. Aircraft engines?"

"Yep. It would be a pretty good fit after what I'd been doing."

"Grandma's killed the fatted calf."

"With mashed potatoes and rolls?" Trace chuckled.

Grandpa's voice carried through the screen door. "Get in here, boys. We're not heating all of Crittenden County."

"We've got our orders." Trace draped an arm around Eli's shoulders. "I'm glad you're here." And he meant it.

"Mainly because you're not the only one having to climb up into the attic for the rest of the outside Christmas decorations." Eli slapped his brother on the back. "When I got here, I noticed Grandma's started an extensive 'honey-do' list for us."

Trace groaned. "I had a feeling. I saw her scribbling on a notepad and swiping it off the counter when I came in the kitchen this morning."

"Gotta pay for our room and board."

Pulling on the screen door, he ushered Eli in ahead of him. "And I'm so hungry I would sell my birthright for that roast beef I'm smelling."

Chapter 13

Sunday, December 15

Mandy invited Trace and Eli to her Sunday School class—the "singles" class. Last week Trace had begged off and just shown up for the worship service. She'd put the kibosh on that idea.

"You don't exactly have the excuse of not knowing anybody," she'd said.

And Hannah will be there.

Following the directions to the classroom, he entered a half-full room. He knew about a third of the attendees—mostly those related to him and a few who worked for RenoVations Inc.

Mandy, seated next to her boyfriend, Clay, waved across the room, gesturing for them to sit by her.

Trace caught a glimpse of Eli, who had that fresh, bright smile on his face.

Of course, he did.

It always did a good job of making Trace just a little grumpier, especially when he saw Hannah sitting nearby.

Would she give him the cold shoulder at church, or was that just a work thing?

"Hey guys, glad you could make it. Is Sam coming down next weekend?" Mandy, the youngest of the Reno cousins, was also the most social and seemed to love everyone in her sphere equally. She gave them each a hug before they could sit.

Trace nodded. "Friday's her last day of school, and she said she was driving down Saturday."

"Yay!" Mandy clapped her hands quietly. "I think you've met everybody, Trace. But Eli, I want you to meet some of my friends." She sat, pointing to the circle of people around her. "These are my best friends, Caryn and Hannah, this is Caryn's beau, Ben. Of course, you know Clay." She smiled extra-brightly at him. "We're celebrating the Twelve Days of Mandy again this year." She pointed out the necklace she wore, with two doves delicately hanging from a silver chain. "It matches the bracelet he got me last year."

Poor Clay was turning all kinds of red but didn't seem to mind too much.

"Silly me. Of course, you know Hannah, Trace."

Hannah didn't say a word, just gave him a perfunctory smile and turned back to her conversation with the person behind her. Avoiding him.

Mandy kept talking, in explanation for Eli's sake, although unnecessary, in Trace's opinion. "Trace sat next to Hannah at Del and Darcy's wedding reception, and now they work together. Isn't that great?"

Trace cleared his throat and snuck a glance at Hannah, whose face was almost as red as Clay's. She seemed to enjoy the attention even less than him.

The teacher chose that moment to wave to get everyone's attention. "Good morning, campers. Looks like we've got more Renos here. Care to introduce our visitors, Mandy?"

"Sure. Everybody, this is Trace and Eli, my cousins. They're twins."

Oh, yeah, tell people that. It always seemed to instigate comments and questions about twins others knew or were related to, how much Trace and Eli didn't resemble one another, or an opinion on whether or not twin telepathy was a thing.

Trace certainly hoped not, or he'd be in all kinds of trouble. Before he knew it, Eli had somehow inserted himself between Mandy and Hannah, leaving Trace to sit on the end of the row, next to Clay.

He had to figure out how to keep Hannah from falling for his brother. The thought had crossed his mind at different times of their lives, but now? Now it was on.

WAS IT RAINING RENOS, or what?

Hannah was surprised when Eli wanted to sit by her and was a little perturbed at the attention. As if one Reno—Trace—wasn't enough, now there were two of them. Twins.

And from all appearances, about as different as daylight and dark.

She should have been listening to the lesson, based in Genesis—all about God's promise to make Abram a mighty nation and about how Abram and Sarai weren't convinced when things didn't happen as quickly as Abram and Sarai thought they should,

Her Bible was open in her lap. Instead of meditating on the Word, she was doing a mental comparison of the Reno brothers, Trace and Eli. Why, she didn't know.

Daylight—Eli. Dark—Trace. And yet, Eli had dark hair, and Trace's was ginger—light. Pleasant disposition—Eli. Grumpy?

Trace, hands down. Although he'd been pretty nice to her all week when she had tried her best to freeze him out.

Not that she was interested in either Reno brother. There were more guys out there than those in her little Sunday School class, even if none of them had crossed her path lately. And beyond that, why did she care? She'd embraced her singleness and decided to focus her energies on her new house and building a life for herself, apart from her parents.

She took a deep breath and nodded her head decisively. When she glanced up, she caught Trace watching her from the other side of Mandy and Clay, an amused expression on his face. That's when she knew—he could tell what she was thinking. Not good. Not good at all.

Could she not get away from this man?

Okay, Hannah. Time to listen. You'll never hear God speak if you don't get quiet and focused.

Another deep breath, and she determined to get her act together, not shifting her eyes anywhere but straight at the teacher.

"What chapter?" Eli whispered to her.

"Thirteen." She whispered back.

"Thanks."

"You're welcome."

Hannah ground her teeth. Trace wouldn't interrupt a Bible study to get directions.

After a lesson on Abram and the consequences of taking on a problem without the Lord's guidance, the message was on waiting for God.

Exodus 14:14, to be exact.

The LORD will fight for you: you need only to be still.

It was almost irritating.

Heading home for a quiet afternoon of lunch and a nap on

probably the last "free" Sunday she had before Christmas, Hannah wanted to tell God what she thought, but that wouldn't be in the spirit of the message thematic scripture, would it?

Hadn't she always been the "good girl," the one with all the Sunday School answers? She'd come in first at the Bible Drill competition. Spent her summers doing mission trips instead of hanging out at the pool in Marion. She only dated guys she knew could be trusted.

Okay, except for the one time, in community college, but did that count?

Ugh. Yes.

The one guy she thought was different, Blaine Peters, absolutely was *not* someone she could trust. By outward appearances, he was top-notch. Met him at the campus ministry center handing out invitations to the regular weekly service. He was, she thought, the poster child for "good guy." Come to find out, he was dating another girl Hannah knew nominally, at the same time he was dating her, and getting more from that relationship than Hannah could fathom giving. When she didn't "comply" with what Blaine expected from a relationship, and he pushed the issue just far enough to scare her to death, she cut him loose.

She'd never met anyone like him. People-pleaser at heart, when she didn't meet his expectations, blame ate at her, and he egged her on. It was a hard lesson to learn about being an adult.

Even then, knowing she had God on her side, living inside of her, the internal dialog was strong. She kept telling herself if she couldn't handle Blaine, who'd had her fooled into thinking he was an actual, bona-fide "good guy," how could she trust anyone else? How could a truly good man trust *her* if she could choose so poorly? It was obvious she had no discernment when it came to men, so she kept her distance and wondered why she didn't have a relationship.

Where was the verse about God fighting for her, then?

Uh, Hannah, it was in Exodus 14:14, the same as it is now.

So, the idea was to be still. Another translation read, "You must be quiet."

Sure, being *physically* still was one thing, but to stop the words from coming out of her mouth or into her thoughts? That was another.

And, why did Trace Reno, who she did *not* find appealing—really—seem to come to mind every time she remembered she'd sworn off dating and planned to be a happy spinster the rest for of her life?

Okay, God. I'll be quiet now.

FOR TRACE AND ELI, a pretty December Sunday afternoon meant finishing up the outside illumination on the elder Reno home. Grandma's honey-do list for her grandsons, instead of her husband, was specific.

All the family would be together this year, so Grandma wanted to pull out all the stops. After all, who knew when there might be a Christmas when she wasn't able to host the Reno holiday?

"Where is Nick putting you this week?" Trace was up on the ladder, untangling the big multi-color lights he remembered from his childhood. Finding bulbs wasn't easy, but it could be done.

"Eddyville project. You?" Eli was wrestling a sleigh and reindeer across the yard to put in the usual spot in front of the porch.

"Same. We're still working on some electrical."

"So, Hannah will be there?" Eli arched a brow when Trace glanced down.

Great.

"Yeah. Hey, don't forget the spotlight for the manger scene."

"Is this a remodel or new construction?"

"Remodel. It's quite a transformation. It'll be like a new house when it's finished. Are you going to work with Charlie and Nate?"

Please, let him have to deal with those two yay-hoos.

"Nah. Since I'm with the Carpenter's Union, I get to play with the grownups." Eli laughed.

"Must be nice." Of course, Eli got preferential treatment. He was Eli, after all.

"It is. I'll trade you, though. You do carpentry, and I'll work with Hannah."

"Heartbroken over Carrie, aren't you?" Trace let the sarcasm shine through. Did anything faze his brother?

Eli shrugged. "No use crying over spilled milk."

The front screen door creaked as Grandpa stepped out on the porch to check their project. "How's it going?"

"Good."

"Got a question for you boys." Grandpa was out without a jacket in the 65-degree weather.

"Shoot." Eli stopped what he was doing and looked up at him.

"What happens if you eat Christmas decorations?"

Trace felt a groan coming on. "I don't know, what?"

"You get tinsel-itis." After a pause, Grandpa's laugh rang across the yard.

"Hey, Grandpa, what do you call an old snowman?" Trace wasn't usually the jokester, but he'd been hanging out with Grandpa a lot.

Grandpa chuckled. "No idea."

"Water."

"Pretty good." Grandpa nodded his approval. "Maybe by the time you have kids, you'll appreciate what they're calling 'dad jokes' now. We used to just call 'em jokes."

"Maybe." Probably wouldn't happen. After the sermon yesterday, he'd made a new resolution: When it came to Hannah, he was going to let the Lord fight for him—and he'd be still.

If it's meant to be …

"Grandma wanted me to tell you she's got pie in the kitchen when you get ready for some."

Trace immediately came down the ladder, and Eli dropped what he was doing and stood.

"And it looks like I caught you right at breaktime." Grandpa shook his head, chuckling and turned to go back in the house.

HOVERING OVER THEM, as usual, Grandma refilled their coffee cups from the fresh pot she'd made while the pie was baking.

"Grandma, this may be the best I've ever eaten." Eli closed his eyes and rubbed his belly.

"I second that." Trace looked up at her and grinned.

She seemed pleased. "An exaggeration, but I'll take the compliment. You know, Mandy learned how to make a good piecrust last winter when she was with us."

"You don't want us to learn pastry skills, do you, Grandma?" Eli's nervous question was dismissed by the mischievous glint in his eyes.

"Wouldn't hurt you any, but no, I'd just as soon you two tag after your grandpa. I'll stick to the spoiling." She winked as she took their plates and put them in the dishwasher. "You've worked hard this afternoon, and I appreciate it."

"It's nice out, so I'm glad to do it today. Makes me wish for spring, and it's not even officially winter, yet." Trace took the list Grandma made and studied it. He could cross off hanging lights—almost. It wouldn't take more than a half hour to finish.

What was this? *Young People Party.*

Grandma, what are you up to?

"Care to tell us about this one?" Trace held up the list.

"I didn't tell you?"

"Tell me what?"

Her grin was sheepish. "I thought it might be fun to host the young adult Sunday School class."

"Um-hum." Trace narrowed his eyes at her, shaking his head in disbelief when her lips twisted in a smile.

Eli was oblivious. "Sounds like fun. Everybody seemed pretty great in the class this morning."

"Was this Mandy's idea?" Trace had a feeling.

"She may have mentioned it, but I thought it sounded like fun. It's a good bunch of kids." She put her hands on her hips and faced her grandsons. "I haven't said anything to Robbie yet, so if you think it's a bad idea, we can forget it."

"I didn't say it was a bad idea. I just don't want you to overdo it." Trace got up from the table and kissed his grandmother on the cheek. "We're here to help out, not to aid and abet."

Grandma swatted his chest and slipped her other arm around his waist. "And I love you for it. I've been promised by Mandy that she and Caryn can do the cooking. They mentioned getting Hannah in on it, as well."

Trace's attention was snagged. Would having Hannah there, where he was living, be awkward?

Maybe for her. For him, it would be another opportunity to see just how nice he could be without raising suspicion that he was interested in her in a romantic sort of way.

"I haven't had Mandy's cooking in a while. I hope it's improved since her mac-n-cheese phase." Eli's forehead crinkled. "Not that I don't appreciate a good mac-n-cheese ..."

"She's improved. I think she may be cooking for Clay Lacey some." Grandma's eyebrows went up conspiratorially. "I wonder if she'll get a ring this Christmas?"

And, as usual, the conversation went back to coupling, pairing, matchmaking. Why was the idea of marrying people off a major topic in a family of grown children and grandchildren?

Ah, that was it. Grandchildren. Trace decided to be non-committal, although if the affection between Clay and Mandy in Sunday School was any indication, they might show up for Christmas married instead of engaged. "I just don't know."

"Well, Clay isn't getting any younger." Her point was not lost on her grandsons, who avoided her gaze.

Chapter 14

December 16

If Trace didn't know any better, he'd think someone had been pilfering his truck. Monday morning, after a Sunday with temps in the sixties, dawned cold and frosty. A front had come through, leaving every vestige of what he'd hoped would be a mild winter behind.

"I don't have time to go to town, get a battery, come back and put it on, then head to Eddyville." Trace was grousing as much to himself as to anyone within earshot.

"Why don't we ride together?" Eli took one last swig of coffee and set his cup on the counter. "I'm not sure exactly where the place is. You know how those roads are around there. The curves have curves."

If it had been a week ago, Trace would have called Hannah to see if she could pick him up. No ulterior motive, just a good chance to spend time with her.

That was before Eli came and threatened to sabotage his plan. His plan to kill Hannah with kindness. It would be difficult, if not impossible, to carry it out with Eli around all day on the finishing crew.

Trace relented. "Sounds good. Let me pull the battery and put it in your truck, and then I can swap it out as we're going through town. I don't like being without my wheels." He picked up his lunch and headed for the door.

"I'll be outside."

He grabbed his tools and popped the hood of the truck. When he tested the battery, sure enough, it was dead. He'd have it tested again at the shop.

Had Hannah done any demo this weekend? She'd mentioned her dad was going to help her. Trace wanted to offer but felt funny. After seeing the place, he admired her vision. If only it weren't so remote.

He'd agreed to let it go, and he would. As much as possible.

Wiping the mess off his hands with a wipe designed for use with automotive grease, he was ready to climb into Eli's truck when he came out with his lunch bag.

"I wasn't counting on Grandma fixing lunches." Eli grinned as he swung into the driver's seat.

"She's a regular one-stop-shop for taking care of her grandkids."

"No joke. She asked me if we'd have access to a microwave, and I told her I didn't know, so she warmed up some apple pie and put it in an insulated dish." Eli shook his head as he put the truck in reverse. "Where do people come up with every little thing that could possibly be used in a kitchen?"

"People who are smarter than us, probably." Trace snorted. "Don't forget I need to stop at the corner to leave the battery."

"Got it."

They rode in silence for a while. It wasn't like Eli to be quiet this long, although Trace was enjoying the time to think.

"I'm thinking about asking Hannah out."

And there it was. Eli gunning for the very girl Trace was interested in. It never failed. On the other hand, Hannah was trying very hard to push him away. Shouldn't he take that as a signal to back off?

"Okay."

"You've known her longer than me. She seems nice."

"She is nice." Trace wanted to come up with something, anything, to get Eli's attention from Hannah. What to say about her? "She's pretty independent. She's bought a house and is renovating it."

"Wow. That's cool. How old is she?"

"Mandy's age."

"Huh." Eli grinned over at his brother, his eyes sparkling a little. "She might be too smart for me."

Trace came very close to telling him she was definitely too smart for him, but that was yet to be seen. What if she did go out with Eli? Should he write her off, then? He took satisfaction in having a plan—preferably with a checklist of what could happen in any given situation. It came from years of working in an industry with strict rules and codes. One of the reasons he liked working with wood was that to do it well, the craftsman must be precise.

He must have paused too long because the next thing Eli said was, "Do you really think she is?"

Was Eli's confidence shaken?

That's new.

"Ask her out. See what she says." Trace shrugged.

And then he did something he knew drove Eli crazy. He clammed up. Not in an "I'm mad, and I'm not talking" attitude but in a "You're a grownup, figure it out" way.

Okay, God, I'm just going to be quiet …

WORKING on the job site with both Trace and Eli was different, but they were the least of Hannah's worries right now. She wanted, so badly, to move into her house.

"Trace tells me you've bought a house." Eli was quite the conversationalist at lunch, while Trace had hardly anything to say. Up to now, Hannah had tried to push him away, and he must have finally gotten it.

"I have. My dad and I ripped out the kitchen over the weekend." She took a bite of her chicken salad sandwich. Mom did make the best.

Glancing over at Trace, she saw a spark of interest in his eyes. When she gave him the "grand tour" of her little house a week ago, he'd been very interested in her vision for the place.

"I ordered the cabinets the day after I closed on the house, and they should be ready by the end of the week."

"That's a quick turnaround." Eli's brows raised, which made her smile.

"When you order Amish-made cabinets locally, you get good service. I went to pick out door and drawer pulls, and he had most of the boxes done already." Hannah loved telling outsiders about the efficiency of their Amish cabinetmakers. It was always a surprise.

"Do they even use electricity?" Eli pulled a napkin from his bag and wiped some mayo off his hands. "I mean, it's kinda their thing, isn't it?"

"Not exactly." She was thoughtful. "The Amish—at least the ones around here—don't have electricity from the grid. They have generators. So, yeah, they use power tools."

Eli nodded.

She couldn't stop herself from glancing at Trace, sitting on the five-gallon bucket on the other side of Eli.

Studiously indifferent. The phrase popped into her mind, and stuck. She stopped and waited, and, sure enough, he glanced her way and met her eyes. A slight grin crossed his lips, inspiring an immediate, similar response on hers. What was she doing? When the realization hit her, it must have shown on her face because the gentle smile he'd had disappeared, and a flash of disappointment crossed his features.

And then, it was gone, and 'studiously indifferent' came back into play.

Men.

"Hey, Trace, when you learn everything Grandpa knows, maybe you could open your own cabinet-making shop." Eli laughed, finishing the cookie Grandma had placed in his bag. "I tell you what, I'll miss Grandma's lunches when I leave."

"*If* you leave."

He speaks.

'If you leave,' spoken to Eli with what she thought a pointed statement, was three of approximately ten words Trace had said all day. His typical response when she'd given instructions was a curt nod, and he was off to complete the task. Hannah hated to admit it, but he was catching on quickly. If he weren't looking for a job in his engineering field, it wouldn't take him long to pass the electrician exam.

"Yeah. I haven't decided." Eli leaned forward, elbows on his knees and hands clasped in front of him. "Not much for me back home. Mom and Dad are down here, and I no longer have a girlfriend to stay for."

"I'm sorry. Is it a recent thing?" Hannah sympathized but didn't exactly feel pity for him.

"Thanksgiving."

"That's about as recent as it gets." Hannah shook her head.

"Yeah." For once, Eli was quiet.

"Ready to hit it?" Trace spoke again. He'd been so obviously taciturn all day that it was, once again, a surprise to hear his voice.

Hannah cleaned up her lunch containers and stood, brushing her hands to get the crumbs off. "I'm ready."

As she said it, the front door closed, and in came Nick. "Hey guys, how's it going?"

Hannah spoke up. "Good. I'm down to installing outlets and the vent fans in the master and the same in the guest bath."

"Good." Nick nodded approval. "Because I need to pull Trace to help out on another project. I'm putting a safe room in the basement of the café. After the trouble we've all had surrounding the tunnels, Del wanted his family to be safe."

"What's up?"

The relief on Trace's face irritated her. Was he so happy to get away from her?

"I need you to run cleanup with Charlie and Nate, finish up some minor carpentry, then later we'll come in with the finish crew. I've got the security system crew coming to scope it out, so I want the framing done before they come." Nick looked over at Hannah. "Can you spare your assistant for the rest of the week?"

"Sure. We know Charlie and Nate need all the help they can get."

"I'm working with them on their attitudes. I didn't like the last time I heard them harassing you."

A warm feeling came over her. Yes. Some men noticed. Men who cared for the women in their lives. "I appreciate it."

"Not at all."

Trace spoke up. "Anybody heading back to Clementville? I rode in with Eli."

"I am." Nick's slow smile became tender. "I need to work in

the office some, and then Lisa and I have childbirth classes in Paducah tonight."

"Aww." Hannah sighed. "That's so sweet."

"I don't know. I understand tonight is 'the video' everyone keeps talking about." A slight hint of uncertainty crossed Nick's face.

"It'll be great. I have a feeling."

Someday? Would she, someday, be in the enviable position of being obviously in love? Married, pregnant with her first child?

Not at this rate.

THE DRIVE back to Clementville was quieter than the one to Eddyville that morning with Eli. Trace liked Lisa's husband. He fit into the family well.

"Hannah says you've done a good job working with her."

Nick's statement surprised Trace. A lot.

"She said that?"

His surprise must have been evident in his question because Nick laughed out loud.

"Yes, sir, she did." Nick's eyes narrowed slightly when he turned his way briefly. "Is there something going on between you two?"

Shock jolted Trace.

"N-ooo."

The lift of his tone at the end almost made it a question.

Nick nodded. "Just wondered."

"What gave you that idea?" Was he wearing his heart on his sleeve? If so, then his feelings were all over his face today, of all days, with Eli there—and Eli was the one person who came nearest to reading him like a book.

With a lift of a shoulder, Nick paused, thoughtful. "I'm not sure. Just a feeling I get. Same vibe as Del and Darcy."

Whoa.

"Have you been talking to Grandma?" Must have been.

"Nope. Just observation."

They rode a few miles without talking, almost to Fredonia, between Eddyville and Marion, before Nick spoke again. "I could see it."

Did Nick have any idea of the impact his words had? Was there any way on earth to stop this conversation before he spilled his guts—something he'd never done with a human being in his *life*?

"How so?" Trace tried to put the grumpy back in his voice because when he even thought about Hannah, he could hear his own voice getting softer. It was disgusting.

"Can't put my finger on it, specifically. You two are just different when you're together than when you're apart."

Interesting.

"It's for sure Hannah's made it abundantly clear can't stand me."

Nick nodded. "She's projecting that, isn't she?"

"Without a doubt."

"Oh, I have doubts." Nick arched a brow and sent a half-smile to Trace as they arrived at the one stop sign in Fredonia. "I've never seen her as oppositional as I have since Thanksgiving, and I've been around her a while now."

Really ... So, maybe the sunny disposition he'd heard about is hiding down there somewhere?

"And you ..."

"What about me?" Was it wise for Trace come off as irritated when he wanted to pick Nick's brain? It was for sure he felt different.

"Ever since I got in the family, all I've heard is how grumpy you are." He grinned. "Said in a perfectly loving way, of course, by the female Reno cousins."

Trace scoffed.

"But when *Hannah* is around, you're ..."

"Off-balance?" Trace spoke before he thought.

"I hadn't thought of that, but yes."

"Great."

"Hey, I don't think many other people have picked up on it."

Was Nick trying to be supportive of his pursuit of Hannah? *Wait a minute ... pursuit?*

"I can see you two together," Nick said, all joking aside.

Trace took a deep breath and relaxed. *Exactly what I wanted, needed to hear.*

Changing the subject abruptly, Nick asked about the very thing Trace had been wrestling with ever since he met Hannah.

"What do you think about her moving to the Durbin place?"

"Not good." Trace had a hard time putting his thoughts into words. "It feels ... dangerous."

"I agree." Nick shook his head. "She wants to move in this weekend."

"She hasn't said anything about it. She said her kitchen cabinets were pretty much ready."

"Knowing Mr. Byler, they're ready." Nick laughed. "He's amazing. Always pads his finish-date by at least a week and always has the order done early."

"Not a bad trait in a cabinetmaker." Trace chuckled, both at the subject and with relief that the topic had turned away from relationships and onto work.

"Hannah's dad called me and wants me to help him get her bathroom finished this week. You game? Secret project. He doesn't want Hannah to know until Friday when her cabinets are supposed to be installed."

"I'm in. So was the safe room a ruse to get me away from the job site?"

"No. I need you at the safe room today. Tomorrow, while everyone thinks you're going to the café to work, you'll go to Hannah's house, instead."

"Perfect." Trace snorted. "If there's one thing I can do, it's keep a secret."

"I knew I picked the right man for the job," Nick said. "Her dad's finishing tearing it out today and getting the materials so he can tile tomorrow. I need a plumbing and electrical assistant."

"I'm your man." Trace thought a moment. "Did her dad say anything about the dresser she wants to use for a vanity?"

Nick tilted his head, then shook it. "No, but I remember her mentioning it. Good catch."

"I try," he said, regretting his attention. "Do you think it would be okay if I take it to Grandpa's workshop?"

"Perfect. We can stop by there on our way to Clementville and pick it up in my truck." Nick made the left turn onto Highway 91.

Trace hadn't noticed when they got into town. "Sounds good. I'll get it under wraps in Grandpa's shop." He laughed. "And then I'll start watching YouTube videos on how to transform an antique dresser into a vanity."

"Sounds like a plan. It's a nice place."

"It is. Just lonely."

Nick nodded. "I see a security system in the future for her house too."

And while we're there, I'll pick your brain about the wisdom of me renting the cabin on her property. As a safety measure, of course ...

Chapter 15

Tuesday, Dec 17

Tuesday, at lunch, Hannah couldn't contain her excitement any longer.

"I'm moving in on Saturday." She did a seated happy dance with her feet. "My cabinets are being installed Friday, and I can live with the bathroom the way it is for a while. It works."

"That's awesome." Eli held his fist up for a bump. "Need help?"

"Sure, the more the merrier. Mom and Dad, my brother-in-law, and Ben, Caryn, and Mandy have all signed on."

"I'll see if Trace is available."

She widened her eyes, then pulled herself together. Chill, Hannah. "Oh. That's okay. I'm sure he'll be exhausted if he's working with Charlie and Nate all week."

"I've heard they're a couple of chuckleheads."

"Good description."

Would Trace come and help? She had to admit, she wanted to show him her new kitchen since he'd seen it in the before stages.

The idealist in her would love to walk in the door on Friday and see a fully-appointed kitchen, along with the rest of the house being done—*but that's not happening.* Her ideal scenario would be her love meeting her at the door with a bouquet of roses and a home-cooked meal. *That's not happening, either.*

Hannah heaved a sigh, her excitement dissipating as she resigned herself to reality. The practical side of her knew she had several weeks of living in chaos ahead of her.

What was I thinking?

She tried to brighten up. "Anyway, Saturday is the big day. After that, I'll no longer be another twenty-something living with her parents."

Which is also the reason Mom keeps a tissue handy. Her nest is about to become truly empty.

"Hey, nothing like your parents moving away to reinforce the idea of not being able to move home again." He chuckled. A brief shadow crossed his face. "Not that I was living at home anyway. We've all had our own apartments since we got our first jobs. Mom wasn't real happy about it, but Dad certainly was."

"Didn't you work with your dad?"

"Oh, yeah, all of us did. Once we started working full time, he knew his free labor source had dried up." He laughed. "He wasn't exactly a tyrant—he kept us in nice clothes, cars, vacations, and a good education. Can't put a price on all that."

"I understand." She tilted her head. "Was it different with Samantha? Only having a sister, I can't fathom the dynamic of having brothers."

He paused. "Maybe? Sam didn't do farm work, but she started working with Mom at a young age—on wedding stuff."

"Oh, that's right. Your mom is a wedding planner. What's she doing since she moved?"

"Making contacts. She says she wants to semi-retire, which

is interesting since she's also trying to establish relationships with bridal salons and the other trades in the industry." He shrugged. "So far, she's only got a couple of events booked, but she doesn't seem too upset about it. She's decorating her empty nest house and loving every minute of it."

"I can imagine. That's the fun part."

"Well, speaking of the fun part, I've got crown molding to cut."

"And I have a vent fan to install." She grinned. "Don't tell Trace, but I'd kinda gotten used to not having to climb up and down the ladder every ten minutes."

DECEMBER 18

Trace ran his hand across the sanded surface of the dresser Hannah wanted to use for a vanity. Nick had brought over the marble top he'd salvaged from another job, and it fit perfectly. It wasn't level, but what is in an old house? He could cheat the distance when it was installed.

Grandpa approached the workbench. Fortunately, Trace saw him in the large mirror that hung in his sight line. It saved being startled when the woodworker was using loud equipment and someone came up behind him.

He had on his good clothes. It was church night. How had he forgotten?

"How's it coming along?"

"What do you think?" Trace stood back, watching closely as Grandpa checked the surface and the joints, shaking it a little to make sure it would be sturdy enough to hold a marble counter and a sink. It didn't budge.

"Coming along nicely." Grandpa adjusted his bifocals and nodded his approval. "Stain or paint?"

"It's Oak veneer, so I thought about just clear-coating it." Someday, Trace would have enough confidence to make a decision and stick with it, but for now, Grandpa was his go-to guy.

Grandpa nodded again, like Trace, a man of few words. "I think you're on the right track. No more than a light sanding. What about the feet?"

"The metal wheels were rusty and would have scarred the floor, so I removed them, and I'm making some bun feet to go under the legs. It'll lift it up slightly too."

"Good idea." Grandpa studied the false drawer he'd fixed to make room for the sink and pulled on the other two drawers. "This is some good work, Trace. Drawers are sturdy ..."

Trace laughed. "They oughta be—I had to rebuild both of them." He dipped his brows as he pointed out the configuration of the middle of the three drawer fronts. "To make room for the plumbing, I had Nick mock up the drain pipe and water supply so I could get it to fit without hitting it every time. I wanted her to still have as much storage as possible."

"Good thinking. I've always been a little leery of making a vanity out of a dresser. Seeing this, I can imagine it working well. This is a solid piece of furniture. That helps."

Trace nodded. "I forgot about Wednesday night church. Will Grandma be upset?"

"Don't worry about it. You've got a project going, and it's time-sensitive if you're going to surprise Hannah on Friday." Grandpa quirked a brow and studied his grandson. "What shall I say if said lady inquires?"

Like she'll ask.

"She probably won't. If she does, just tell her I'm worn out from working with Charlie and Nate." Trace winked at Grandpa and took his tack cloth to wipe down stray particles of wood from the sanded surface. "I plan to get the first coat on tonight, then come out here and put on a second coat in the morning so we can install it later tomorrow."

"Ambitious, but I think you can do it. You warm enough out here?"

"Yep. I'm working up my own heat."

"I hear you." With a lift of a hand, Grandpa slipped out the door of the workshop.

Every time Trace paused in his work, he got nervous and started second-guessing his ability to carry off the surprise. Plus, he missed Hannah. It wasn't as if they'd worked together for years or anything, but even when she was aggravated at him, he'd rather be fetching and carrying for her than doing just about anything else

Good grief, I'm going soft.

DECEMBER 20

By the time cabinet day arrived, Hannah was chomping at the bit to get to her house after work. Nick had kept her busy enough, and between work and a couple of shopping excursions with Mom and then with Mandy and Caryn, it had been a week since she'd made an appearance at what was to become her home.

Pulling up, she saw the RenoVations Inc. box truck pulled up to the kitchen door. She had to make herself calm down before she made a fool of herself in front of everybody. Nick's truck sat next to the big pine and Trace's. Trace was here? She expected him to be in town working at the café. Eli had been non-committal about whether or not Trace would help with the move on Saturday.

Hannah met Trace at the door as he came out to grab another piece of cabinetry to carry in.

The startled expression on his face annoyed her, his words even more. "You're here."

"Why wouldn't I be here? It's my house, after all."

His eyes shifted. "Sorry. I was just expecting you later."

Weird, but then Trace often did weird things.

If he's so weird, Hannah, why did you miss him every day this week? Huh?

Why wouldn't her internal voice leave her alone?

"What's left to bring in?"

"Lowers and some drawers. They installed the slow-close hardware at the shop, so all we have to do is put them in the cabinets."

Hannah wanted to hold on to her irritation with Trace, even as her insides jumped up and down. Surely she was maintaining a calm, cool, and collected demeanor. She cleared her throat and lowered her voice. "Sounds good."

Trace laughed. "Can't wait to see it, can you?"

It was obvious that her attempt at stoicism had not succeeded. She took a deep breath and then tilted her head. "My poker face isn't serving me well today, is it?"

"Poker face?" He grinned, regarding her with what could be misconstrued as tenderness.

She wasn't even going to think about deciphering Trace Reno's smile. Not now, anyway.

"I'm torn. Part of me wants to watch the installation, and the other part wants to help install it. Does that even make sense?"

"It makes perfect sense. I don't think there's room for another person in there. What's the latest on the countertop installers?"

"They're set to come this afternoon." She tried to get

beyond him, but he kept bobbing when she bobbed and weaving when she weaved. Finally, she put her hands on her hips and attempted to glare at him. "Trace. Let me into my house. Please."

Will the glare work on him? It will tell me a lot if it does …

Crossing his arms over his chest, he narrowed his eyes. "Are you sure?"

"It's been a week since I've been out here. Nick has kept me all kinds of busy. Yes, I'm sure. Now get out of my way, or I'll go through you." She intensified the glare.

He looked properly frightened. On second glance, he was fighting the urge to laugh again. She growled and shoved her way past him.

"There's the woman of the hour." Nick appeared as excited as she did. Contractor or homeowner, something about cabinet-install day made you feel like a project was really happening.

"Hey. Everything fit all right?" She chuckled when everyone just looked at her. "What am I saying? Of course, they do."

"Had to shave a little off the back of the pantry to get it in the door. That part doesn't show anyway." Mr. Byler ran his hand along the polished wood. "I think they turned out real nice." Amish craftsmen didn't often brag about their work, but there was no question. The smooth maple finish was perfect.

"I think nice is an understatement."

Hannah's phone vibrated. She turned to them, holding it up. "Here's the countertop guys from Evansville. Give me a minute."

The work crew, consisting of sons and grandsons of Mr. Byler, went about their business of installation as usual, not paying any attention to her. They had a system and weren't easily distracted.

When she came back into the room, she was amazed. Every

cabinet was in place. All she needed was the counter installed, plumbing hooked up, and then her stove, dishwasher, and refrigerator delivered.

Hannah's phone dinged. "They're on their way now."

Nick beamed. "I figured they'd get here early. When do the appliances arrive?"

"This afternoon. I was worried I'd have the countertop and appliance people here at the same time. I lucked out."

Nick shook his head, then observed the activity around him. "No luck involved. I think God's blessing you with this house."

Her cheeks warmed. Honestly, she hadn't stopped to consider her home a blessing from God. What was she thinking? Did God only care about her when it came to relationships and other internal, personal decisions?

There isn't anything more personal than where I lay my head at night. Hannah would take every ounce of blessing she could get.

"Thanks, Nick." Oh, boy. She'd be a blubbering mess before this was over. "I think I'll explore a little bit."

Trace was busy helping to install the drawers. His head jerked up when she turned to go through the doorway into the dining room and living room.

She was tempted to roll her eyes but didn't want to give him the satisfaction. Her eyes were too full to roll, anyway.

Oh, well.

She stopped when she got to the living room. Something was different.

The walls, patched and ready to be painted, hadn't changed. The floors were covered with paper so they wouldn't get paint on them before they brought in the sander to refinish them. She glanced toward the small hallway to the three bedrooms—no, two-and-a-half, because one was too small to be anything except perhaps an office or nursery—and the one bath in the house, then turned back to the living room.

That's when she knew what was different. No tub or toilet was sitting in the middle of the floor.

"TRACE? NICK? COME IN HERE, PLEASE."

Hannah's voice carried through the house even with the cordless drivers doing their job installing cabinet doors.

"Do you think she'll be mad?" Would she take their work in the spirit in which it was offered, or would she rather have the opportunity to do it herself?

"I guess we'll find out." Nick shrugged.

When they got to the bathroom door, she turned, eyes wide, tears running down her face.

Oh, boy. She's upset.

"You guys ..." She choked up, gesturing in the direction of the completely-finished, brand-new bathroom. "It's perfect."

Relief flooded Trace, leaving his knees almost weak. She wasn't upset.

Hannah started laughing and crying at the same time. "Do you have any idea how much I dreaded moving in here with that horrible bathroom?" She went in, running her hand along the tiled tub surround, and then she gawked at the sink and covered her mouth with her hand.

Trace thought it came out okay, but would Hannah see the imperfections?

"If it's not right, we can take it out, no problem."

She turned on him, eyes wide. "There is no way anyone is taking my gorgeous vanity out of this house." She turned to Nick. "Did you do this?"

Nick shook his head, then pointed to Trace, who just shrugged.

"Your dad was in on it, and he had the dresser in his shop, so we took it to Grandpa's workshop and did a little work on it."

Nick scoffed. "There was no *we* involved. The only thing I did was provide the countertop and sink from another job and hook up the plumbing. Your dad installed the tile. The vanity was all Trace."

"Thank you." She ran her hand across the antique marble, then touched the glass knobs Trace put on there to replace the mismatched wood ones that were there before. She tested the smooth glide of the two lower drawers he'd rebuilt, shaking her head in wonder. "How did you know exactly what I wanted?"

He shrugged again, no clue what to say.

"I listened, and your dad listened. We wanted it to be nice for you."

"Nice?" Hannah snorted. "This is beyond nice." She clasped her hands in front of her. "This is the best Christmas surprise I've ever had."

No pressure, Bud.

He hadn't noticed Nick's absence until he came back to the door to get Hannah. "Countertops are here."

"Is it just me, or does this day keep getting better?" Yes, there was a bounce in her step he hadn't seen before, and Trace discovered he reveled in it. In someone else, it might irritate him, but Hannah?

Every aspect of this woman drew him in further and further, and he wasn't sure how he felt about that. Falling in love with Hannah could be dangerous. For one thing, she might not be able to stand him, but the bathroom project may have scored him a few points.

Well, Lord, the ball's in Your court now.

Chapter 16

Nick left Trace at Hannah's house to help out where needed. Three deliveries and installations in one day was a lot, but the work went smoothly. Nobody was in anybody's way, and through it all, Hannah's eyes sparkled like Christmas lights.

Did she have Christmas lights?

The weather turned out to be beautiful, which was great for the deliveries and installations. Trace had gone outside to get some air—too many workers in one spot for his taste—before his claustrophobia got the better of him. It cropped up at the oddest times.

He'd made his way to the back of the house where the cabin stood. Good shape for a building that hadn't been used in years.

Must have a good roof on it.

Trying the door, he found it unlocked, so he stepped inside. It was old, obviously, but it had good light. The ancient sofa and chair were covered with dust sheets, and he saw through to the one bedroom where a bedstead, also covered in cloth, had a patchwork quilt hanging down underneath. The fireplace was stone, probably from the property, because the hearth was one large rectangle of rock. How had someone maneuvered it in there?

An idea started niggling at his brain, and he kept shooing it away. She'd never go for it. It would be presumptuous, and if he wanted to make any progress with her, he needed to keep his distance as much as he could.

What had this been used for? And how old was it, exactly?

"Hey!"

Trace started when Hannah's voice came from just behind him in the doorway. Either she was extra quiet, or his mind was occupied with other things. Such as her, for instance, which made no sense.

"Cool cabin."

"It is. I can see landscaping around it to bring it into the yard more."

"What will you do with it?"

"I've got a few ideas, but most of them would require spending money, and for now, that's a big fat no." She smiled. So, *this* was the Hannah everyone had told him about.

He found himself smiling back. "It would make a good rental."

She crossed her arms and narrowed her eyes, thinking. "It's been mentioned—by you, if I recall correctly." Her eyes sparkled.

His face scrunched into a grimace. "Pretty presumptuous of me, wasn't it?"

She held two fingers close together. "Just a smidge." She grinned. "It might be a good way to pay for some of the other renovations I'd like to do. I don't know if I want to deal with it, though."

"What would be the downside?"

"I'd always have someone coming and going on my property. That's a little disconcerting."

"There are always background checks. Rent it to someone trustworthy." Trace felt a tiny spark of hope.

"True." She gestured toward the bright windows. "It would make a great studio."

"Do you paint?"

"A little." She mumbled the words.

"I didn't catch what you said." He arched a brow at her and she frowned at him.

"I said a little."

He considered her for a moment. He'd only known her a little over two weeks, and he'd never seen her do anything badly, or halfway. If she painted, she would be good at it. "I have a feeling I'd hear differently from other people."

She shook her head. "It's been so long, my paints are probably completely dried out."

"There's this thing. I think you're familiar with it. A store? A store that sells, like, art supplies?" He laughed at the way her lips twitched as if fighting hard not to smile.

"Very funny." Shrugging, she continued. "I'll have to give it some thought."

"When is the security system being installed?"

The deep breath she took should have clued him in that he was treading on dangerous ground.

"Are you still planning to move in this weekend?"

"I'm not just planning to move, I'm *going* to move in, if I have to move every stick of furniture in by myself. If I wait until everything is perfect, it'll be after the first of the year before I move in."

"Would that be so bad?"

She stood there and glared. It was as if every bit of progress he'd made with her was crumbling in his hands. One step forward, two? Three? No, make that ten steps back.

"UGH."

Hannah had unloaded on Mandy, who was patient and kind, and who did nothing—yet, anyway—but listen.

"Who does he think he is to question whether or not I should move? I mean, really?"

Cutting in paint onto the walls and trim of the living room and primary bedroom was beginning to work its magic in calming her.

Beginning to.

Mandy kept rolling, and Hannah tried not to watch as she painted every which way, unlike Hannah's precise *W*s. The paint was getting on the wall, which was the main thing if they were moving her stuff tomorrow.

"He's just being Trace." Mandy glanced her way as if to check her mood.

"I know."

She stepped onto the ladder to cut in around the ceiling. Leaning on the top of the ladder, she rested, looking down at her friend. "Is there something wrong with me?"

Mandy turned toward her, eyebrows raised. "Wrong? Not that I know of." Then she bit her lip, hesitating.

A huge sigh escaped Hannah and she closed her eyes. "Tell me."

"Well, you've been ... um ... a little manic since fall. I guess since you decided to buy the house."

There was a part of Hannah that wanted to rear up and tell Mandy she didn't know what she was talking about. Part of her was sick to death of people thinking they could count on her to take criticism in the sweet, agreeable manner Hannah Buckner was known for.

Mandy didn't deserve to get the brunt. But then, neither did Trace. He just knew how to push her buttons.

Closing her eyes for a second, she whispered a prayer in her head. *God, grant me wisdom. And patience. And love.* "I'm sorry, Mandy."

Mandy set her roller gently on the edge of the pan and walked over to Hannah. "Time for a break."

"We don't ..."

"Yes, we do. We have time for a chocolate chip cookie break."

"I don't have ..."

"Yes, you do. I brought cookie dough, a cookie sheet, and a spatula."

"You are the best, did you know that?"

"I hear it on occasion, but it's always nice." Mandy wrinkled her nose and winked, making Hannah laugh.

"I need to wash my hands before I do anything." Hannah held out her paint-spattered hands for inspection. "Latex paint isn't harmful, but it's not very tasty, either."

"So true." Mandy pulled off the nitrile gloves she'd donned to protect her manicure.

"Smart."

"No, just don't want to have to spend money on another trip to the salon." She shrugged. "Now, go wash up, and I'll put the cookies in."

Hannah shook her head, confused.

Mandy laughed. "I preheated the oven while we were in the kitchen eating pizza."

"I still say it ..."

Mandy waved her off. "Oh, go on with you ..." When Hannah didn't respond, Mandy repeated, "I said, go on ..."

The two young women dissolved in giggles as they hugged.

"I don't know what I'd do without you and Caryn to keep me straight."

"Somebody's gotta do it." Mandy grew serious. "Hannah, really, it's going to be okay. I just have a feeling."

Hannah nodded, tears close to the surface as they'd been all day since seeing the dream for her kitchen come to life and then seeing the bathroom so expertly done. Flitting to the bathroom in question, she closed the door and turned on the water, then stood, leaning on the counter as she stared at herself in the mirror.

Chill out, Hannah. You can prove to everyone that you are mature enough to buy a house and move out on your own, but not if you go off on people who are trying to help. Even if they need to mind their own business.

She once again took in the beauty of the little bath. The gleaming white tile made the room glow, and the lighting? It was perfect for makeup. She knew without a doubt. Nick was great, and she knew finishing out the bathroom was his and her dad's brainchild, but her instincts told her it was Trace who put the little potted poinsettia on the counter to decorate it for Christmas.

DECEMBER 21

Saturday dawned bright and clear at an unseasonably warm sixty degrees. Hannah couldn't have a better day to move.

Moving day would be tough, but there was no way Trace was going to miss this opportunity to help. Not if Eli was going to help. Hannah hadn't seemed interested in his twin, but stranger things had happened.

Forewarned is forearmed.

If only he'd known that idiom around the time of his junior prom.

Fortunately, "promposals" weren't a thing yet, but just when he'd worked up the nerve to ask Lauren Carmichael to be his date to the prom, Trace witnessed, with his very eyes, his brother handing her a rose in the hallway before fifth period.

It was his own fault, dragging his feet and dreading the possibility of rejection. He hadn't told Eli what he wanted to do. As usual, he'd kept his thoughts to himself. If only he'd known about planning ahead.

Come to think about it, he remembered seeing Lauren's expression when she saw Trace over Eli's shoulder.

Wait a minute. Was she disappointed?

Carrying in a heavy box of kitchen equipment with items Hannah had gleaned from her mom and sister, Trace shook his head, trying to get his attention back in the game. The moving game.

The past was in the past, and last he'd heard, Lauren Carmichael was married with three kids and one on the way.

She never dated Eli again after prom.

Okay, I feel better.

When he came through to deliver the box to the kitchen, Hannah's mom stopped him. "Trace, you've been a Godsend."

"Um ... thanks, Mrs. Buckner."

"Don't you Mrs. Buckner me. Call me Kristi."

"Yes, ma'am."

She smiled at him. Now he knew where Hannah got her smile. "The vanity looks so nice. She was so proud she was in tears when she got home last night." Kristi sighed.

Were they tears of happiness and gratitude, or irritation at a man who couldn't seem to go a day without messing up?

"I'm so happy for her. Not crazy about her living out here,

but she's dug in her heels more than I've ever seen her." She shook her head. "I've just got to learn to let go and let God—and realize I'm not in control." She chuckled. "Here I am, talking your ear off, and you're standing there holding a box. Put it on the table, and I'll sort it out."

"Yes, ma'am." Trace obeyed and vamoosed as quickly as possible, running straight into Hannah as he wheeled around the corner. "Oof."

He steadied her with both hands on her elbows. "We need a traffic light here." Trace tried his best to keep it light and friendly. Letting go of her arms, he stuffed his hands in his pockets.

"Yeah. Well. I thought I'd better check on Mom."

"She's putting away kitchen stuff."

Hannah closed her eyes, took a deep breath, and released it slowly. "That's what I was afraid of. She's putting everything where she thinks it should go, and it's my house."

"She's just trying to help." Trace wanted to see Hannah relax and enjoy the day. It was, after all, her big day.

He saw her visibly attempting to calm down. "I know." She closed her eyes again.

"I think she knows you're stressed, and she's trying to keep busy and out of the way."

"You think so?" Her face crumpled. "I don't want her to feel left out."

She turned to go into the kitchen, and Trace touched her arm. She stopped short and turned back to him. "What?"

Now he was uncertain where he was supposed to be. Support Hannah above all else, or help her see the truth?

"Hannah ..."

"What?"

He swallowed. "It's not up to you to make your mom happy."

Her mouth fell open, and she stared at him, saying nothing. He felt bad when he saw tears gathering in her eyes. "I know, but I feel like it's always been my job to keep everything going smoothly."

Shaking his head, he took her hand. "It's not. I know exactly how you feel, but I'm not as empathetic as you."

She pulled her hand away and swiped her cheeks with her forearm. "Thank you."

"For what?"

"For keeping me from making a mountain out of a molehill."

"I'm here to help." He winked at her, and she didn't move away. She was so close. If she moved a little, and he moved a little ...

"Where can I put these lamps?"

A bucket of cold water couldn't have startled Trace more.

Thanks, Eli.

WHAT JUST HAPPENED HERE?

Hannah's mind was going in ten different directions at once—no, at least eleven.

Did he understand her? She'd never thought about it being important that someone understand her because it was her job to serve everyone else. Wasn't it?

After she was distracted by Eli and the lamp query, she turned around, and Trace was nowhere within sight.

Okay, I can do this. I'm not responsible for other people's happiness. Not even my parents.

It was a tough pill to swallow. Trace was right. She'd read enough on birth order and, yes, oldest daughter syndrome, to know he was. Sure, she was a perfectionist, but wasn't she supposed to be? Shouldn't she strive for perfection?

If Mom puts my stuff in the wrong spots, I can always move it.

Entering the kitchen, Mom smiled from atop the two-step stool she used to reach the upper shelves.

"How's it going in here?"

"Well, I'm probably putting things in the last place you'd put them, but it's getting put away and boxes emptied. I figured that was the goal." Mom stepped down and faced the box Trace had just left. "These are Grandma Buckner's dishes. She always wanted you to have them, so I've had them boxed up and ready."

Tears pricked again. Was Hannah going to be a slobbery crying mess by the time this day was over? She pulled out a cup and saucer from the top. "They're so pretty."

"She said you'd always liked them, so as the oldest grandchild, you should have them."

Hannah walked over to her mom and hugged her, burying her face in her mother's shoulder. "Thank you, Mom."

After an extra squeeze, Mom leaned back to study her face. "What's the matter, Hannah?"

She shook her head and shrugged, tears still smarting. "Honestly, Mom, I don't know." She sniffed loudly and held her hand out for the paper towel her mom offered. "Thanks."

"You're welcome."

"I think the only thing I know for sure is that I love this house, and I know it was the right thing for me to buy it."

"Then that's all there is to it."

Huh? Mom had stayed suspiciously quiet ever since she broached the subject of her getting her own place.

Mom may have kept quiet, but Dad talked enough for both of them.

Mom poured herself and Hannah a cup of cocoa. When had

she had time to make it? Didn't matter. Mom was a wizard in the kitchen, and Hannah knew knew it would take a lot to live up to her legacy.

The warm cocoa eased down her throat. This time, it wasn't for beating the cold. It was for comfort, pure and simple. "So good, Mom."

"I thought it might hit the spot. We'll offer some to the rest after a while. Dad's busy putting the bed together, which is good—it keeps him in one spot and out of our hair." Mom's slow grin—the smile that matched Hannah's—made Hannah giggle.

"What is going on with him?" She hadn't wanted to ask, but now was her opportunity. "I've never seen him so opinionated in my life."

Mom sighed. "I know, sweetie." She shook her head and tilted it a bit. "Daddies don't like to think they're losing all control of their household."

"But, when Heather ..."

"I know. When Heather wanted to get married so young, it just about killed him. She stood up to him and told him she was getting married with or without him."

"I remember." Hannah shook her head in wonder. "I could never figure out where she got the guts to face him."

"It floored him too. Sweet little Daddy's girl had a mind of her own, and she'd found the one she'd been looking for, even if she was just eighteen. If it makes you feel better, I'm sure Vi will be more like her Aunt Hannah than her mother. That's what happens when parents only have one kid, and they do all their trial and error with one little person."

"I'm not sure if Violet being like me is a good thing or a bad thing. I've seen that little crinkle of worry between her eyebrows."

"I know. You and Vi want everyone to be happy." Mom

tilted her head. "I think you're realizing that in taking care of everyone else, you've neglected yourself."

Hannah nodded. "I was told recently that I was not responsible for other people's happiness."

Mom nodded. "Trace was right." She grinned.

Was there guilt written all over Hannah's face?

"I may have overheard a little of the conversation."

Oh, no. She heard her angry words about Mom putting her things in the wrong places. *Hannah Buckner, you are an awful person.* "Oh, Mom, I'm sorry."

"Listen. The only constant in this life is change. We either roll with it, or we spend our lives letting it knock us down."

When did Mom get so smart?

Hannah gave her an extra hug. "Thanks, Mom."

"That's what I'm here for." After another squeeze, she said, "Now get back in there and tell those men where to put your furniture. Use 'em while you've got 'em."

Mom's practical side always won out.

ONCE AGAIN, Trace found himself walking around outside, enjoying the mild weather. It was due to change in the next few days. He felt pretty superfluous inside with more help than room, once the boxes and furniture were offloaded. Hannah didn't have much stuff.

But the cabin ...

It stood there, calling to him. He was almost afraid to bring it up again.

"Hey, Trace."

Hannah was calling him. Before wondering what she needed, he decided to enjoy the sensation of his name on her lips for a few more seconds, then, "I'm coming."

He could tell her face was freshly scrubbed, all traces of tears gone except for the slight tinge of red around her lashes. It didn't detract from how pretty she was.

"What can I do for you?"

She smiled, more relaxed, knowing the task was almost done. "Ask not what you can do for me, but what I can do for you." She pointed at him and laughed. "Roxy's put together a huge to-go order. Food in exchange for retrieval?"

"That sounds like an offer I can't refuse." He'd tried his best gangster impression, but it only made her laugh harder.

"Please, never try to imitate a Chicago gangster again." She continued laughing. "Promise me."

"Promise? Forget about it ..." Trace paused for effect, not having any idea where this was coming from. "See what I did there?"

Hannah was still laughing. "I see what you did. I may have to rescind my invitation to stay and eat."

Trace held up a hand. "I promise."

"Awesome." She held out some cash.

"Now you really can forget about that."

She frowned. "But I ..."

"My treat." When she tried to interrupt, he held his hand up, and she stopped. "I succeeded in something I didn't think possible today."

"What's that?"

"I made you laugh."

The pink on her cheeks was attractive in the dimming light. She stood there, saying nothing. Would he get the last word?

"Thank you."

"I only ask one thing."

She looked curious.

"Think seriously about renting out the cabin. And while you're thinking about it, consider renting it out to me."

She stiffened and opened her mouth to speak.

Trace held his hands out to slow her down. "Ah, ah, ah, I just said think about it." He nodded toward the house. "I think it would make your dad feel better about the remote location. Just sayin'."

Turning toward the cabin, she wrapped her arms around herself. "I'll think about it."

"Good." He paused for a moment. "Right. I'm off to see Roxy." Then he turned to walk to his truck.

"Hey, Trace." She spoke quietly. When he turned, she was still standing in the same place, looking right at him. "Thank you."

"Welcome."

Chapter 17

December 24

"I thought they'd never leave." Trace took a deep breath.

"You sound relieved." Working on the new security system, Hannah smiled as she stripped the wires she needed to connect this phase of the assembly.

"Maybe a little."

"How was it working with them this week?"

"Not as bad as at first. Let's just say I'm glad this project is almost done. I'll be glad to get out of this basement."

"Me too."

"Are you settling in?" Trace kept busy, sweeping up the debris from the carpenters until Hannah needed something.

"I am."

"Not too quiet out there?"

She was concentrating but still grinned and glanced up for a second. "I'll admit it was pretty quiet the first night. Once I got that one under my belt, it was better." She chuckled. "I left on every outside light."

"Smart. You probably need another security light out there."

"Maybe." She put down the needle-nosed pliers and stepped to the tool bench outside the small room. "I'm running low on these connectors, and I need some more twenty-two AWG wiring."

"Two or four-stranded?" He was glad he was learnng the lingo.

"Bring down some of both, if you don't mind."

"Yes, Boss."

"And don't you forget it." She glanced up with a smirk then returned to the task at hand. "I'm grateful to have my assistant back today."

Finally, she had relaxed. If she looked up again, would she see a goofy grin on his face? "Alrighty-then. I'll be back in a flash."

"Thanks, Trace."

He went out the door, looking at his phone and then laid it down on the workbench next to hers.

"Hey, Trace?" Hannah called out to him as he hit the bottom step.

"Yeah?"

"While you're out there, could you get my Thermos from the truck?"

"Sure thing, Boss."

"Ha-ha," she called back, deadpan.

It was Christmas Eve. They were both a little giddy at the prospect of a week off. At Thanksgiving, Trace had faced the impending family celebrations with dread, but now there was a buzz inside him. He wasn't sure if it was because of Christmas or spending time with Hannah today.

Christmas was about family. Tonight, the whole Reno clan

would be together. It had been a long time since the full family had gathered.

His sister, Samantha, had arrived on Monday, and they'd had some kind of baked treat every day since. She was determined to learn how to cook like Grandma.

He wasn't complaining.

The clouds were lower and thicker than when he'd been out earlier. It had been warm the last few days—warm for Christmas week, anyway. After being snug and warm in the café, the cold hit him. His imagination and the age-old desire to have a white Christmas were playing tricks on him. That could not be a snowflake.

Maybe if he hadn't been distracted by the thought of spending the day with Hannah, he'd have remembered how quickly the weather could turn in this part of the country.

He pulled the supplies Hannah requested then reached into the cab and retrieved her Thermos. He'd ask Roxy to fill it for him. Then he'd be returning not only with what Hannah asked for but also with a treat. Maybe Roxy had some leftover cookies going begging?

Warmth enveloped him as he stepped inside. Instead of heading down to the basement, he walked up the few steps to the café kitchen. Roxy was zipping up the bank bag with the day's receipts, having sent everyone else home to start their holiday. He'd heard the side door shut earlier when Jimmy left. They would be closed for a few days, as well.

"Hey, Trace." Roxy smiled broadly. "What can I do for you?"

"I wondered if you had any coffee left over to fill Hannah's Thermos?"

"I most certainly do. I hate throwing it out." She bustled about, dumping what was in the container and rinsing it out before filling it with fresh coffee. "I'm glad you came up—I waited to pour out what was left, just in case." She grinned. "I have a few cookies left too."

"You read my mind. Really." Trace smiled at his aunt. He stood by his opinion that Uncle Steve had done well marrying Roxy.

She pulled a bakery box from the shelf and put a dozen cookies in. "They'd just go to waste. They have pecans, and my grandchildren turn up their noses at any form of nuts."

"I will gladly take them off your hands." He grinned. "And I'm sure Hannah won't argue, either."

"You two don't work so long you're late for Christmas tonight." She handed him the box, which he set down to hold out her coat.

"Thank you."

He grinned. "I didn't want to stand in the way of whatever you're bringing to Grandma's tonight."

"Smart boy." She laughed. "Y'all wrapping things up down there?"

"We've only got a couple of hours' work to finish up, and then we're both out of here."

"Good. See you at Sylvia's tonight."

"Yes, ma'am." He gave her a salute and headed back down the stairs to the basement, determined not to drop the most important cargo—Roxy's cookies.

HANNAH HEARD THE CONVERSATION UPSTAIRS, and her mouth watered at the prospect of fresh coffee *and* cookies. "It's a Christmas miracle," she said to herself, then laughed.

Trace came clomping down the stairs talking to the items he carried.

She called out to him, "You should have taken a bucket to carry all the extra stuff."

"Wish I had." He laughed.

He got into the safe room, hands full, stumbling on some conduit. Before he could recover himself, he dropped the wire and connectors, hanging on to the cookies and Thermos. In the melee, he kicked the doorstop holding the door open, and it closed with a decided slam and a click.

"Whoa, there, partner." Hannah laughed at the sight.

"At least I held on to the important stuff." He set the box and Thermos down carefully, then turned to open the door to let in more heat.

Except it wouldn't open.

"Everything okay over there?" Hannah didn't usually laugh at other people's misfortune, but seeing Trace stumble in, dropping everything *except* the cookies and coffee, still tickled her.

He didn't say anything. Just kept rattling the doorknob.

"Trace?"

After a few more seconds, he stood there, his back to her, hands on his hips in what screamed frustration as he looked up at the ceiling. "We may have a problem."

"What problem? The cookies survived, didn't they?" She chuckled as she measured out the amount of wire she needed for the last round of connections.

"The door won't open."

"What do you mean, the door won't open?"

He wasn't kidding.

"I mean, unless you know something I don't, we are locked in."

She got up in a hurry. "No, that can't be. This is a safe room, designed to be locked from the *inside*, not the *outside*."

Rattling the doorknob, she studied it. What in the world?

She stared at the door. "Okay, we can figure this out."

Would staring at it help?

"This is basically a closet. According to code, a closet door must be installed to be opened from the inside." She repeated it. "It's not code if you can get locked in."

"Right."

"This was one of the last things done before we started the electrical, right?" Hannah knew her eyes were rounded in panic.

Trace nodded.

It was the doorknob. It locked automatically.

"How ..." She frowned.

Then it came to her.

He spoke up. "The lock is on the wrong side."

Hannah straightened her spine. Troubleshooting was one thing she was good at. "Okay. First, we don't panic." She felt her back pocket. "Where's my phone?"

"It's out there," he said, pointing to the door, "right next to mine."

"No, no, no, no, no." She checked around her. Surely one of the random tools at her feet would dislodge the door.

"Can't go through it. Solid steel door." Trace had been figuring too.

"We cannot be stuck here in this basement on Christmas Eve."

"Sounds like a Hallmark movie, doesn't it?"

She glared at him. "You wish."

Remain calm, Hannah. It was a mistake. Everyone makes mistakes.

Hannah covered her face with her hands. "Trace, tell me something." She pulled her hands away and looked him in the eye. A more uncomfortable expression she'd never seen.

"Trace," she said calmly, she hoped, "who installed the doorknob and lock system?"

Trace shifted his stance. They were both distracted when the work light flickered.

She closed her eyes and repeated herself. "Who installed the doorknob and lock system?"

"Are you asking who actually *did* the work, or who was responsible for the work?"

"Isn't that the same thing?" She was beginning to get frustrated.

Trace raked his hand over his face. "Okay. I installed it under the supervision of Charlie."

She swallowed thickly, nodding. "Trace?"

"Yes, Hannah."

"Had you ever installed a doorknob or lock before?"

"Never in my whole life had I ever installed a doorknob. Until today."

Laugh or cry. That was the question.

TRACE, *you idiot. Any progress you've made with Hannah just crashed and burned. YOU have crashed and burned. Forget it. Forget any chance you may have had with her. You, my friend, are dead meat.*

Trace stood there, wondering when the explosion was going to take place. Instead, Hannah stood there, obviously thinking. She scanned the small room, tapping her chin with her index finger. Calm, cool, and collected.

Probably a very good trait in a person who installs electricity.

"Okay, what do we have here?" She paused her survey of the room and looked directly into his eyes.

"Besides cookies?"

He regretted the levity as soon as he said it. She closed her eyes and took a deep breath. Was she counting again?

Hannah raked her hands over her face. "Okay. We know we could dig ourselves out of here easier than breaking through that steel door." She blew out a breath. "Unfortunately, the door to the tunnel system, along with our phones, is outside of this door."

"I'm sorry, Hannah." *Will that help?*

"I know, Trace." She shook her head, her lips clenched in a firm line. "Who's at fault is kind of the least of our worries. We're stuck."

Considering the four walls were beginning to close in on Trace, he agreed. Had he ever mentioned, in passing, that he was claustrophobic?

"Roxy left right after I took the cookies, so the café is locked up tight." He was still mortified. Because his hands were full of cookies, he'd stranded them down here.

"Nobody is in the café. Nobody is in town. Even the bank branch took off a half-day today."

The lights flickered again, and Hannah grimaced.

"I sure do wish I'd finished hooking up the lights down here."

No cords. "What do these portable lights run on?"

She arched a brow. "Rechargeable batteries."

"Oh, no."

"And these aren't the newest of batteries. I've got extras plugged in—out there on the workbench." She took her hands off her hips long enough to gesture to the offending door.

"How long ...?"

"They usually last about six to eight hours. These? These last about five."

"And we've been down here?"

"About four and a half."

Trace cringed. Hannah was putting a good face on it. She was, by nature, a problem-solver. He was to a degree, but Hannah? She'd made it an art form. She was so good, he wasn't sure if she was angry or not.

"So, we know the lights are going to go out in just a little while," Trace reiterated.

"Yes. We have three, so let's turn off two of them and save the batteries."

He pointed at her and moved to turn off one, while she shut down the other.

"Of course, powering them off, and then on again will deplete the batteries." Hannah shrugged. "Sorry."

"Nothing for *you* to be sorry for," Trace scoffed.

"Very true." She glared at him a little. "It buys us a little time with lights." She paced for a few more seconds, then stopped in front of him, hands back on her hips.

"Did you not ...?"

Trace held his hands up. "As I said, I have never installed a door or a doorknob. I just followed the instructions on the package and tried to stay out of the way." Shaking his head, he said, "And I guess that was my first mistake." He rubbed the back of his neck. "If I'd been inside the room, in the way, Charlie and Nate would have noticed, or I'd have been working from the correct side. I guess this, literally, is a matter of perspective."

Trace began to pace, the walls getting closer and closer. Suddenly, he had sympathy for inmates in a six-by-six cell. The room was so small he walked five steps before having to turn around. He finally stopped, because it was getting him nowhere either physically *or* mentally.

"I guess we can keep working as long as there's light and we've got materials." Trace didn't want to be the cause of them not getting the job done. "When were you expected at your parents' house?"

"Five."

"Ouch."

"Yeah. What about you?" She went back to work on the connection she'd started before the door debacle.

"I usually get to Grandma's before five, but the folks aren't arriving until six or six-thirty." He checked his watch. "That means we'll be here ..."

"At least four hours. Maybe an hour and a half of light."

Trace watched Hannah closely, frowning at the paleness of her face. Was she going to pass out? And if she passed out, and they were here long enough for his claustrophobia to take hold and *he* passed out, where would that leave them?

"Are you okay?" Trace reached out to touch her elbow.

She nodded. "Just thinking ahead to the lights going out."

"You know what my grandma would say to that?" Maybe if he kept her talking, she'd relax.

"Probably the same thing mine would—don't trouble trouble 'til trouble troubles you." She smiled weakly, trembling.

"I give up." Trace finally stopped pacing and leaned against the cold, concrete wall, sliding down until he was in a sitting position.

"What do you mean?"

Draping his forearms on his knees, he shook his head. "There's nothing we can do. The upside is we know we won't die down here because there are people who know where we are. On the other hand, we're stuck until those people have time to notice we're not where we're supposed to be." He snorted quietly. "And I, for one, am not the one they'll miss immediately."

HANNAH WAS STRUGGLING. She wanted to be angry at him. Why wasn't she? For some reason, when she realized they were going to be locked in the safe room for a while, a strange calm came over her.

She did have a few unrealistic expectations. One, a man should have basic carpentry skills. Was she asking too much? Was she projecting a bias because she was in the building trade? Did that make him less of a man?

Of course not.

Would she dismiss even friendship, out of hand, because he installed a doorknob backward?

That would be ridiculous—and wrong. Nobody should be shunned for a skill they'd never been taught. Would she be dismissed because she couldn't bake a soufflé?

Compassion won out. He hadn't balked at anything she'd asked him to do. Everything she'd asked of him had been done with grace and almost eagerness.

When the first light began to flicker, the panic hovering at her edges built. Trace said nothing but rose from his spot on the floor to turn on the second light.

Had she told him she was afraid of the dark? No, because that sounded like something a four-year-old would have to admit, not a twenty-five-year-old woman.

She'd offer an olive branch. "Want a cookie?"

His lips lifted on one side. "I'll never refuse a cookie, just so you know."

"I had a feeling." She brought the box over to where he was sitting and sat next to him, the box of cookies between them.

"Coffee?"

He chuckled softly. "I hope you remember that we don't exactly have 'facilities' down here."

"If we ever build a safe room again, we outfit it with a refrigerator, microwave, and bathroom."

"That could be a thing." He nodded, munching on the white chocolate macadamia nut cookie. "These are so good."

"I'd put Roxy's cookies up against anybody's."

"Yeah, I think everybody's glad she and Uncle Steve married—and not just for Uncle Steve's sake if you know what I mean."

Hannah nodded. "I'll bet potlucks with the Renos are amazing."

"And now we've got Darcy too." He raised his eyebrows when she laughed.

They were quiet for a few minutes, but they'd both relaxed somewhat. Trace had seemed nervous before. She understood and knew the signs. He'd broken out in a cold sweat. Same. Shallow breathing. Same.

When the second light started to fade, Trace once again got up and turned on the third—and last—light.

She swallowed thickly and took a sip of the cooling coffee. "Want some?"

"If you don't mind me drinking out of the same cup."

She handed him the Thermos and cup. "I'll chance it."

"Thank you. I was beginning to think I'd have to start spitting out the cotton balls forming in my mouth."

"Me too. It helps." She perused the room they were stuck in. "Did you hear about Lisa and Nick getting caught in the tunnels under Nick's house during the tornado a few years ago?"

"Yeah, they took me down there and showed me the tunnels." He paused. "I'm not sure how I would have done in their situation."

Hannah arched a brow and turned toward him. "We're kinda in the same situation. It's just cleaner."

"I guess so." He cleared his throat. "I'm not a fan of close spaces."

The last light flickered. They might have about ten minutes of light left. The dread of what would soon happen was tempered by the fact that she wasn't alone.

"I can identify." She wasn't ready to disclose her fear. Not yet. It still felt so immature and needy—the last image she wanted to project.

The next surge of light left the light lower as the battery powered down.

Chapter 18

Trace felt Hannah stiffen when the light glimmered weakly and grew dim.

"Did I mention I got to go to Space Camp when I was a kid?"

"No, but I always thought it would be fun."

He blew out a breath. "It was. I always wanted to be an astronaut."

She turned toward him, her voice closer to his ear. "Really?"

"Mm-hmm. I read everything I could on rockets and space travel, and when Eli and I were green-lighted to go to Space Camp between seventh and eighth grade, we jumped on it."

"Did Eli want to be an astronaut too?"

He leaned his head back, staring at the ceiling, and smiled. "No, but he was afraid he would miss a good time, so he applied too."

"I can see that."

So, she's noticed Eli's attention-hog tendencies?

"Yeah. I did great for most of it until we got to the module simulator training." He didn't tell people about his experience. Just going to Space Camp gave him some cred in the geeky crowd he ran with—if you could call it running. Images of the Dungeons and Dragons group he met with twice a month made him grin.

"What happened?" She was relaxing, fixing her sight at him as the lights grew dimmer. Eyes closing for a few seconds, she opened them and held his gaze as if she were hanging on to him.

Which would be more than fine with me.

Taking a deep breath, he continued. "I was the last one up for the simulator. I'd seen every kind of reaction from the other kids. A few came out and threw up."

"Yikes."

"Seriously. A few were dizzy the rest of the day, and then there were the ones in line to do it again immediately." He peered down at her. From her expression, he probably came across as pretty disgusted. "That was Eli."

"Figures." She chuckled gently.

The lights buzzed a little, then went off, plunging them into thick, complete darkness. When Hannah inched closer to him, he moved the cookie box out of the way and reveled in her nearness.

"Anyway, I was last, and somehow Eli learned that when a certain button was pushed, the door would lock."

"Oh, no."

"Yep. He locked me in, and it took a little bit for the instructors to get me out. They thought the door had jammed, but it hadn't. Once they figured out it was done on purpose, they were determined to get to the bottom of it."

"Did they figure out it was Eli?"

"Nope." Trace shook his head even though she couldn't see it in the darkness. "And I didn't tell anybody. Since then, closed-in spaces just about do me in. Elevators, any room with no windows, and please, don't ever make me go into an escape room. Tried it, didn't work."

"I'm sorry, Trace." Her shoulder made its way right up next to his, her warmth more of a comfort than the most open of spaces.

"Thanks. Just one of those things that happen when you're a kid."

"What about your aspirations of being an astronaut?"

"I still wanted to, but eventually, I realized that I'd never pass the initial evaluations." He shrugged. "I thought about aerospace engineering, then realized electrical engineering would be more practical."

PRACTICAL. When Hannah heard the word, she shook her head. If she'd followed her dream, there would have been no way she'd be in this dark box right now. "I was practical too."

"Hannah, practical doesn't begin to describe what you do. With you, electricity is an art form."

Wow. The darkness frustrated her. She wanted to see his face, read his expressions, to see if he meant what he said.

"I mean it, Hannah."

I guess that answers my question.

"Thanks. I never really thought of it like that. It's just something I decided to do when I convinced myself Interior Design was the most *im*practical career I could choose and still live in this area."

"Why? Lisa's made a career out of it."

"I know, but she's Lisa. I always thought she was amazing. It was pretty awesome when she moved to Texas to be on a television show." Hannah sighed again.

Trace laughed out loud. "Do you remember Lisa when she was in high school and college?"

"Of course I do. I thought she was cool, anyway."

Was it possible to hear someone smile? She'd heard that telemarketers were told to smile while they talked because the customer could tell the difference. If so, then Trace was definitely smiling.

"According to Del, she was beyond geeky."

"So? I happen to be partial to geeks."

Now she smiled into the darkness when he choked on a cough.

"Anyway, I wanted to be an interior designer, and I loved art."

"Does Lisa know?" Trace spoke quietly.

"Probably not." She was quiet, pondering. "I think I had in mind showing her by fixing up the house."

"She'll be impressed. The kitchen design is great."

"Thank you, kind sir."

"You are more than welcome."

Hannah hesitated. Trace had told her his deepest fear. Could she be completely honest?

"What time is it?" Her phone was how she kept the time.

Not Trace. He held up his arm and the dial glowed with an analog wristwatch face revealing the time to be 2:45 pm. "You mentioned liking geeks?"

"I'd appreciate them even more if they had a way out of here—or were wearing a smart watch."

"Again ..."

"Don't say it. I know you're sorry. I am too. We'll just have to survive a few more hours. In the pitch dark. Which, by the way, is my biggest fear in life."

Trace didn't say anything for a time, and neither did Hannah. He slid his hand down her arm until his fingers folded gently around hers. She didn't pull away. When he spoke, it was soft. "What do they call that?"

"Fear of the dark? The Bogey-man?" She snorted, disgusted with herself. "It's called nyctophobia."

"Sounds like it should be fear of nicotine." There was that smile sound again.

"It does, doesn't it? I was accidentally locked in a toy box playing hide-and-seek with my little sister."

"How old were you?"

"Six."

"Yikes. How long were you in there?"

"It felt like years. According to my mom, it was just about forty-five minutes. I thought I was going to suffocate."

"Those kinds of experiences stick with you."

"I was a little worried about moving out in the country because of that. I hope it'll help me get over it."

Trace didn't say anything, just sat there and squeezed her hand gently. Was he recalling all the warnings she'd been given about living out there on her own? Would he bring up renting the cabin again? And, did she want him to live right outside her back door?

"We need to get you more security lights."

That's all he said, and she was grateful. He was giving her space.

"Thank you."

"For what?" He even sounded surprised.

"For not thinking I'm silly."

"I'm the last person to judge someone for something they can't help." His voice was directed at her more. He must be turned directly toward her. "Does it help to close your eyes? Maybe fake yourself out?"

"Sometimes. If I were here alone, I'd probably have a panic attack. Since I have to be trapped, I'm glad I'm not by myself."

Neither of them spoke for a few minutes—or was it seconds? In the dark, she had no concept of time.

"Tell me about being a twin." As long as the conversation flowed, Hannah's mind was kept off the oppressive darkness pressing down on her like a weighted blanket.

"Well, you've met Eli."

"I have." She chuckled.

"He's a lot."

"I've noticed. He's about as opposite you as can be."

"That's always the first thing people say when they find out we're twins since we really don't look alike. "You know the show, *Everybody Loves Raymond?*"

Now she laughed. "I do."

"I'm not Raymond."

Hannah laughed out loud. She couldn't help it. Eli was great, but he would irritate her after a while. "Raymond's brother had his redeeming qualities."

Trace scoffed, making Hannah grin in the darkness. "He's a gloomy Gus. Like me."

"I don't think so." Hannah hoped Trace heard the sincerity in her voice. "When my family went to Orlando, did I bring home a stuffed bear? Of course not. I had to be different. I wanted his more serious friend."

"Really?" Now it was his turn to laugh. "He was my favorite too. That is awesome."

"Of course it is." She was feeling good. Not in an 'Oh, wow, this is the greatest day, ever,' way but in a deeper, more satisfying way. When Trace wove his fingers between hers, she held her breath, allowing him to envelop her small hand tighter in his larger one. It fit.

They sat there a few minutes, quietly. She didn't know what to say now, because it seemed her nervous system had a meeting with the rest of her and decided that the hand

Trace held was where all the nerves in her body wanted to gather.

"Tell me about Mandy and Clay. I've heard a little bit, but I figure you had more details." She appreciated his trying to keep the conversation going.

"You know how dramatic Mandy can be, right?"

"Oh, how well I know." He snorted.

"Exactly. When her parents couldn't get home for Christmas, she just about had a come-apart. She had it in her head that Christmas would never be the same again, and, according to her, the world as she knew it was going to end."

"Sounds about right."

There's the smile in his voice again ...

"Anyway, When Clay heard about it, he decided it was up to him to give her the best Christmas ever." She leaned her head back on the cold, hard wall. "It was like he just noticed her, and his biggest fear was that she would think he was too old for her."

"I don't know Clay well, but he showed a lot more imagination than I would have expected."

"No kidding. By the time he was ready for the big reveal, Mandy had fallen hook, line, and sinker in love with him."

"Do you think she'll get a ring anytime soon?"

"If she doesn't, she'll be very disappointed. Maybe not Christmas, but Valentine's?" Hannah wondered when she would want to get a ring.

Hmm.

"That would be a lot to live up to, giving an engagement ring for a holiday or birthday."

"Sounds like you've thought about this."

"Not extensively. Just thinking about the male point of view."

"I agree." She nudged his shoulder with hers. "Just wanted

to give you a hard time." After a few seconds of quiet and pressing darkness, her heartbeat roared in her head, and she could hardly bear it.

Tears were very near the surface, but she tried to keep from sniffling. "Talk to me."

TRACE SQUEEZED HER HAND. He tried to think of the games he and his siblings played on long car trips, trying to kill time. Twenty questions usually worked. But what to ask?

"Twenty questions."

"Okay, you start." He heard her sniffle as she chuckled.

Good call, Trace. Now what to ask?

He dove in. "Worst date ever?"

Seriously, Trace? You went there?

"Oooo. That's a tough one. I haven't had many great ones," she said with a weak laugh.

"Me, neither. I dated this one girl in college—we dated for six weeks. Come to find out, she was dating me to get closer to Eli."

"That's horrible."

"I agree. Anyway, the worst date I had was with her. She was mad. She'd flirted with Eli and got nowhere—he's a good brother, most of the time—so after that, she figured she'd cross both Reno boys off her list."

"That's harsh."

Trace could tell she'd relaxed a little. The muscles in the hand he held had been tense. Now it curled around his as if it were meant to be there. It made him feel pretty good about himself.

"It's a jungle out there."

"No kidding. Mine would have to be when Caryn set me up with her cousin from out of town for a double date."

"A setup is hardly ever the best way to start a date."

"I agree," she said. "From the moment we met, besides being a little handsy, he 'babed' and 'honeyed' me until I thought I would scream."

Trace laughed. "Not a fan of terms of endearment?"

Noted.

"Oh, I have no problem with it—except when it's used within minutes of meeting and totally contrived." She scoffed. "Then, it's just ridiculous."

"Caryn was so embarrassed. She'd only hung out with him around family, so she had no idea how arrogant he was."

The more time Trace spent with Hannah, the more attractive he found her. Had he ever really been in love before? If he had, he couldn't remember it. This moment, right now, was about the most romantic thing that had ever happened in his life.

"I'm imagining the mouth-watering aromas at my parents' house right now." Hannah sounded wistful. They'd had lunch, both of them eating light since they were anticipating major meals before the Christmas Eve service.

"Want another cookie? I'd offer to pour you some coffee, but ..."

Hannah laughed. "The cookie, I'll take. I'll pass on the coffee —mainly because, with our luck, we'd both have it all over us." The teasing note in her voice encouraged him. She'd held him at arm's length, but now she accepted his presence. Maybe his friendship? Trace couldn't count on any more than that. It was insane to think she would fall for him as quickly as he fell for her.

"I'm thinking no more liquids for me until we get out of here."

He handed her the cookie, feeling his way, and her hand ended up on his wrist and hesitated. "Where's the cookie?"

"You've got my wrist."

She maneuvered until she got to the cookie. "Ah. Got it." After that, she went quiet, and Trace's hand felt cold and sad. "How much longer?"

"Couple of hours if we're missed before suppertime."

He heard her take a deep breath, or was it a yawn? "This is making me so drowsy, which is odd. Usually, I would be in panic mode because of the dark, but I think this time the dark has triggered sleep."

"Get comfortable and sleep if you can. I'm feeling it too." He felt her wriggle next to him. "Feel free to use my shoulder for a pillow."

She stopped abruptly. "That's okay. I think I can doze a little like this."

They didn't talk for a while. Occasionally one or both of them would shift positions, and finally, after about fifteen minutes, he felt her head slide to his shoulder.

Trace shifted around and pulled her closer, leaning his head on top of hers.

He could sit on this cold, hard floor forever if it meant she would stay right there.

Chapter 19

Lisa had no more than taken her coat off before Grandma appeared, apron on, spoon in hand. Something was wrong.

Her first thought was Del and Darcy. Their flight had been delayed once. Were they going to be even later? Had something happened?

Grandma started asking questions before they had a chance to.

"Where on earth is Trace? Was he supposed to be working late, and on Christmas Eve, of all times?"

Lisa's brows drew together as she shook her head. "I don't know. Have you not heard from him?"

"No, and I don't want to think of him in a wreck, unconscious in a ditch somewhere."

Grandma wasn't usually the one who panicked.

Ginger and Tom, Trace's parents, came in right behind them. "What's this?" Ginger cut her eyes toward Grandma.

"Trace isn't home yet."

Lisa bit her lip. "Nick?"

Was there a hint of tears in Grandma's eyes?

"He was fine when I saw him earlier today. Maybe he and Hannah ran into a snag, and he's running late. He put a new battery on his truck the other day." Nick checked his phone. "I haven't had any calls from either him or Hannah."

"I talked to him this morning, then I texted him this afternoon and never got an answer." Ginger, Trace's mom, was holding it together, but a wrinkle divided her forehead.

Tom went to his wife and put his arm around her.

Eli handed her a tissue. "He'll be okay, Mom. He's a big boy."

Ginger sniffed, swatting him as she pulled out a tissue. "I know, but he'll always be *my* baby. Just like you."

While everyone checked their phones for missed calls, Lisa's phone vibrated and played "Jingle Bells."

Maybe this was Trace. Lisa touched the screen to answer the call. "Hello?"

"Lisa, this is Kristi Buckner. Has anyone heard from Hannah? She was supposed to be here over an hour ago, and she hasn't called. She always calls. She's not answering her phone."

"Don't worry. We're on it—Trace hasn't shown up at Grandma's either."

Lisa had a fleeting thought ... no, she was being ridiculous. Trace and Hannah barely tolerated each other. No way they would choose Christmas Eve, of all times, to run off together. Lisa chuckled to herself at the very thought of this particular cousin "running off" with anyone. Ever. He was too stolid, methodical, level-headed.

In the meantime, she had a worried mom on the line, and, feeling a tiny kick into the region of her ribs, Lisa realized that someday she might be in the same situation. "Hang on a minute, Kristi. Nick's checking to see if he's had any calls or voicemails."

"Yes, I can wait."

Lisa heard Kristi Buckner, on the other end of the line, take a deep, shuddering breath.

Her heart squeezed in sympathy. "I'm sure they're both fine."

Lisa held the phone to her chest and whispered urgently to Nick. "We've got to find them."

That was the moment the newlyweds made their dramatic entrance. Could the evening be any more convoluted?

As soon as Del read the room, he caught Benji in a hug and pulled Darcy and Ali into the middle of it.

Lisa caught his gaze and whispered, "Trace and Hannah are missing."

Mandy sidled up to Lisa and whispered, "You don't think …" She frowned at Clay, who was suddenly very serious.

Lisa shook her head, knowing, as usual, she and Mandy were on the same wavelength. "I don't think so. They barely know each other. I don't think Hannah even likes Trace."

Mandy didn't say anything, but she shrugged and tilted her head, brows arched. Did Mandy know something the rest of them didn't know? Judging by the expressions going back and forth between Mandy and Samantha, she wondered.

Clay took out his phone and punched in a number, then waited. "Ben, sorry to call you out on Christmas Eve. Hannah Buckner and Trace Reno are missing." He pulled the phone away, speaking to Nick. "Where were they working?"

"Café. Finishing the wiring in the safe room." Nick put his phone back in his pocket. "No missed calls, no voicemails. He's not answering my call, either."

Lisa could not let this poor mom wait any longer. "Kristi,

Clay's here, and we're narrowing down where we think they could be."

Del spoke quietly. "After everything that's happened in those tunnels …"

"Exactly." Nick nodded at Del, and then turned to Clay. "I'm heading to the café."

"I'm coming with you." Eli displayed almost as much concern as his parents.

Clay nodded. "Let's mount up."

The four men left in Clay's sheriff's vehicle, and Lisa then remembered she had Kristi on the phone. "Kristi, I'm sorry you've had to wait so long."

"That's okay. Have you heard anything?"

Lisa's heart hurt for her when she heard the tears in Kristi's voice.

"No, but I'll call you as soon as I hear anything, okay?"

"Thank you, Lisa. I've been so worried about her living alone and in such a remote place. That was the first thing I thought of."

The queasy feeling in the pit of Lisa's stomach was either worry, lack of food, or baby Woodward doing calisthenics in her belly. "The last time Nick saw them was at the café, so they'll start there. Since they're both missing, I figure they're at the same place. I'll call Nick and tell him. If they're not at the café, maybe they're at Hannah's house."

"Just let us know. We can't have Christmas without Hannah."

"I know. Same here with Trace." She tried to put comfort in her voice and her words. "It's for sure we want to be able to attend the Christmas Eve service together."

"Amen, Lisa"

They ended the call, and Lisa chewed on her bottom lip for a few seconds, attempting to squelch the tears building in her eyes before her brand-new sister-in-law came up and hugged her.

Darcy tilted her head and looked her in the eye. "It'll be okay. They'll find them."

"I know. For some reason, things hit me harder these days."

She laughed and pointed to Lisa's baby bump. "I think we both know why."

"I'm sure glad you're home, Darcy." Lisa started to relax. "I need to have more faith, don't I?"

"You do." Darcy had the smile of an extremely happy woman. Now she had her husband, her children, and the whole family, all in one place—well almost. When they came back with Trace, they'd be together.

TRACE WAS HAVING the most marvelous dream.

I'm lying on the beach—I had tickets for a Caribbean cruise. Wait, didn't I cancel those? Get my money back? But wait. The most beautiful woman in the world is lying here next to me, napping in the sunshine.

The palm trees are swaying full of twinkling Christmas lights. That's different. I'm so sleepy ... It's odd ... I can see the Christmas lights twinkle in the bright sunlight. Whatever ...

I'm feasting my eyes on my companion, lying on my side, leaning my cheek on my fist so I can have a better view. Hannah's dark blonde hair has lighter streaks of sunshine from spending time in the equatorial sun. Her sunglasses are hiding her eyes, but she smiles. Is she watching me?

Busted. I don't care. I want to spend the rest of my life here, with her ...

"When is the guy going to come and move the umbrella? The sun is bright today ..."

Trace heard noises and woke abruptly to a cold, not-as-dark basement room. No more sunshine. Regret filled his soul for a few seconds. Was there any way to sneak back into his dream?

Hannah moved against him, snuggling deeper into his arms, and he finally realized he wasn't basking in the warm Caribbean sun. It was his cousin, Del, shining a beam of light into his face. He jerked, waking Hannah, whose eyes grew round as she struggled to get up off the floor.

"Great way to spend Christmas Eve, huh?" Eli had been laughing quietly, but now he released a loud guffaw.

Trace shook his head to finish waking up and caught sight of Hannah. She had that deer-in-the-headlight look. As much as he had enjoyed it, had being caught in this position ruined the headway he'd made earlier?

"How in the world did you two get locked in here?" Nick asked him.

Trace was saved from answering by more footsteps coming down the stairs.

"Hannah?"

"I'm okay, Mom."

Kristi Buckner pulled her daughter into her arms, tears in her eyes. "We were all so worried when neither one of you answered your phones. I had visions of the two of you unconscious in a ditch somewhere. Oh, Hannah." She hugged her daughter again.

"We both had vehicles here, Mom. We wouldn't have been together."

"That's why Dad and I are here. Nick let us know when they found both your trucks in the parking lot of the café."

Trace and Hannah's gaze met for a few seconds. He lifted his mouth in a one-sided grin, and she licked her lips nervously.

She didn't look away. At least not immediately.

"Great door installation, brother." Eli was examining the incorrect placement of the locking mechanism.

"I never claimed to be a carpenter."

I'll know better from now on, that's for sure.

And yet, he didn't regret the hours he'd spent with Hannah. They were themselves while they were down there, trying to overcome nervousness and fear. "We knew y'all would find us when we didn't show up."

Eli stood next to Trace, his lips twisted curiously. "Not a bad setup." He pointed to the cookies and Thermos of coffee.

Trace turned to him. "No, it wasn't bad—except I'm claustrophobic." He quirked a brow at his brother, who had the grace to look a little embarrassed. "I guess Hannah being with me made the difference."

Nothing would pull out of him the secret of Hannah's aversion to darkness.

HANNAH JUST WANTED to drive her truck home and take a shower before heading over to her parents' house for the celebration. Mom threatened to come with her, but Hannah assured her she'd be there within the hour, and that this incident had nothing to do with where she was living.

Not much Mom could say to that.

The shower warmed her and helped her to put things in perspective. She'd been scared at first, but by the time it was truly dark, she was comfortable with Trace.

Maybe comfortable wasn't quite accurate. In some ways, she was very *un*comfortable. She'd allowed him too much access inside her head. Inside her insecurities, needs, and wants.

Maybe instead of "comfortable," the correct word was closer to "safe," the way a princess feels when the prince slays a dragon for her. Cared-for. Protected. When she woke with her cheek lying firmly on his broad chest, she wanted to snuggle in and stay longer.

Until she realized they had an audience and was completely humiliated.

Was this going to be something she'd never live down?

Ugh.

From the moment he took her hand as it got darker and darker, the icy wall she'd tried to build around her heart began to thaw.

Not thaw. Melt.

Just thinking about his arms around her snatched at her breath. *Wow.* Holding her hand to her cheek, she felt the warmth of the blush she was sure stained her face. She had about five minutes in the truck before she would arrive at her parents' house.

Five minutes to get a grip, Hannah.

The little golden cross hanging from her rear-view mirror sparkled as she drove by one of the few streetlights in downtown Clementville.

Had she even thought to pray when her fear began to loom in front of her? Had she put as much energy into trusting God with her fear and anxiety about her future as she had in building a melty, faltering, man-made wall?

She'd been angry. Convinced that if God hadn't worked by now, He was leaving her behind. After all, Caryn and Mandy both had their men, so why couldn't she?

It seemed impossible that just when she'd decided to give up on finding "the one," God dumped Trace Reno in her lap.

Actually, I was basically in his lap. And I liked it.

All this time, Hannah had resented her friends having

found "the one," and she couldn't decide if Trace might fit into that category or if they were "two ships passing in the night" to show her that she had the ability and desire to feel these things.

Things inside herself she thought she understood.

She didn't.

Chapter 20

If he'd had it his way, Trace would have slid into the house without anyone noticing. He came in behind the rescue crew, which was a mistake. It gave the guys time to get the word out about Trace's ineptitude in carpentry.

Grandma and Mom were there, waiting at the door for him.

"We were so worried." Mom pulled him into a hug, which he returned.

"I'm sorry for worrying you. We were safe, just stuck." He shrugged and tried to smile. "Let me jump in the shower. It won't take me fifteen minutes." He spoke to his mom quietly. "Don't let Grandma hold everything up for me, okay?"

Mom patted him on the cheek. "I'll tell her." When he pulled away, she stopped him with a hand to his arm. "Trace, don't mind Eli."

Forewarned is forearmed?

"I won't. I guess I should be used to him by now, shouldn't I?" He grinned, relieved when she smiled back.

"You run on, now."

As quickly as possible, he made it up the stairs and to his room to get his clothes, only to be waylaid by the peanut gallery, mostly made up of Mandy's nieces and nephews.

"Hey, Trace, where you been?" Four-year-old Robbie Jr., met him in the hallway.

"I got stuck for a little while, but I'm back now."

"Eli said you got trapped in a room with a girl."

The expression of horror on the young man's face made Trace laugh. "I'll tell you a secret, Robbie."

The boy whispered so loudly Trace was sure they heard him downstairs. "I can keep a secret."

"Eli was right, I did get stuck in a room with a lady, but guess what?"

"What?" The boy's eyes widened.

"It wasn't too bad."

"I'd hate to be stuck in a room with my sisters."

"Oh, well, that would be different. I don't think I'd like to be stuck with Samantha, either. Hey, don't tell her I said that, okay?"

"Is she pretty?" Robbie tilted his head.

Trace thought for a minute before answering. How did he explain to a four-year-old that he'd just been locked in a room with the most beautiful woman in the world? Then it hit him. Truth is always the best answer. Simple. To the point. "Yes, she is very pretty."

Robbie nodded his head. "I have a girlfriend."

"Oh, do you, now?" This conversation was not going in the direction he anticipated, but he'd admit, it was getting interesting.

"Maggie."

"That's a pretty name."

"Umm. She's pretty too." He was very solemn. "What's her name?"

"Whose?"

"The girl you got stuck with."

Trace had to get him off the idea of being "stuck" with somebody. "No girl would appreciate us saying we got stuck with her."

"How come? Isn't that what happened?"

"Well, yeah, but it was an accident, and we couldn't get the door open."

"Sounds like you were stuck, to me."

"Her name is Hannah."

"I know Hannah." The boy nodded solemnly, his eyes flickering in recognition. "You gonna marry her?"

Trace wouldn't admit it to Robbie Jr., but the thought had crossed his mind. "I guess we'll just have to wait and see."

Robbie nodded his head. "I get it. I'm not sure about Maggie, either."

"Can't rush into these things." Trace eyed the staircase where Mandy had been listening in on their conversation the entire time. "I better get cleaned up or Grandma will tan my hide for holding up Christmas dinner."

"And presents?"

"Definitely presents."

Distracted by the idea of opening gifts, young Robbie scooted back to the family room.

"You gonna marry her?" Mandy quoted her nephew in a sing-song voice and grinned at him.

"Cute." He regarded her seriously. "It wasn't all fun and games. We were a little worried for a while."

"I'm sorry. Is Hannah okay?"

"I think so. Just embarrassed, and she has nothing to be embarrassed about."

"That's her, though. Get cleaned up. We got dinner on

hold, cousin!" She walked away, phone out where she texted quickly.

Hannah, maybe? What he wouldn't give to have access to that conversation.

IN ALL, there were twenty-four people at the Reno Christmas celebration. Easy enough to stay under the radar.

The family had a few laughs at his expense. It could have been worse. There were tables all over the place, and everyone had a seat. Ten in the dining room, five at the kids' table, a couple of toddlers toddling around with no interest in organized dining, and then a table of seven set up on the enclosed back porch.

When everyone was stuffed to within an inch of becoming comatose, the tables were cleared, and everyone gathered in the living room—a spacious room, usually, but with twenty-some-odd Renos in one place? Cozy, to say the least.

Trace held back in the doorway between the dining room and living room, pulling a dining chair forward to sit in while Grandpa read the Christmas story. It was the time he treasured most, when everything got quiet for just a few minutes. Grandpa, usually a man of few words, would always recap the blessings of the year, they'd pray, and then the gift-exchange melee began. They'd learned a long time ago that it was best to let the kids open their presents first.

This time, after Grandpa read the scripture, he changed it up.

"I'm told that someone here has something they want to say—apparently he needs witnesses—so Clay, you have the floor, realizing these kids have waited a while for their Christmas presents."

All eyes shot to Clay and Mandy, and a collective gasp rose when Clay got down on one knee.

"Thank you, Mr. Reno." He cleared his throat nervously, and his face shone a brilliant red.

He knelt before Mandy, whose cheeks were flushed and eyes sparkled, fixing his gaze on her face. "Mandy, the past year has been the best year of my life. You taught me what it was like to love someone more than myself and to let myself be loved in return. Last Christmas Eve, I think I knew you were the only girl for me, and while I don't have eleven pipers piping this time ..." He paused, smiling as a chuckle came up from the spectators. "... this Christmas, I want to ask if you would, if you could, love me for the rest of your life as much as I love you."

Mandy covered her mouth with her hands when he pulled out a box in the shape of a tiny drum, again completing the Twelve Days of Christmas cycle. He hit a button on the side, and it popped open, revealing a diamond solitaire ring inside. "Marry me, Mandy?"

She threw her arms around his neck and kissed him.

Cradling her in his arms as if they were the only people in the room, he grinned. "Is that a yes?"

Laughing and crying at the same time, she said, "Not until you put the ring on my hand, Sheriff Lacey."

He slid it carefully on her ring finger and kissed her again. "I love you."

"I love you, Clay." She placed her left hand gently on his cheek, smiling broadly when he pulled her palm to his lips, then pulled her closer as she slid her arms around his neck. When applause broke out, Mandy groaned, giving her new fiancé a quick kiss. She took Clay's hand, pulling him toward the sunroom, turning to the spectators in the room—her entire family. "All right, people, the show's over. Nothing to see here."

Grandpa chuckled, suspicious moisture in his eyes. "Well,

looks like we've had dinner and a show, so let's bow in prayer, thanking God for His many blessings." He surveyed his family. "Del, I think you can identify with blessings this year, can't you? Lead us in prayer?"

"Yes, sir, I sure can." He took in his family seated around the room, then beheld Darcy and the twins—his new family— by his side. "Join me in prayer."

Bowing, the room became still. Even the youngest were aware that this was a special time.

"Dear Father, we thank You for the blessings of this year. There have been good times and bad, but You have made a life for us beyond anything we deserve. I thank You for my wife and family, for the children here and to come ..." Trace peeked as he saw Del peek up and wink at his sister, Lisa. "... and the new families that will be created before next Christmas. Thank You for sending Your Son, Jesus, to die for us on the cross, be buried, and then rise again victoriously. And it was all for us. Help us to be humbled by the grace You've given us and to make life better for those around us. In Jesus' name, Amen."

After a round of "Amens," Grandma stood. "Now we're going to be organized in this present opening this year."

"Mama," Steve, her oldest son, began, "you've been trying to organize us for fifty years."

"Well, eventually, it's going to happen." She laughed. "Where on earth is Mandy?" Grandpa cleared his throat and pointed to the sun porch where Mandy and Clay were celebrating their engagement—on their own.

"I think Mandy is otherwise occupied." Grandpa chuckled, pleased.

Grandma smirked. "I was going to ask Mandy and Samantha to do the honors of passing out the presents, but I think Mandy is busy."

"Eli and I can do it, Grandma." Samantha glared at her

brother, who had started to protest. "Hey, you do know how to read, don't you?"

"Yeah?"

"Then quit grousing and get over here. The next youngest from Mandy is six, and she's just a trainee, right, Lizzy?" She grinned as young Lizzy, Cassie's oldest, stepped up to the plate. Samantha was the next-youngest grandchild, Lizzy the oldest "great." Trace grinned at his sister, thanking her silently for not dragging him into it. She'd seemed a little at loose ends the last few days, but they hadn't had time to talk.

While he waited for the official gift opening to begin, Trace's mind wandered to Hannah's house. She left the café without a word. How would it be when they met again?

There was a slight gnawing in the pit of his stomach and watching his cousin Mandy get engaged right there in front of him did little to ease the nervous energy filling him.

Once the presents were opened, Trace was restless. Now the family would spend the next year talking about nothing but weddings. His mom, the wedding planner, had already cornered Mandy and Clay, tossing around dates.

If she was this excited about her niece's wedding, how would she be for one of her children?

Trace slipped out to the porch to get some air. Mandy and Clay were a good couple. Clay was a little older and more settled than his cousin, but compared to when he had dated Lisa, Mandy brought out a tender side to him that made him pause.

Was that how it was when a man found "the one"?

Stop it, Trace. Not gonna happen.

He pulled out his phone. Neglected on the workbench all afternoon meant he had more battery left than usual, but he hadn't checked his email since early in the morning.

Scrolling through newsletters and ads, he hit delete, delete, delete.

Then, something caught his eye.

From: G.E. Aviation, Madisonville Plant

Was it another, "Thanks for applying, but no thanks" email?

He opened it up, his heart pumping harder the longer he read.

When he went on the interview a few weeks ago he couldn't have said whether or not it was successful. The job offer, though? Besides the interview, it was based on his education and the recommendation of his former employee. They wanted to talk to him next week, if possible.

Oh, it'll be possible.

If Trace were the kick-up-his-heels-and-shout type, now would have been the time. He wasn't. Instead, he'd smile and revel in it for a little while before he told anybody.

It was the exact job he wanted. Forty miles from Clementville, good retirement benefits, very good pay.

The few times he'd prayed about his move to western Kentucky, one of the signs he'd asked for was that he find a job by Christmas. Did this happen today just so God could make sure Trace knew it was Him? His schooling and former employment were factors, but even that was God.

It's all You, Lord. I'll take this one step at a time. Give me the patience to accept the life You have given me and help me learn to watch for signs of You all around me. Forgive me for resenting the happiness of others—it's not their fault they've found someone. If You have someone for me ...

He paused. Was it asking too much? Did he have the right to ask for "Special Dispensation" from the Lord of Hosts?

God, if You have someone for me, could it ... might it ... be Hannah?

Trace put his phone in his back pocket. He wasn't one to demand attention for himself, so he decided to make one announcement about the job and be done.

He went in, the squeaky screen door giving him away to those close by and decided to go for it. "Hey, y'all." He waved to get their attention. "I got a job."

He didn't expect applause, but he got it.

Mom hugged him. "Oh, Trace, at least one of my babies will be close by." She paused. "At least I hope so. Is it around here?"

Trace draped his arm around her shoulders. "It's in Madisonville, at the GE plant."

"Good job, Trace." Dad was all smiles. He'd been worried, Trace knew, because Trace wasn't one to put himself out there if there was any other way to get something.

"It's the one I hoped for. I've met several guys who either work there or have retired from there, and they have good things to say about the plant."

"Congratulations, Son."

"Thanks, Dad."

HANNAH WAS DETERMINED to get through Christmas without anyone having a clue that something was wrong. Mom was watching her closely, so Hannah acted as bright and cheerful as a girl could be.

When Hannah got Mandy's text with a picture of her engagement ring, she was glad for her, but it dampened her spirits a bit. Caryn would be next, undoubtedly. Mandy sent her another picture of the Reno crowd, mainly of the kids. Trace was there in the background. She enlarged the picture.

Everybody was having a good time except Trace. With him, it was hard to tell.

Taking a deep breath, Hannah pulled her mind away from the Reno family and smiled at each thing Vi brought to show her.

Her niece, three-year-old Violet, was over the moon excited for presents because, of course, she had the most under the tree. They'd all watched, ooh'd, and ahh'd over her gifts. Vi wanted to tell each one of them about every present she got, individually. Since she was the only child in the family, they did tend to go overboard.

"Y'all have got to cut back next year, you hear?" Heather sighed when she saw the mountain of gifts stacked by the door to go home with them. She looked over at her husband, Clark, shaking her head. "We've got to get a bigger house."

Clark's grin caught Hannah's attention. There seemed to be a lot of extra affection going on between those two. Maybe a little brother or sister for Vi?

"Anything you don't have room for, we can keep here for her to play with," Mom said with a dismissive wave of her hand.

"Like that's going to happen. Vi prefers to have all her toys within sight, all the time." Clark laughed and goosed his little daughter in the ribs, sending her off giggling.

Everyone had leaned into the "Hannah's a homeowner, now," vibe when buying presents, which was great, but she fancied the usual clothes, jewelry, and gift cards too.

Oh wait, here's a gift card ... to the local hardware store ...

"Thanks, Dad." She jumped up and kissed him on the cheek. "Do you plan on helping me spend it?"

"I'll be glad to. You need a good toolkit for something besides electrical work."

"You mean my hammer and screwdriver aren't enough?" Hannah laughed. Fortunately, when she needed more than electrical done, there were others around who had the equipment.

"Sometimes you'll have to figure out some stuff on your own ... with help from YouTube, of course." He winked at her. Dad figured out, with the help of the Internet, a person could learn how to do just about anything if they found enough online videos and tutorials.

That, and the *Reader's Digest Fix-It-Yourself Manual*—which happened to be the next gift Hannah opened. "It's the updated one!"

"Back in the day, the nineteen-eighty-five version was my main source of instruction. Still comes in handy from time to time."

"I love it." Taking in the treasure trove of gifts, and then her family, Hannah felt a little emotional at the blessings she'd been given. Who was she to be annoyed at God when He'd given her so much?

Heather took Clark's hand and nodded up at him. "Mom and Dad, Hannah, there's another present we want you to open at the same time."

Hannah arched a brow. They opened the small box, all of them exclaiming when they read the missive on the coffee mugs. Hannah's said "Best Aunt Ever, x2," and her parents' said "Best Gran and Grandpa Ever, x2."

"I knew it! I knew it!" Hannah's smile was so wide it almost hurt. It would be her turn someday, but today it was all about a new baby in the family.

"How did you know?" Heather looked dumbfounded.

Numbering the evidence on her fingers, Hannah shared the facts as she'd seen them. "One, there's been a lot of lovey-dovey going on between you two—get a room, guys. Two, all these comments about needing a bigger house. And three, since I know you very well, I can see the same glow you had when you were expecting Vi."

After a round of hugs and kisses, Hannah picked up Vi, who was still enamored of the doll furniture Dad made for her. "What do you think, sweetie? Are you going to have a brother or a sister?"

Vi stared up at her, solemn as a judge. "I'm gonna have both."

When Hannah's eyes met her baby sister's, she started laughing and shrugged her shoulders. Sure, this was all Vi's idea. There was nothing to back it up.

You never know ...

Chapter 21

Once the presents were opened at the Reno celebration, it was time to get ready to attend the Christmas Eve service at Clementville Community Church.

Trace and Eli were put on table-leaf removal duty, pushing the two ends of the table back to normal.

"Looking good, kids." Grandma came out of the kitchen where she'd been putting the butterscotch pull-apart rolls together for Christmas morning breakfast. The rest of the family spent the time rounding up scraps of wrapping paper in the trash bag while setting useable bags aside.

Lisa held one up that had seen its share of Christmases. "Hey, Mandy, check out this one."

The small bag, covered in illustrations of cats and dogs with Santa hats, was a keeper. "Didn't Grandma start using that one about ..." Mandy put her finger on her chin, thinking "... fifteen years ago?"

"Oh, definitely. It's a little worn, but I can't throw it away."

Nick happened to walk by about then. "Sweetheart, do we need this?" He lifted it, noting the tear on one side and residue where a sticker had been used on it—which was usually strictly forbidden. Somebody, at some point in time, had done it anyway.

Trace caught a glimpse of tears in Lisa's eyes. "Lisa?"

Lisa swiped the tears off her face. "Oh, I'm fine. It's these baby hormones. I look at anything with even the least sentimental value and break down."

Darcy came up to her and patted her on the back. "Oh yes, I remember it well." She nodded with sympathy. "Once the third trimester kicks in good, you'll be somewhat back to normal." She paused. "Note I said *somewhat*."

Lisa grabbed the bag out of Nick's hand and held it to herself. "If I can use pregnancy hormones as an excuse to do crazy things, I'm keeping it." Her side eye dared her husband to tell her differently.

Nick held up his hands in surrender. "I can accept that the bag is going home with us."

"Good." Lisa tucked it in with the rest of her presents. "Next year, I'll give it to someone who is deserving of the spirit of the gift bag."

Trace couldn't help it. He laughed, only to get a glare from Lisa.

"You, dear cousin, are not on that list, but with that new job, you'll be able to afford to buy us all new ones."

Cassie, Rob, and their three kids loaded up and made their way to the church, the rest of the family following suit as they gathered their things. Somehow, Trace ended up last, with Grandma and Grandpa.

"We'd better get a move on if we want to get a seat." Grandpa was always worried they'd be late and have to traipse in and sit in the front. Trace understood. He hated the feeling of being observed.

"I'll be ready just as soon as I put on my lipstick."

"It's a candlelight service. Nobody's going to be checking to see if you've put on lipstick."

"Christmas spirit, dear." She stopped at the mirror beside the door and smoothed on the finishing touch. "Now, I'm ready."

Trace grinned as he saw Grandpa kiss Grandma on the cheek. "I'll have the prettiest girl there."

She laughed and swatted him. "Oh, you."

If that's what sixty years of marriage looked like, Trace was in.

THERE WAS A CROWD THERE. Trace figured the mild temperatures helped.

The Reno contingent had claimed three pews about halfway up the aisle, and they were already crowded.

Turning to see where there were more seats, his gaze met Hannah's, and he smiled. It was automatic. He didn't think, *I need to smile at Hannah*. He just did. He made his way over to her. In his peripheral vision, Eli waved at her, pointing to a minuscule spot on the pew next to him.

But Trace was closer. "It seems your family pew is full too."

Hannah's face colored as she tugged at her bottom lip with her teeth.

"There's room for us over on the other side of the sanctuary. Sit with me?"

She still seemed unsure. After what was probably a fraction of a second, she returned his smile. "Sounds good."

He put his hand on the small of her back, guiding her through the crowd to get to the spot he'd seen. He hoped it was still available when they got there.

Ushering her into the pew, it was a squeeze, and Hannah

She leaned back and punched him in the arm gently. "Good for you!" Then she paused, heaving a fake sigh. "Now I'll have to break in another gofer ..."

"Maybe I should turn it down." Trace grinned when she punched him again.

"I'm happy for you, Trace. Will you move to Madisonville?" Her eyes drew him in.

"No, I think I'll stay around here."

The smile on her face did something to his insides. Had God seriously allowed him to both work *and* live the life he wanted? Had He given him a chance with Hannah? Every step he'd made, all his life, even when things didn't go as planned —like not becoming an astronaut—led him to this moment.

HE WAS STAYING, and he appeared to be happy about it.

Hannah was happy too. She didn't think for one minute there would be anything come of their friendship. Those kinds of things didn't happen to her.

Did they?

Could they?

Okay, so maybe she did think about it for a minute. Or two.

Sitting so close to him made her think of how she woke in his arms earlier in the safe room. She was utterly content until she realized where she was and what had happened.

Trace was so sweet about her fear of the dark. He kept her mind off it, talking to her, and from what she'd been told, he wasn't a talker.

Hc'd shown her a completely different side to him, and she liked it. Oh, sure, he was still a bit of a grump, but somehow it looked good on him.

The service was coming to a close. Every time she glanced

over at him, his body language indicated he was a little more content. Could people say the same about her?

After the closing prayer, everyone started getting up to leave. Before she stepped out of the pew, Trace stopped her. "Are you okay after the little ordeal?"

"I am." She paused, then remembered. "I forgot to tell you—Heather's expecting again."

He smiled and took her hand. "I'm happy for her, and for you. I'll bet you're a great aunt."

She felt the heat on her face. "I hope so." Just then, Vi crashed into her legs, almost knocking her over. "Whoa, Nellie."

Vi frowned deeply. "I'm not Nellie. I'm Vi'let."

"Oh, yeah, you're that little girl who calls me Aunt Hannah, aren't you?"

"You're silly."

"Not as silly as you." Hannah hugged her.

Vi peered up at Hannah, and then at Trace. "Who's this?"

Hannah stole a glance at him. "Violet, this is Trace Reno."

Trace held out his hand. "How do you do, Miss Violet." He was treating the meeting with the utmost respect, which made Hannah smile even more. She wasn't sure how much he'd been around kids, since nobody in his immediate family had kids yet.

"I'm good. Do you want to see my dolly bed Grandpa made me?"

He knelt, getting down to Vi's level. "I would love to see it sometime. I like to build things too."

"Trace fixed up the dresser I have my bathroom sink on in my new house."

Vi looked confused. "Why do you have a dresser in the bathroom?"

"Because it's prettier than a plain ol' cabinet, and because

Trace made it for me." The glance between them held. She hadn't said it out loud until now. As much as she loved the vanity he'd configured, she loved it even more because he'd done it.

"Oh." No question about it, Vi was rapidly losing interest in the conversation.

"Violet, I've told you not to run off from me."

The little girl put her hands on her hips and frowned. "I wasn't running *off*. I was running *to* Aunt Hannah." Vi's withering, much-too-mature expression indicated she was in despair of the intelligence of both her mother and Hannah.

"Okay, this time. Next time tell me where you're going. Promise?"

"I promise." Vi looked up at the grownups. "Mama, this is Trace."

"So, you're the Trace who got stuck in the basement with my sister." Heather grinned, curiously observing the two of them.

Trace stood, holding out his hand. "Guilty."

"In more ways than one, but who's counting?" The lightness Hannah felt was a relief. All her life, she'd striven to please people and make them think she was happy.

Now? She was happy. For real.

"Little girl, we've got to get home or Santa won't have time to stop at our house. We wouldn't want that, would we?"

Vi shook her head solemnly. "No. I'm ready." Violet started pulling her mother toward the front door. "Let's go, Mama."

"It's a shame I can't use the threat of Santa every night at bedtime."

"That might get expensive." Hannah hugged her sister. "Merry Christmas, Heather."

"Merry Christmas, Hannah."

WHY WAS it so hard for him to say "goodnight?"

The crowd was thinning, and the majority of people lingering were Renos and Buckners. They were waiting for Hannah and him.

"Why do I have the feeling our families are trying hard to give the two of us time together?" Hannah whispered with a quiet giggle on the side.

Her words lifted the pressure from him.

"Like we haven't had enough time together today." Trace arched an eyebrow at her when she looked at him quickly. Did she think he was being serious? "I'm teasing."

"I'm beginning to figure out your sense of humor."

"I'm told it tends to the dry side." He couldn't stop his smile. "My grandpa is the same way."

"I've been treated to his, and yes, I can see the resemblance in more than just looks." She appeared to be studying him.

He grinned. "I'll take that as a compliment."

"If that's how you want to take it ..."

Did she ...?

Trace narrowed his eyes as her face bloomed in a smile, a rosy color on her face. "You got me."

"Turnabout is fair play."

"How are things at your house?"

"Good. Settling in. While we're off next week, I want to get some pictures hung and curtains on the windows."

She eyed her parents, who kept glancing at them.

"I'd be happy to help. I don't start work until after the new year." He shrugged. "It'd give me something to do."

"Maybe."

The brightness in her countenance gave him hope—but not too much. She was being very careful. He appreciated her reticence. He wasn't exactly confident in relationships. Not that this was one.

Not yet, anyway. They had shared a stressful time, locked in a dark basement. Did having something in common, a shared experience, create a relationship of some kind?

He would have to think about that one.

"Is it okay if I check with you after Christmas?"

"Yes, that would be great."

"Goodnight, everybody," Del shouted over the group. "Gotta get the kids to bed." Carrying the two preschoolers in his arms, Del showed proof he was as happy as Trace had ever seen him.

"How about that?" Trace intended it as a rhetorical question, but Hannah sighed next to him.

"It makes me think maybe God is still in the miracle business."

Chapter 22

Watching the newlywed Reno couple and their children made Hannah sigh inside. Or was it out loud?

When she glanced up at Trace after her comment about the miracle business, she found his gaze on her.

"Maybe He is."

Her attention was diverted when her parents approached them. She sneaked another peek at Trace to find a quizzical expression on his face.

"Hannah, sweetie, are you coming back home with us or heading to your house?"

It was something she hadn't considered. Where was "home" now?

She paused, then made a decision. "I think I'll sleep at my house, but I can come for breakfast if that's okay?"

Mom's face bloomed. "Of course, it's okay. I'm making pull-aparts."

"My favorite."

Hannah laughed when she and Trace spoke at the same time.

"Grandma makes them every Christmas too. The years I haven't been at her house, Mom made them." Trace grinned.

"Great minds think alike," Hannah's dad teased, then grew serious. "Keep an eye on the weather. We might have a little snow tonight."

"Snow? Can't be much with this warm weather." He noticed his grandparents making their way to the car. "Looks like my ride is heading back to the farm. Is your truck here?" Trace's eyebrows drew together.

"It is, and I'll be fine."

"Okay. Be careful."

"I will." Hannah smiled, studying his face. "Merry Christmas, Trace."

"Merry Christmas, Hannah." He took her hand and squeezed it for a split second. It was over so quickly she wondered if she'd imagined it.

He left, and she missed him.

Was it possible that in the span of twelve hours, she'd fallen for the one man she was determined not to fall in love with?

Had she misread him the whole time? Had she been so determined to be her own woman that she nearly missed a great guy?

Kissing her mom and dad goodbye and waving at the others and shouting, "Merry Christmas" to everyone in general, Hannah walked to her truck.

She started it, smiling at the slight roar of the engine, then pulled out of the parking lot. The warm weather they'd experienced made a white Christmas impossible, though the temperature had dropped since they'd entered the church an hour ago. Surely Dad had heard wrong.

A low rumble surprised her. Thunder? At first, she was startled, and then she laughed at herself.

It was December. Of course not. But it was the warmest December on record so far. She hadn't seen any weather reports since she'd been incommunicado all afternoon and evening.

Wait, hadn't she heard of "thunder-snow?"

All she saw was light rain. Light rain that was turning into light slush by the time she got to her house.

The thunder was there, all right, and the cold wind had changed direction between the time she left church and got home. As soon as she entered the house, she pulled out her phone and found a string of weather alert notifications on the screen.

When the lights flickered, she immediately went to where she thought she kept her flashlight.

No, it's where she was *going* to keep it. It hadn't made it there yet.

Great, Hannah.

Phone. There was a flashlight app on the phone. She turned it on, a little concerned when she noticed her battery was at twenty-four percent. Using apps would make the battery go down quickly, and her phone didn't hold a charge well on a good day.

She would use it long enough to find her flashlight, saving her battery if the power stayed out.

Her phone chose that moment to ring. Dad. She put it on speaker so she could continue searching.

"Are you okay, Hannah?"

"I'm fine. Looking for my flashlight." So far, no luck.

"Did you check your truck?"

"On my way there now."

A crash of thunder and lightning lit up the woods around her house, revealing a sheen of ice coating everything.

"The weather is turning icy, Dad."

"I know. I don't like you being out there alone."

Here we go again.

"I'm fine, and hey, if there were any bad guys out to get me, they'd have a hard time getting here in this weather." Maybe if she stayed light, Dad would too.

She got to her truck and opened the door, hearing the tinkle of ice breaking. It was quickly accumulating on the grass and trees. Feeling around behind the driver's seat, her fingers wrapped around the Maglite flashlight she'd been searching for. She needed to get an extra to keep in the house.

"Got it. Going back inside now."

"Call if you need me."

"I will, Dad. I'm a big girl."

She heard the snort on the other end of the line. "To me, you'll always be my Hannah banana."

"Love you, Daddy. Be there bright and early."

"Call before you leave."

She looked up and took a deep breath. "I will."

By the time she made it back to the porch and into the house.

"Lord, for those who prayed for a white Christmas, that's much preferable to an ice Christmas."

She rifled through her junk drawer in the kitchen, found some matches, and lit some candles on the nightstand in her bedroom. It wouldn't be very bright, but it would be better than total darkness.

Now if she just had the gas logs she'd ordered two weeks ago. If the power didn't come on in the next few hours, she was going to be cold.

WHEN A FIERCE GUST of wind and a drop of slush hit Trace's face on the way to the door, his first thought was of Hannah.

Was this going to be an actual weather event?

As soon as they got in, removed their coats, and began putting things to right before they went to bed, the power flickered, and then went out. Grandpa immediately reached under the sink, pulled out the battery-operated lantern, and set it on the table.

"I'm glad I got the Butterscotch Pull-Aparts put together." Grandma laughed. It was an old family joke.

"Might be hard to bake 'em if there's no power in the morning," Grandpa said.

"Oh, do you think it'll last that long? It was so warm all day." Now Grandma was starting to worry.

Grandpa patted her on the back. "Fear not. I can get a fire going and cook them in the Dutch oven." Grandpa sounded more confident than he appeared.

"We'll have to hope for the best."

Trace pulled out his phone and saw the notifications for weather alerts. He'd had his phone turned off since earlier this evening and hadn't thought to check the weather between being locked in a basement and having Christmas with his family.

"I'll get you boys some extra blankets."

The house was still plenty warm. Trace had a feeling it would take a while to cool it down to what he considered a comfortable sleeping temperature.

"Thanks, Grandma," Eli said, also checking his phone.

"Did you know about this forecast?" Trace asked Eli.

"Didn't even think to check." Eli continued looking at his screen. "They're calling it a 'whiplash' event."

"I believe it."

"Nothing we can do about it now. May as well go to bed and save the phone battery." Eli trudged up the stairs to the room they shared.

Trace had already decided that if Eli decided to move down here, he'd have to find his own place. There was only so much room two grown men could share.

"I'll be up in a bit."

Eli nodded. "Merry Christmas, bro."

"You, too, bro." Trace grinned, then stared at the screen and decided to go for it.

> Are you okay?

Nothing for a few seconds, and then the dots indicating her typing started to bounce.

> I'm fine. Got a flashlight and candles going. Where did this weather come from?

> I guess we were a little out of the loop today, lol.

> Ya think? Ha!

> Just wanted to check on you.

> Thanks. Dad called as soon as the power went out, said he could get here if I needed him.

Oh yeah. She has a dad who can do those things for her.

Why did Trace think it would be up to him to care for her? To make sure she was safe and peaceful?

Because you're an idiot, that's why.

> Good deal. Just wanted to make sure you got home okay.

Thanks, and Merry Christmas. :)

Merry Christmas, Hannah.

No bouncing dots. Conversation over.

He missed her already.

HANNAH GRIMACED when she saw the charge on her phone. Fifteen percent. If she didn't use the flashlight, it might last until morning. If it was dead when she woke up, she'd take it to the truck and charge it.

The thick darkness pressed on her—except when the lightning struck, and then it was a glittery, beautiful, scary mess. One bright flash revealed her truck, completely glazed over with ice.

It was dark, but it certainly wasn't quiet. The trees were creaking and cracking. How many limbs would be down by morning?

Mandy:

Are you alone at the house??

Hannah shook her head. She didn't have a chance to get lonely.

Yes, and I'm fine.

Just checking. Clay just texted he'd
been called out to an accident already.
Why are people out traveling in the wee
hours of Christmas morning?

It wasn't Santa, was it?

I heard no report of injured elves or
reindeer, so I'm assuming that's a no.

Whew.

Seriously. Anyway, going to sleep now,
wondering what I'll wake up to.

Thanks, Mandy.

No prob. Merry Christmas!

Merry Christmas!

Ten percent. Hannah sighed. May as well go to bed and wait it out—it was only a few hours until daylight anyway.

A loud crack in the wooded area between her house and the highway startled her. Had a tree fallen?

Chapter 23

Hannah could sit there and worry or realize that God loved her and was in control. There wasn't a thing she could do about it.

Thank you, Lord.

Leaving a jarred candle lit on the table next to her bed, she contemplated other times she'd been caught in the dark. This afternoon it had been darker than it was now, without power—which reminded her she needed to always keep a flashlight in her toolbox. She hadn't been as worried as she expected because Trace was there.

She lay there, eyes closed for the longest, her mind running over the last few days, her thoughts consistently turning back to Trace.

Opening her eyes, she stared at the long shadows flickering in the candlelight. Were the feelings she had real, or were they part of the fear she experienced in the dark? Was it just gratitude?

"Ugh." The growl she articulated made her feel better.

Then Hannah realized something. She wasn't alone. She had Someone to talk to.

"Okay, God, we need to talk. I will admit, I've been a little irritated at You, and I know that's wrong. I'm confessing, okay? I know when Jesus came, He was fully human, but somehow I doubt He sat around and wondered why all this was happening to Him. Did He?

"Oh, He did ask for the cup to be passed from Him, if possible.

"Is that even the same thing?

"I guess, for me, it's not even that I think I've missed opportunities for relationships, but that everyone around me seems to be in a relationship with Your blessing, and I feel like I'm left out."

Oh, great. I have fear-of-missing-out with God. How childish is that?

"Forgive me, Lord, for putting You in second, third, fourth, and beyond places instead of where You are supposed to be, which is in first place. Forgive me for being jealous of my friends. My very best friends. I'm happy they're in love.

"I guess I just want it to be real for me too.

"Thanks for listening. Amen."

Hannah drifted off to sleep as the wind howled louder and the house creaked all around her.

THE LIGHT SHINING in Hannah's bedroom window made the entire room glow. The candle, flickering cheerfully when she went to sleep, had burned out, and her breath made little white clouds in the air.

The bright light coming in her windows made her happier than she could explain, even to herself.

She'd survived the night, in the dark, alone in her house. Now, if she could talk herself into getting up and leaving the comfort of the bed she was snuggled in.

Picking up her phone, she saw she still had about five percent battery, which was a Christmas miracle.

Two text message alerts displayed on the Lock Screen.

Dad was the first one.

And then Trace. When she saw "Grumpy" appear, she laughed.

Change it? No, not yet ...

As much as she appreciated Dad checking on her, Trace's text made her feel warmer than the covers pulled up to her chin.

Dad:

You okay out there, Hannah-banana?

> Just fine. Haven't left the bed yet.

News flash: it's cold.

> No joke. I'll be there as soon as I can get dressed.

Do you have any de-icer?

> No, thought I'd take some hot water if the door's iced shut

LOL—good luck with that.

> Oh, yeah. Okay, I'll be there as soon as I can.

No rush. Be careful.

10-4

She grinned. No power, no hot water. She'd figure it out ... after she read Trace's text, sent about an hour ago.

Grumpy:

Good morning. Everything okay?

> Merry Christmas! Yes, everything is fine. I survived the night in the dark.

I knew you would.

She slowly pulled the cover back and hurried to the window. The sky was still gray, but the snow and ice made everything brighter. Sure enough, a crystalline glaze covered every surface.

> Now to get the door of the truck de-iced so I can get to Mom and Dad's house.

2 parts rubbing alcohol, 1 part water, drop of dishwashing detergent in a spray bottle.

> Awesome. My first thought was warm water, but ...

Yeah, good luck with that, lol

She laughed out loud. Dad and Trace. Great minds?

> Thanks.

Welcome. Merry Christmas again.

> Lol, Merry Christmas to you again too.

He ended the conversation with a smiling emoji, which made her smile right back.

The house was cold. She looked longingly at the empty fireplace but decided it was just as well since she needed to get dressed and get to her parents' house. It was already 8 am, and their house had a generator, which meant breakfast would be ready by the time she got there—and there would be hot water.

Yes, I'll be installing a generator—and soon.

ONCE BREAKFAST WAS devoured next to the wood stove Grandpa had fired up earlier, plans were made to pack up and head to Mom and Dad's house—brand-new and equipped with an alternate power source.

Trace had wondered if it was worth the expense, but as an adult, a power outage wasn't as much fun as it was when he was a kid. He couldn't figure out why Grandpa hadn't installed a generator after the ice storm of 2009 left them with no power for three weeks.

"As long as I have a wood stove, wood to burn, and kerosene for light, we'll be just fine," Grandpa said after the power went off.

"I'd just as soon be able to cook with my electric oven if it's all the same to you," Grandma returned.

Grandpa didn't have much to say after that, just helped her get stuff together and made sure she had her metal cleats on her boots so she didn't slip.

Grandpa agreed to let Trace drive them in his truck, so they loaded up Eli's vehicle with stuff and Grandma and Grandpa in the truck.

When they arrived, Dad had the fire on full-blast in the fireplace, and Mom had both double ovens on, so it was plenty warm.

"Merry Christmas!" Samantha met them at the door and helped Grandma and Grandpa unwrap from their coats and scarves while Eli and Trace brought in the pies and coconut cake Grandma had left from the night before.

"Merry Christmas, sweetheart!" Grandma kissed Sam on the cheek. "I'm so glad to be with all of you this year. It's been a while."

"I know."

"I'm glad to not have to leave my house this morning." Mom laughed. "The last Christmas we had with my parents, it snowed, and I took everything over there to cook." She hugged Grandma, who returned the embrace.

"I know you miss your folks."

"I do." Mom's eyes were teary, but she was smiling. "But I'm happy to be down here with you and Grandpa."

"We're glad to have you too." Grandpa put an arm around her shoulders. "Now Tom here ..."

"... is just like his daddy, so don't mind him." Grandma huffed a little, attempting to hide a smile.

Mom laughed out loud. "And Trace takes after both of them."

"Hey, there, When did I get pulled into this?" Trace set down the last of the foodstuffs on the counter and kissed his mom on the cheek.

His mother pulled on his beard, grinning. "I think about the time you decided to grow this mess."

Trace stroked his nicely-trimmed ginger beard with pride. "And here I got all trimmed up just for you, Mom."

Mom's arched brow let him know she didn't believe that for one minute. "Oh, you're nicely trimmed," she said, inspecting him from one side to the other. "Something tells me you had someone else in mind when you did it."

Eli sat back on the bar stool, grinning. "Yeah, I think he stayed up texting after we all went to bed last night."

"That so ..." Tom's brows went up.

Samantha slipped her arm through Trace's. "Was it Hannah?" She had a knowing look on her face.

"I was just …"

Samantha lowered her brow and spoke seriously, deepening her voice in imitation of her brother's as much as possible, but it was belied by the sparkle in her eyes. "… making sure she got home all right …"

All eyes were on him. He was so far outside of his comfort zone. His first instinct was to deny it. "I wasn't …"

Mom smiled gently. "You don't have to explain one thing, Trace."

"Thanks, Mom." He shook his head at his siblings. "First power outage in a new house, especially out where she lives, I wanted to make sure she was okay."

"I get it, son." Dad nodded. "You were being a gentleman."

Trace shot a glare at Eli, silently warning him to keep his mouth shut.

"Since we're all here, and lunch is underway, why don't we go in the living room." Mom directed their attention to the beautifully decorated tree with presents piled underneath. "I think Santa may have come."

"And boy, was he noisy last night." Sam quipped. "Just sayin'."

"Mom, I think you can stop …"

"Who, dear?" Mom's brows raised, and her eyelashes fluttered.

"I mean, I think Santa …"

Dad whispered loudly, "I told you three not to tell Mom there was no Santa …" Then he laughed.

"Thank you, Trace." She nodded and gestured for him to continue.

"I think Santa can probably stop filling our stockings any

year now." He twisted his lips. "Preferably before we turn forty?"

"Tell you what." Mom eyed her three offspring. "You get me some grandchildren, and I'll pass that word along."

Mom knows how to shut us up—and quick.

HANNAH'S CHRISTMAS was much like it had been for the last few years since Heather and Clark married. They ate a big breakfast, a light lunch, and then pulled out the leftovers from the night before when Heather, Clark, and Vi stopped by on their way home from Clark's parents' home in Paducah.

Vi came bursting in the door and went straight to the Christmas tree.

"Well, hello to you, too, Miss Vi." Mom laughed.

"She's looking for her stocking." Heather's weariness caught her attention.

Mom went to hug her. "Then she's come to the right place."

"You know she doesn't have to have a stocking everywhere she goes." Heather tilted her head at her mother.

"I know. Is there any reason I can't enjoy my only grandchild?"

Clark grinned as he brought in what was left of the food they'd taken to his family's Christmas celebration. "Remember, next year you'll have double." He turned, catching Hannah's eye. "And who knows, two Christmases from now ..."

"Hold it right there, Buster." Hannah loved her brother-in-law dearly, and having him around made her wish she'd had a brother in addition to her sister. Now, however?

"I'm just saying, you never know what a year can bring, do

you?" Clark had all the smugness of a married man about to have not one, but two children. "Oh, and it's started snowing."

She wrinkled her nose at him and changed the subject as they all went to a window to check out the precipitation, ignoring his question. "I've got the turkey and dressing heating in the oven, so we can heat the rest of the stuff in the microwave."

"Can I wait about an hour?" Heather's eyes were bulging. "I think I've eaten more in the last twenty-four hours than I have all year."

"At least you're keeping it down, now."

"Yes, and thank you for keeping that part of your pregnancy a secret." Hannah winked at her.

"You're welcome." She sighed. "Actually, I wasn't as sick this time."

Mom lit up. "You're having a boy."

"What?" Heather stared at her mother like she'd grown two heads.

"It's not scientific, but if one pregnancy is dramatically different from another, chances are you're having the opposite sex."

"Old wives' tale," Dad weighed in, voice raised, from his recliner in the next room.

Mom shouted toward the living room. "Well, I'm an old wife, so I guess it's okay, then." She pursed her lips to hide her grin. "Claims he can't hear when I call him from the next room, but he can hear conversations he's not even a part of." She shook her head. "That man."

Hannah giggled. As much as she loved having her own home now, she also loved it when they were all together.

Mom spoke again. "Let's go sit in the living room until we're ready to eat. It's warmer in there."

Maybe Hannah would appreciate her family more by not being with them all the time. Did Trace feel the same way?

Oh, good grief. Here we go, thinking about him again.

"Hannah, how was your first power outage in your new house?" Heather snuggled next to her big sister on the couch.

"It was fine." Hannah thought for a minute. "The power went off just as I was getting home. Then I had to go to the truck to get my flashlight before my phone died."

"Ouch. I'm glad ours didn't go out this time. I was not up to that."

"The worst part was not having any heat." Hannah shrugged. "I made it okay."

Mom couldn't contain herself any longer. "Hannah said Trace texted to check on her."

Dad's reading glasses were down on his nose as he read yesterday's paper. He never looked up, but all other eyes were on Hannah.

"Oh, reeeealllly." Heather's sing-song voice had Hannah covering her face with her hands.

"He just texted to see if I got home okay," Hannah said, a slight pleading in her voice begging, 'Please, don't go there.'

"It was very nice." Mom had Vi in her lap, rocking her and her new doll.

"Oh, it was nice, all right." Dad's voice was a cross between irritation and suspicion, with a little dash of humor. He ducked the paper and peered at Hannah above the glasses. "Anything we should know about you two getting stuck in the basement together?"

Hannah was horrified. "Daddy!"

His good-natured wink gave him away.

Chapter 24

"I don't think it's a good idea." Hannah was emphatic. It didn't matter how many times Trace brought up the idea of his renting the cabin from her, she intended to say no.

It would be too weird.

"It would only be temporary until I can find a place. I've taken advantage of Grandma and Grandpa long enough."

Hannah forced herself not to laugh. She knew Sylvia Reno. The woman doted on her grandchildren.

"Trace." She put her hands on her hips and tilted her head at him.

He took a deep breath and shifted his eyes, twisting his lips in humor. "Okay, so chances are Grandma will be sorry to see me go, but it's looking like Eli might be moving down, and I hate for her to have both of us."

"Or do you want to get out before Eli gets too comfortable?" She chuckled at the guilty expression he wore.

"Maybe a little." He grinned.

It would be a bad idea. She knew it would. Was she developing ... feelings ... for Trace?

"What's wrong?" Trace narrowed his eyes.

She didn't have a poker face. At. All. If she weren't careful, she'd give it away, and that was the last thing she wanted. She wanted to be in control of herself and the situation, and the idea of having him that close gave her pause.

"Nothing." She consulted the instructions provided with her new gas log set. Fortunately, the power outage only lasted a little over a day. The van delivering the logs the day after Christmas slipped and slid down her driveway, but he came, and she'd give the company kudos for delivering on time.

When Trace called to see if she needed any help at the house, her first instinct was to say no, but she wasn't as comfortable hooking up a gas line as she was a power line, so she asked him to come over and spot her while she connected it to the gas logs in the fireplace. After consulting with both Dad and Nick, she felt pretty sure of herself. If Nick gave her his seal of approval, she was confident that she could do it.

Hannah leaned back and double-checked the burner connected to the gas line. She wanted to test the burner before placing the logs. "The moment of truth." She looked up at him. "Fingers crossed?"

"I feel like we should pray or something." He gave a low chuckle.

"Probably not a terrible idea." She glanced up, whispered a prayer, pushed the gas button, and then the striker button to start the pilot.

"So far so good." Trace had squatted down next to her. "Turn the burner up and see how it does."

"Do you smell gas?" The last thing she wanted was a breach in the connection from the line to the burner assembly.

"No." He glanced at her. "Do you?"

"Nope." Hannah took in a deep, satisfying breath as she turned the flame to the highest setting, then off again.

"It's perfect." Trace shook his head at her. "Is there anything you can't do?"

She scoffed. "Plenty." She placed the logs carefully in the locations specified by the instructions, aligning them perfectly on pins that held them in place.

"Got s'mores?" Trace quipped as she turned the burner back on and settled it into what had all the appearances of a perfect wood fire.

She shrugged. "I may or may not have prepared for just such a time as this." She scrambled up from the floor. "You put away the tools, and I'll get the s'mores ingredients."

TRACE DID as he was bid, and when Hannah returned from the kitchen, he'd spread a picnic-style throw on the floor.

"Nice!" Her smile shone with approval.

"Keep a little padding between the cold floor and ..."

"Exactly." She laughed.

She handed him skewers and set out the ingredients before them.

"This is a professional-looking setup."

"I hesitate to say this, but s'mores are my best dish." She turned red. "Cooking was never my thing. I can function, but who has time for the niceties?"

"Hey, if you can make s'mores, it shows you know how to plan ahead." He shrugged as he turned his marshmallow with precision, pulling it back when it began to smoke, watching as it puffed and turned a delicious brown.

"I guess. When I was in high school, I was all over what I was doing in trade school during the day and doing art the rest of the time."

Trace glanced around at the cozy living room and at the

different things hanging on the wall. "Did you paint some of these?"

She nodded, slowly looking from one to the other as if they were old friends.

"Do you still paint?" Trace wanted to know. Who was he kidding? He wanted to know everything about her.

"I haven't in a long time." She concentrated on assembling the gooey treat. "I took a few classes at community college, but I didn't have time to expand on it."

He had only to tip his head back to study the painting above the fireplace. "What about this one?"

She glanced over at him with a smile. "Yes. It's my favorite."

It was a landscape. Trace thought he recognized the area. Was that Lisa's house? It was from across the field, so the house wasn't the main subject, nor was the barn. The land was. There was a clump of trees and a creek on one side, fence rows and crooked posts marking off the different pastures, and in the far left-hand corner, it was brighter, as if the sun had just risen and cast a golden glow on the farm.

"I can see why. "It's beautiful."

"Thanks." There she was, blushing again. It was interesting. All the times he'd tried, in vain, so far, to express interest in her, the deepest flush of emotion came to her when he complimented her art. It was that important to her.

"I painted two at the farm, and I gave one to Lisa and Nick when they got married." She shrugged, smiling.

"I thought I recognized it. Lisa paints too."

Hannah nodded. "I admired her, growing up. She always seemed to know what she wanted and wasn't afraid to go for it."

He looked at her askance. "Is this Lisa Reno we're talking about?"

"Yes, and I know what you're going to say."

"Oh, really?" His lips tipped in a smile as he waited for her to continue. "I'll admit, her art has more spatial awareness than her body." He laughed at the indignant expression on Hannah's face.

"Not everyone is beautiful from day one like Mandy."

"True. Mandy must have gotten it from the other side of the family," he teased.

Hannah shook her head. "I've seen pictures of your grandmother," she said. "Mandy looks just like her."

"Okay, truce. They're both pretty amazing. If you tell them I said that, I'll deny it, you hear?" Was his glare 'glare-y' enough, or was the twitch of his lips as he fought a smile giving him away?

"I hear, and I won't say a word." She snorted. "Boys."

When she gave him the side-eye with a hint of a good humor, he knew.

He knew it more now than he'd known the first time he realized he had fallen for her. How did this feeling continue to grow? Would it eventually grow so big that it would get out of control?

What he thought of as "love at first sight," was, instead, an attraction to this woman slowly blossoming into feelings far beyond physical attraction.

And he didn't quite know how to deal with that.

WHEN TRACE LEFT SOON after the S'mores snack, Hannah was a little deflated. He was a hard one to figure out. Was it worth the trouble to have any kind of relationship with him—even as friends?

They'd been talking about her art, and then all at once, he

was glazed over. Somewhere in the conversation, a switch flipped, and he left soon after.

Washing up the skewers and plates they'd used, she couldn't get him out of her mind. She'd scoffed at the idea of him liking her. Sometimes, like when they were trapped together and she was scared and in the dark, he was so tender it was impossible not to be drawn to him. Other times, he was distant and broody. How was she to know which Trace she was going to encounter on a day-to-day basis?

Crush on Ron Weasley notwithstanding, Trace had niggled his way into her affections. It was a crush, pure and simple. Had to be. It was brought on because she'd claimed a moratorium on dating, and she knew that when a person prayed for patience, guess what? God would give said person a reason to have patience, so that person could learn from it.

The last time she'd felt anything like this was when she was crushing on James Carrino, her family's neighbor down the road. They rode the same school bus. Who was she kidding? *Everybody* in Clementville rode the same school bus. He was "older," a senior in high school when she was a sophomore. She laughed at herself. She'd thought herself in love. When he asked her to be his date to the prom, she had been beside herself.

When she found out he asked her because his out-of-town date canceled on him, she was disappointed but ignored it and had a good time.

Looking back, she saw it for what it was—a fun evening. They danced, they talked, they laughed at each other's jokes. When they got back to school the next Monday, he'd asked her out, which was the icing on the cake.

The funny thing was, what she'd thought was enduring love with him had dwindled to friendship by the time they went out a third time. It's probably why she never believed in love. Why she thought maybe it had passed her by and she wasn't meant to have it.

But Trace? She denied being attracted to him. Refused any attempts of his to impress her.

Had she hurt his feelings?

Maybe that was why he left so suddenly. Did he come to realize she wasn't the girl he thought she was?

Why, then, did she have these feelings? These memories of being snuggled next to him in the dark. Of contemplating his lips and wondering what they would feel like on hers?

Chapter 25

Trace was spending most of his off-time in Grandpa's wood shop. He'd done some research, and he was determined to finish this project before he had to report to his new job on the third of January. While he sanded and stained the wood, he had time to think and to listen. It seemed like God had been waiting for Trace to be still long enough to get through to him.

This wasn't all about Trace and his relationship with Hannah. It was about a relationship with God, and His blessing on a relationship with Hannah.

"Love at first sight" wasn't real. He'd known it. He'd fought against it, then fell for the rhetoric of the world that told him physical attraction was all he needed to start a lasting relationship.

What he'd once thought was love was a major crush, But now? Now it was deeper. Now it wasn't just about what it would be like to kiss her, to touch her, to spend time with her. Now it was about how to care for her. How to anticipate her desires.

If he thought too much about it, it made him crazy, because the two were so intertwined he had to distance himself from her to get his head on straight.

Did she have any feelings toward him? They had fun together. While they were stuck in the basement, the trust she had in him was sweet, and he reveled in the physical contact she allowed because she was scared and because she was asleep. If she'd been awake and unafraid, it might have been totally different.

"How's it going?" Grandpa had sneaked in.

"Hey, Grandpa. Pretty good." He kept working, head down, putting some nuts and bolts in place to hold the project together. "Do you have any light chain?"

"How light?"

Trace held his fingers up, measuring it with his eye. "Oh, about a half-inch to three-quarter?"

Grandpa rifled through a bin of random metal objects. "How much do you need?"

"How much have you got?" Trace chuckled.

"About four feet."

"More than enough."

Grandpa fished it out and set it on the workbench. "Here you go. Anything else you need?"

Trace considered his grandfather, the man he'd been told he was like. Besides his dad, Grandpa was the man he trusted most. "Got a minute?"

"Got an hour if you need it."

Trace glanced up with a half-smile, then cast his gaze down at his feet, frowning. How did he ask this question? Was he a seventh-grader? At twenty-eight, that was embarrassing.

"Something on your mind, son?" Grandpa made himself comfortable in the old rocking chair he kept in the shop for rest breaks. "Pull up a bucket."

Trace put down his tools and found the five-gallon bucket Grandpa indicated, turned it over, and sat. "I'm trying to figure out how to ask something."

"Take your time."

Trace nodded, leaning his elbows on his knees and lacing his fingers together loosely. "Here goes." He swallowed, then dove in. "How do you know the difference between physical attraction and loving somebody?"

Grandpa sat there, rocking back and forth, seeming to ponder his answer. When he looked up at Trace, there was a light in his eyes. "It's all about patience."

"Patience?" That wasn't what he was expecting—and he didn't want to be patient. He wanted to get on with life.

Grandpa rocked some more. "When I met your grandma, I was in eighth grade, and she was in seventh. It was her first year of junior high," he said, shaking his head, "went to the junior high in town, no less. All I knew was that she was a pretty little thing. We weren't either one of us thinking about romance. She'd come from the other side of the county, in Mattoon, so the only time we would have had the opportunity to meet would have been in town or at the fair. Somehow, we never met, or if we crossed paths, it didn't stick."

"Hannah said she'd seen pictures of Grandma, and that she looked just like Mandy when she was younger."

"She did indeed." Grandpa shook his head. "When I saw her the first day of school? It stuck."

"What did you do?" How had he never heard this story before?

"Absolutely nothing." Grandpa laughed. "We were thirteen and fourteen years old. It was the sixties, not the dark ages."

Trace nodded. "When did you know?"

"When did I know the torch I'd carried for her since the first day I laid eyes on her was the real thing?"

"Yeah."

"When I got drafted into the Army to go to Vietnam right after I graduated from high school."

His wartime experience wasn't something Grandpa talked about much. More in the last few years as his grandchildren grew up and became curious. Grandpa told Eli and Trace a few stories about his time over there that Dad had never heard.

"What did you do?"

"First, I thought about what it meant for me to go to war." Grandpa took a deep breath and expelled it. "When we both got to the high school, we'd become friends. Had study hall together. She was a cheerleader, and I was on the basketball team, stuff like that. We kidded a lot, but I'd never had the nerve to ask her out on a date."

Grandpa grinned. "That day, I called her. I knew it might be the wrong thing. What if I didn't come back? I'd known several who didn't. It was a different war than we'd been taught, growing up."

"What did she say?" Trace was mesmerized.

"She very graciously said she'd go out with me and then asked me what took me so long."

They laughed together. Sounded like Grandma.

"See, son, I'd had my eye on her for a long time, but because of our ages, we were forced to be patient. There was no way her papa would have let her go out with me until she was sixteen, but even then, I was too intimidated to ask her. She turned eighteen a few weeks before my draft notice came in."

"Seems like it was kind of meant to be." Trace held his grandfather's gaze.

"When it's right, that's how it is." Grandpa pulled a handkerchief from his pocket and blew his nose. A sheen of tears glistened in his eyes. "The initial attraction I had as a young teenager grew into loving her and wanting to care for her and do things for her."

"How long did you get to see her until you went to basic training?"

"Six weeks." He smiled broadly. "Six of the happiest weeks of my life, up to that point, anyway."

Trace did some math, knowing when his grandparents' sixtieth wedding anniversary had been celebrated, and how old they were now. "You two got married before you left."

"That we did." Grandpa stood and put his hand on Trace's shoulder. "I told you it takes patience, but I didn't say you had to wait forever." He gave him a wink and whistled all the way back to the house.

Trace had met Hannah about five weeks ago, Thanksgiving weekend. They'd spent the better part of Christmas Eve together and become friends, which is much more than they'd been before.

An idea formed in his mind. He still had a few days until Del and Darcy's New Year's Eve party. In the meantime, he wanted to do something for Hannah. Building the easel for her was a start.

He hoped he knew her reasoning for wanting to keep their living arrangements farther apart. Could she possibly be as attracted to him as he was to her? She'd been so careful, so noncommittal, and yet he'd caught glimpses of his feelings mirrored in her eyes.

If that was the case, as much as he would relish living ten yards from her back door, it wasn't a good idea. He didn't want to play on the attraction he felt for her. He wanted to build on it—but only if she felt the same. He'd watched Eli date one girl after another, none of the relationships until Carrie lasting long enough to call it serious. Oh, there'd been an attraction, but Eli didn't let it last long enough to think it through.

Patience. That was Grandpa's advice.

Maybe "love at first sight" was just the first step to a lifetime of so much more.

Smiling as he cleaned up the shop, Trace dusted off the hand-made artist easel he'd built for Hannah, making sure no splinter marred the surface. The pieces were smooth to the touch. It would work perfectly in her new cabin-slash-art studio.

Hannah was awakened early by the *clunk* of items being pitched into the bed of a truck or a trailer. Grabbing her robe, she peeked out the back door. Trace's truck *and* a trailer backed up to the door of the cabin.

Hadn't she told him plainly that she did not want to rent the cabin to him? Had she not made herself clear?

The weather had warmed up a bit from the Christmas cold snap, but in those places where it was shady, patches of snow and ice lingered. She stomped into her bedroom and pulled on jeans and a hoodie, hat, boots, and coat, then went out to ask Trace Reno just who he thought he was.

She paused. First, she'd turn on the coffee maker. And maybe make a little more than usual.

And pre-heat the oven for biscuits ...

Hannah, you wimp.

Once the coffee maker started working, she pulled her gloves on and marched right outside.

This was *her* place, wasn't it?

"Good morning, Hannah." Trace was cool as a cucumber.

At thirty degrees, he should be.

She stood there, hands on her hips, legs spread apart in a power stance—or at least she hoped it was. The whole body language thing confused her.

"What do you think you are doing out here? Didn't I tell you I didn't want to rent out the cabin? What were you thinking to just haul a trailer in here and start emptying the building? I mean, really?"

His smile grew broader as she kept talking, which made her even madder. "Seriously? You're going to stand there and smile?" She knew her eyes were bugging now.

"Good morning, Hannah." He gestured toward her, pointing at the area of her mouth. "You're gonna catch flies in there if you're not careful."

"It's winter, and it's thirty degrees out here. I don't think the flies, or me, are in danger."

"Fair enough." He walked toward her, and she bristled.

"Well?" This time, she crossed her arms and jutted her chin, in what she hoped was also a power move.

"I didn't have anything to do today and thought I would help you by clearing out this cabin. You mentioned wanting to use it for an art studio." He stood there, daring her to object, waiting.

Hannah twisted her lips and raised her eyes to the sky. Why, oh why, did he have to go and do something nice? "I said I wasn't sure what I'd do with it."

Well, that was pouty, Hannah.

"After seeing your work, I will be disappointed if you don't use this space to paint more." He grinned, a mischievous glint in his eyes. "Unless you want to rent it to me to live in?"

She shot him a glare. "Why?"

He hadn't dropped his gaze from her since she'd come out, and it was a little disconcerting. "Why, what?"

"Why are you doing this for me—without being asked, I might add."

"Because I start a job next week, and I'm going crazy doing nothing."

"But ..."

"But what?" He took a deep breath and walked closer to her. "Hannah, I saw something that needed to be done, I had the time, and I thought maybe you could start using the space now instead of waiting until warm weather to do it by yourself."

"Because you're such a big, strong, tough dude and can work in below-freezing temperatures?"

"Ah, Hannah, your sarcasm is showing." His grin was infectious.

"Trace Reno, what in the world am I going to do with you?" When his eyes dipped to her lips, her breath caught.

It was so quick, his expression. Had she imagined it? Had she imagined those other times when his face tendered?

He cleared his throat. "Well, I have a few ideas."

Another glare shot his way, but it missed its mark.

"There are a few pieces of furniture in here. Have you gone through any of it?" Back to business.

"A little." She glanced behind him. The days had been so short since she bought the property that she hadn't had time to explore as she wanted to.

"Listen," she began.

"I'm all ears." He was finally beginning to exhibit that I'm-cold-and-need-to-move-around stance he'd contained until now.

"Have you had breakfast?"

He shook his head. "Got out before anybody talked me out of coming over."

"First, I'm going to cook breakfast ..." She waved away his

refusal. "Don't get excited. It's the one meal I do well. I've already put on the coffee."

"If you insist."

She sighed and turned toward the house. "Come on. It's warmer in there than it is out here."

TRACE COULDN'T HIDE the grin on his face when he stepped into her kitchen behind her. He was reverting back to the kill-her-with-kindness tactic that he was counting on to work this time. They had a history now—a shared experience. They'd gone through a stressful event and come out as better friends than they were before.

Now? Now, he was determined to spend as much time with this woman as humanly possible without her throwing him off the farm. He pulled off his gloves, hat, scarf, and coat, hanging them next to hers on the available hooks next to the back door. *Handy.*

"How do you like your eggs? Please say scrambled. My fried eggs are still in process." She wrinkled her nose as she pulled the eggs, sausage links, and canned biscuits out of the refrigerator.

"Scrambled for me." He tilted his head until she looked at him. "You don't have to do this, you know."

"I know."

She sounded exhausted. Was it worth it to wear her down? Would she resent it? Maybe she had plans today.

"I guess I should have asked if you had other plans today." He twisted his lips and shrugged.

"Maybe you should have," she said, "but I don't. I might have frittered away the day if you hadn't come."

"And maybe those can be plans too?"

"Caryn and Ben are going to Nashville for the day, and Mandy and her mom are going wedding dress shopping."

"I'm surprised you're not going with them."

Hannah grinned. "Pretty sure her mom wanted the first trip to be just the two of them. I think it's sweet."

"Aunt Chris wasn't here last year when she and Clay started dating, so it's good she's able to throw herself into her wedding." He chuckled. "Mom is tickled pink."

"Well, that's good, because Mandy *loves* pink." She sent him a withering look. "Not my favorite color, but I'll wear it for her."

"You'll look terrific."

She glanced back at him in surprise from her stance at the range, then turned back to the task at hand. "I think they're planning a fall wedding."

"Wow," Trace said. "Mom always said you need to allow a year for the kind of wedding I figure Mandy will have. That's quick."

"As Mandy said, no point in being silly about it."

Trace looked even more surprised. "That is a very un-Mandy-like sentence."

Hannah laughed. "Right?"

"Huh. Maybe she *is* growing up."

"Mandy and I are the same age, you know."

"Yeah, but she's my baby cousin. She'll always be a teenager in my eyes."

"Well, she's not." Hannah frowned, a tinge of ... something ... unsettling her.

He stared, mouth open, for a minute. "No, and you aren't, either."

As she considered him, a flush crept up his neck and into his cheeks. The beard didn't hide everything, bless his heart.

She coughed, clearing her throat, suddenly feeling uncomfortable—but not in a bad way.

"So, you've decided I need an art studio?" She pulled the biscuits from the oven and then slid the eggs onto two plates.

"Thank you," he said as she set it in front of him. "Good coffee."

Shaking her head, she curtsied and said, "And again, I say thank you."

"I got to thinking about the pictures you showed me the other day, and since I've given up on the idea of renting the place, I thought it might be nice for you to have a place to be creative in." He shrugged. "If not, at least the junk will be gone."

She hesitated a few seconds before picking up her fork. "Bless it for us?"

"Glad to."

They bowed, and Trace prayed a simple prayer. A prayer of thanksgiving, of forgiveness, and asking for God's protection on them for this day.

Not his first rodeo.

After a few bites, she spoke. "I'll admit, the thought had crossed my mind. The windows are on the side of the house with the best light, and if I added a couple more windows ..."

"If you replaced all of them and added some, you'd have a lot more insulation."

"True. I think using it as-is for a while would be better. I can save up and cash flow extra projects."

"Makes sense." He smiled. "I don't care if you are the same age as Mandy, you're an old soul."

"I'm not sure whether to take that as a compliment or not." She chuckled.

"From me, it's a compliment." Finished with his meal,

Trace set down his cup and paused. "You don't go into things without thinking them through."

"Usually."

"Usually?"

She just nodded. There was absolutely nothing she was willing to say at this point because it would be very tempting to scrap sensibility and let him know she was attracted to him. But she wasn't brought up that way.

"Hannah," he began, then paused to re-fold his napkin. When he looked up, his eyes were narrowed, as if he was having a hard time getting his thoughts together.

"Trace?"

He blew out a breath and then raised his eyebrows, checking her plate, which was clean. "Ready to get out there and see what treasures we find?"

She had the distinct feeling that treasure-hunting was so not what he had on his mind, but she'd give him a pass.

This time.

Chapter 27

*T*race, *you idiot.*

He was mentally kicking himself. Right after he complimented her on being "an old soul" and thinking things through, he decided to ask her out for the party, then and there.

But he didn't.

The timing was off.

Was it?

He'd been rejected enough times that he was very cautious before putting himself in the position to be rejected again. It had limited the number of dates he'd gone on in the last ten years.

However, if he wanted to get anywhere with Hannah, he would have to put that behind him and take a chance. She might be thoughtful and an "old soul," as he'd said, but there was something in her eyes. It made him think maybe she *wanted* the grand gesture, though she'd never admit it. Before now, he'd have never considered it an option. It was something other people did—not him.

Inside the cabin, he took off his knit hat, ran his hands through his hair to get rid of "hat hair," and checked out the job ahead of him. This was doable. Just a few boxes, a few pieces of old furniture, and a ladder in the back corner leading to the attic.

"Do you want to start at the door and work our way back?" Her place, her decision.

"Good idea." She held out a roll of black contractor bags. "I figured trash first, then we can see what's left."

"Good thinking."

They worked quietly for about an hour, starting in the middle and then going in opposite directions.

"Hannah, check this out." He held up a box. "It was underneath the desk in the corner." He imagined her setting up her easel there. It was a wooden crate, hinged, with a homemade latch on the front and a rusty padlock.

"What in the world ...?"

Trace set it on top of the desk and examined the lock. "Well, I'm no lock expert ..."

A bubble of laughter came from her lips. "Don't even go there."

"Cute." He shook his head and looked at her blandly. "I was going to say I don't think it'll be hard to get the lock open."

"I wonder how long it's been here?" She examined the outside of the box. "Do you think it belongs to the Durbins?"

"Maybe. There's no writing on it, though, and you bought the place lock, stock, and barrel—"

"I guess this is the 'lock'?" She grinned.

She was relaxed enough to tease him. Progress. "Yep."

"So, there would be no issue with opening it?" She bit her lip, thinking.

"I wouldn't think so." He examined the lock more closely. "Maybe with a screwdriver ..."

"Whatever is inside, if it's related to the Durbins, we can save for Rebecca."

"Sounds like a plan."

Trace spied a rusty screwdriver on the floor that looked to be about the same age as the box. "Want me to open it?"

Hannah clasped her gloved hands together and nodded with excitement. "I feel like we've found buried treasure."

"I doubt it, but it might tell you more about your place."

She nodded, her eyes lit with anticipation.

He took the screwdriver and used it as a lever to break the lock. "It's tougher than I thought it would be." He kept working on it until *snap*—it came apart. "I was about to think I needed something stronger." Gesturing to the lid, he said, "And now it's all yours."

She bit her lip, then pulled back the latch and opened the crate with a loud squeak.

Inside was a map, a crinkly manila envelope, books, and a few old pictures.

Hannah opened the envelope, the metal hasp breaking off in her hand. "Oops," she said, then carefully pulled out the papers inside.

Trace glanced over her shoulder. "Those look pretty official."

She nodded, reading the header. "U.S. Marshalls."

"Whoa."

"According to this, Trip Durbin's grandfather was part of the Marshalls, working undercover." She swallowed. "This is his presidential pardon."

He focused on her, noting her wide eyes. "Rebecca and her dad need to have all this."

"I agree." She put the documents back in the envelope and unrolled the map. "It's a county map, and look," she said, pointing to red dots on the faded paper. "There's Clementville, the café, the old Woodward place, and the entrance to the caves on the Ohio River."

"Lisa and Nick's place isn't on there, is it?" He leaned down to get closer. "Here's a date —1907." He paused, then, incredulous, he said, "That was pre-prohibition. Their house hadn't been built yet."

"This is something, isn't it?" Hannah was still shaking her head.

Trace took out his phone. "I'm going to call Nick and see if we can come over to show this to him."

"Good idea. He'd know how to get in touch with Rebecca too." She picked up the book on top, flipping through it. "This is a journal, Trace."

TRACE TOOK the journal in his hand, carefully opening it. The handwriting on the inside flap had a definite feminine slant to it. "All I can make out is 'Amelia.'" He squinted, holding the page closer. "Does that look like 'Woodward' to you?"

"Maybe. I'm not aware of any Amelias, but Nick might know." She gave him a half-smile. "My mom's side of the family has connections to the Woodwards."

He laughed. "Of course it does. Is everyone around here kin to everyone else?"

"Pretty much." She smiled. "Clementville is one of those places you don't just *go* to. It's the destination. Not many strangers find their way out here. Since that's the case, it's not that amazing the number of people you're related to."

"We're not related, are we?"

Wouldn't that be just great?

"Pretty sure we're not. When we were in seventh grade, we

had to come up with a family tree, and Mandy and I knew we'd find ourselves distant cousins of some sort, but we didn't."

"So, if you're not Mandy's cousin, chances are you can't be mine, since my Mom isn't from here."

Was it him, or did Hannah come off as relieved as he felt?

She put the envelope, map, and journal carefully in the box and closed the lid.

"Got a voicemail on Nick's number, and Lisa's. They must be out of town." Trace stuffed his hands in his coat pockets and noticed Hannah shivering, her face pinched with cold. "Do we need a coffee break?"

"We need a warming break and maybe some hot chocolate." Her ready smile warmed him more than the chocolate would.

"Sounds perfect."

As Trace bent to turn on the gas logs, his phone buzzed with a text. "Nick." He read what was on the screen. "Lisa had a doctor's appointment. Be home by four-ish, is it okay if they stop by here on their way home?"

"Tell him of course it's okay to stop."

"I told him—he said if we want, they can bring pizza. Lisa's craving it these days." He chuckled.

"That sounds great." She checked her refrigerator, happy she wouldn't have to cook real food. "I'll make some sweet tea, and we'll be set." While she stood there, she pulled out a couple of sticks of butter and some eggs. "I'll soften some butter and make chocolate chip cookies."

"And you said you didn't cook."

"Breakfast and chocolate chip cookies do not a cook make. Heather's the cook in our family—she hung out with Mom while I helped Dad. It worked out great until I realized I'd missed a significant part of my female training."

"My mom made sure we boys could follow a recipe and

feed ourselves. She said no woman should be expected to wait on a man and that we can cook for a woman as well as a woman can cook for a man."

"I love your mom."

Trace laughed. "She's pretty great. It worked out well for her to have boys first." He shook his head. "I almost feel sorry for the guy who ends up with Samantha."

"Oh, you're being mean." Hannah stood at the stove, hip leaning against the oven door, stirring the hot cocoa in a saucepan.

"Maybe a little. She does all right in the kitchen, but she took Mom's philosophy to heart. Whoever gets her will have equal responsibility in the house."

"Does your dad ascribe to her philosophy?"

He paused, thinking. "Grandma just had boys, so they're all pretty traditional, and Dad's always been a farmer, so no, not completely. When Mom started her business, though, he had to pick up the slack on weekends whenever she was in full-on wedding mode." He hitched a shoulder as he leaned against the counter on the other side of the galley kitchen. "We all pitched in."

"Sounds nice."

"Pretty good way to grow up. Dad would get irritated at times, but that's just him."

"Is he a grouch too?" Her arched brow brought a smile to Trace's lips.

"Mm-hmm. I came from a long line of 'em. Grandpa, Dad, and then me. Maybe more further back. Those are the only ones I know."

Hannah poured the steaming milk into two oversized mugs and gestured to the living room. "Let's go in there where it's warmer."

She bypassed the furniture and sat down in front of the

fire, Trace following suit. The firelight flickering over her features assured him he was right where he wanted to be. He leaned his back up to the ottoman behind him, positioned perfectly to see her face.

Tucking a flyaway strand of hair behind her ears, she took a sip and groaned with pleasure. "I may not be much of a cook, but I'm glad I kept making hot cocoa until I got it right."

"It's amazing," Trace said, surprised. "And no store-bought packets in sight." He held his mug up in a toast.

Hannah chuckled. "Mom used to try to pass that stuff off as hot chocolate, and about the time I turned twelve or thirteen, I watched a cooking show where this guy was making cocoa from scratch with some ingredients I'd never thought about."

"Such as?" Trace sipped, trying to identify what was different.

"Maybe I'll keep it a secret." Smug, she took a long sip, batting her eyelashes at him.

She was playing with fire, now.

He narrowed his eyes, pondering the best response.

Patience. Slow and steady wins the race. Slow is smooth, smooth is fast.

Keeping his narrowed eyes trained on hers, he said, his voice lowered, "I'll get it out of you. Maybe not today, maybe not tomorrow, but someday, somewhere, when you least expect it, I will find out what makes this the best hot chocolate I've ever had in my life."

The giggle bubbling from her lips made every bit of patience and waiting worthwhile.

HE WAS STILL GAZING at her, a slow smile growing on his face.

When Trace assured her he would get her hot cocoa "secret ingredients" out of her eventually, it made her shiver. Was it crazy that in twenty-five years, Hannah had never felt this way before?

She choked a little on her hot chocolate, glad when his phone buzzed, this time with a call.

"Hey, Nick."

Hannah studied the fire, trying to find the right words to say. Or maybe say nothing at all. She didn't *always* have to have the last word, did she?

"Sure, we'll be here." He tapped the button to end the call. "They're getting back a little earlier than expected, so they're bringing lunch instead of dinner."

Her brows flew up. "Oh. Okay." She gave a cursory glance around and into the kitchen from where she sat. The place looked fine. A few breakfast dishes in the sink and a throw on the floor where it had covered her legs. She hopped up, folding the blanket as she stood. "I guess I need to get the cookies made, then."

"Nope. He said they were bringing a box of Crumbl cookies. I heard Lisa holler that she knew how it was when you first move into a place."

She put away the eggs and butter. "Then that's that. I'll have the coffee pot ready."

"You've made a mistake making your cocoa for me."

"Have I?"

He had a teasing lilt to his words, but stoic in expression, as always. Nodding, he eyed the dregs in his mug, frowning. "This may have ruined me for coffee."

"I think we both know that's not going to happen. Just think first thing in the morning."

"If it were infused with enough caffeine ..."

"I'll have to put that on my list of things to try." She smiled. "Would you like some more?"

"No, I think I can hold out until lunch." He stopped her with a hand to her arm. "I meant what I said."

"And what's that?" His fingers on her bicep made her want to melt into a puddle of goo. She could not let him know that.

Not yet.

"This is the best cocoa I've ever had."

"No exaggeration?"

He held up two fingers. "Boy Scout's honor."

She narrowed her eyes. "Were you really a Scout?"

"Of course I was." He grinned. "Until I learned 4H was co-ed."

"Has anyone ever told you you're incorrigible?" The urge to laugh was about to get the best of her when he let go, and she passed into the kitchen.

"Mainly Grandma."

"Smart woman." She put the mugs in the dishwasher along with the saucepan and spoon, and then quickly wiped the counter. "It'll be a couple of hours still before they get here, right?"

"Yeah. Want to throw some of the trash onto the trailer before they arrive? Pretty sure none of what we bagged up is worth anything to anybody."

They bundled back up and made their way out to the cabin. With the short winter days, they would only have a few hours left of daylight, and Nick and Lisa's visit would cut that in half.

As they entered the dim structure, she pointed to where they'd ended their task earlier. "Did you see the desk there in the corner, where we found the box?"

Trace nodded. "It was nice. Looked like solid wood. It may need a little tightening up."

"I think I'll keep it in there. If I were to ever do any design work ..."

He spoke, breaking her concentration. "You mean *when* you do design work?"

She bowed to him. "Yes, sir. *When* I do design work, it would be good to have an office outside of my house."

Trace pulled it out from the wall, revealing the beautiful tiger maple front that had been hidden from sight. It was in better shape than he'd thought. "Hannah, you've got something nice here."

He knelt in front of the desk, sliding his hand over the finish on the fine piece of furniture, and she caught the excitement on his face. A strong sense of *deja vu* jolted through her. She'd just had a flash of a possible future ... "Trace ..."

"Yeah?"

Her mind was a jumble. Total chaos.

"Um."

"You okay?"

Hannah cleared her throat. What she wouldn't give for a long drink of water. "Never mind. I agree. It's gorgeous."

He tilted his head a little, a slight frown appearing and then his crooked smile reached in and tugged at her heartstrings. "All it needs is shining it up with a little cleaning and a coat of furniture wax, and it'll be great."

Maybe that's what she needed. A little shining up. Live in the moment—like she did when she bought the place—instead of up inside her head second-guessing every aspect of her life.

Chapter 28

By the time Lisa and Nick arrived, Trace and Hannah had cleared the floor of trash and placed things to donate or investigate in boxes. Next was climbing the ladder to the attic.

"Saved by the Woodwards?"

Hannah laughed.

Trace figured his face betrayed his feeling of relief of not having to climb into a dark attic. He'd rather Hannah didn't when she was here, alone, but he knew better than to make the suggestion she wait.

Lisa and Nick peeked inside the cabin, Nick looking from the loaded-up trailer to the clean floor, whistling. "I'm impressed, guys. There was a lot of stuff in here."

"Yeah, stuff that would have been here come warmer weather." Lisa smiled her face scrunched in disbelief. "What possessed you to do this on the coldest day of the winter?"

"Our bosses gave us the week off, that's what." Trace chuckled. "I start the new job next week, and I had to do something, so I persuaded Hannah that this would be a good project to keep us busy."

"Because far be it from him to promote staying in front of the fire with a good book." Hannah narrowed her eyes at Trace with a hint of glare he'd come to recognize as not anger, but humor trying to masquerade as anger.

Lisa went in and took note of the space. "This is great." When she got to the desk, she sighed. "Was this already here?"

Hannah nodded. "Isn't it amazing?"

"Tiger Maple, no less. Are you taking it in the house when you get it cleaned up?"

Hannah's eyes flicked over to Trace, and he grinned.

"No, I think I'm going to use this as an office and studio," Hannah answered confidently, with a faint question mark at the end of the statement.

"Great use of space." Lisa continued to nod her approval. "It's about time you started working on design. This will be perfect."

"How ...?"

"Honey, Mandy Reno is my cousin. When has she not shared great information?"

"Come to think of it, never. Caryn and I learned a long time ago there were some things better left as a surprise for Mandy."

They all laughed.

"I still can't believe she's engaged," Lisa said, calming down from the laughter.

Trace shook his head. "Was she even looking when she and Clay started dating?"

"No, she had a boyfriend in law school, and when she broke up with him, he basically stalked her, so she wasn't in a hurry to date anybody for a while." Lisa smiled. "He got his act together and came around last Christmas to make amends as part of his recovery program," Lisa said. "I think he's doing well now, but Mandy was ready to move on—she just didn't know how close her destiny was."

"Yeah, Clay, of all people." Trace snorted.

"Don't knock him until you get to know him. He's a good man. He just wasn't the guy for me." Lisa grinned at Nick who came up behind her and cradled her protruding baby bump. "Obviously."

"This is the box we found under the desk. I guess when Rebecca went through things to sell the house, it was left behind." Trace picked it up. "Hannah, do you want to take it into the house?"

"Unless y'all want to risk frostbite, I'd say most definitely." She chuckled. "Thanks, Trace."

"You're welcome, m'lady." Trace glanced at Hannah, a look of surprise crossing his features. Was he surprised at what he, himself, said?

She wasn't sure how to take his comment. It was a little on the possessive scale, but it sounded so natural, as if it came out of his mouth before he'd put his brain in gear.

For some reason, that made her happy.

HANNAH WATCHED Nick's face as he opened the envelope and studied the documents. He shook his head slowly, deliberately, eyes wide.

"This is a gold mine as far as my family history is concerned." Spread out in front of him, he put the correspondence in chronological order, with the Presidential Pardon awarded to Charles C. Woodward likely the last document included. "When we found the tunnels under my house, we learned that alcohol smuggling was the family business from way back. My great-grandfather—Dad's grandfather—was all over it." He glanced up at Lisa and then the rest of them. "According to this, his father, and maybe even his grandfather, worked for the government, infiltrating organized crime. Charles was the good guy, but I guess his son decided to go with the flow."

"Nick, look at this." Lisa had been carefully turning the pages of the journal. "This is hard to read, but I'm pretty sure Amelia Woodward was your ..." She counted on her fingers. "Great-great grandmother?"

"Sounds about right."

"So sad." Lisa held the book up to the light to see better. "They came here from Tennessee. The Bureau of Investigation —is that what turned into the FBI?—sent her husband here undercover as a farmer, but he was killed in an accident. All these papers were what she put away when he died."

"How did they get so mixed up with organized crime, then?" Hannah knew it wasn't any of her business, but at this moment, living history was sitting right here at her kitchen table.

"Gradually, it seems. We've blamed your great-grandfather for being a part of this. According to the dates here, he grew up without a father, like your dad." Lisa had tears in her eyes. "Seems to be a recurring theme."

Nick reached over and took her hand. "A theme we're breaking with this little one."

Lisa smiled, squeezing his hand back. "Here's the question, though. Where do the Durbins come in?"

"After everything that happened last year came out, Rebecca told me she'd been told there were Woodwards in her family, but nobody had ever told her where the connection came from." Nick put the papers down. "When they came back here after the trial—after Trip was released from prison—I was able to talk to him. Come to find out, Amelia married a Durbin after her husband was killed. She had a few more kids after Charles, and that's where the Durbin line started. Kind of a half-cousin thing."

"Genealogy is something else." Trace shook his head. "Lisa, I'm afraid our background isn't nearly as colorful as the one you married into."

"That's fine with me, but I'll admit, it's pretty fascinating." Lisa winked at her husband. "Keeps the relationship exciting."

Nick's lips twitched. "Exciting is what it's going to be around here in a few months."

Lisa sighed, chin in hand. "I wonder how long until Del and Darcy have more kids ..."

The timer went off, alerting them the pizza they'd brought and had to reheat because of the cold temps was ready.

Hannah jumped up. "And with that, lunch is served."

NICK TOOK the box of treasures home with him, promising to contact Rebecca and her dad to invite them into the discovery.

After they left, it was quiet again. Hannah had sent the rest of the amazing gourmet cookies home with Lisa and Nick, because they were so good and she was so full she thought she might never need to eat again.

"What about those cookies?" Trace's eyes were round as he turned to Hannah when she came back into the living room. He'd taken a spot on the sofa. "Aunt Roxy and Darcy could so make those."

Hannah sat in the armchair closest to the fire. "I agree." She grinned, her smile interrupted by a yawn. "But right now I think a nap sounds better. We'd better get back out there and finish up before it gets dark."

Trace checked out the window and scoffed. "I think that ship has sailed. How about I unhitch the trailer, and we finish it up another day?"

Hannah tilted her head, trying to figure him out. "You don't have to do this, you know."

He stared into the fire, not saying anything for a moment, then he looked at her. "I know."

"I could get Dad and Clark and any number of people to help me if I needed it."

"I know." He leaned forward, hesitating. Was he having a hard time vocalizing what he was thinking? He frowned, twisting his lips a little. "I have a sister."

"You do." Hannah sputtered a laugh.

"And I would like to think there were people out there who would be willing to help her if she were living on her own." He shrugged. "I guess—I guess I want to be that kind of man."

Her eyes leveled on him. Sister. Something inside of her broke. He lumped her in the same category as his sister, his baby cousin, or any number of females in his life.

I've been friend-zoned.

"I see."

His eyes and what he'd said didn't match. If this was where whatever "this" was, was going, she'd have to move on. Quickly. She didn't want to involve her heart any more than it already was.

And it was involved. Deeply.

Standing, she fixed her eyes on the floor, hands clasped in front of her, giving him as cold a shoulder as she could. Maybe if she stood there long enough, he would get the hint and leave.

"Hannah."

"Thanks, Trace. You've been a big help today. And finding the box, and the desk? It might have taken me months to unearth it all. Right now ..." She swallowed, looking around at anything but him, trying to stop the hurt in her chest from manifesting itself as tears, "... I need to ..."

He stood up and took the two steps toward her. "Hannah, what did I say?" Again, the eyes and the words.

She gave him her brightest, sunshiny Hannah smile, all the while moving toward the coat rack next to the back door, where his coat hung next to hers. *Don't think about it.* "Not a thing. I'm sure you have things to do before you start your job next week. I guess I'll see you at church."

After she handed him his coat, she continued smiling, her hands clasped in front of her to keep them from shaking. She knew her eyes were bright from the tears burning to be released, and there was no way she was going to give in to it until he was out of her house.

She watched as he unhitched the trailer from his pickup. He glanced back to her door, raising his hand in a wave, but she let the curtain drop and leaned against the frame, back to him, closing her eyes tightly when the truck started and crunched down the driveway.

When her emotions were finally released, they washed over and over her like the surge of ocean preceding a hurricane.

He'd compared her to his sister. She knew he considered Mandy too young to know her mind, but she'd thought he saw her differently. Maybe she'd misread the cues.

But maybe it didn't matter what he thought. She had a house, and she'd take care of it herself. She'd leave word with someone that he needed to pick up his trailer, then she'd thank him nicely and send him on his way.

No way would she pine over a guy she didn't even like two weeks ago and who thought of her and her contemporaries as children.

Her first instinct was right. Bossy, grumpy ... and she knew there were some other words to describe the negative traits she'd seen.

In the meantime, she'd have to remember *not* to remember his good traits.

That will be much harder.

Chapter 29

Trace kicked himself mentally all the way home, trying to call forth what he had said. He wasn't one of those guys who talked so much that he couldn't remember what he said. Trace recalled pretty much every conversation he'd ever had with Hannah.

She was that important to him.

Maybe that was the kicker. She sensed he had feelings for her, and since she didn't, she decided to distance herself from him, and quickly.

It was time to call a spade a spade.

She's just not that into you, Bud.

He pulled up to his grandparents' house. Instead of going inside, he headed to the wood shop.

Hannah's easel was spread out, in pieces, the polyurethane sealer curing before he assembled it. He ran his hand across the legs. Not one splinter. He would still give it to her, but he'd get it there when she wasn't home. No reason to put himself through that again.

"Trace?"

He raised his head when he heard Eli's voice.

"Where you been?" His twin came in and made himself at home in Grandpa's rocker.

"At Hannah's." Trace was still deep in thought. The last thing he needed was advice from Eli. Who knew? Maybe Eli would be the one to make Hannah's heart go pitter-patter.

Ugh.

"I had a feeling."

Trace rounded on him, getting in his brother's face. "Why? Why would you 'have a feeling?'" Trace exploded.

"Hey, hey, hey ..." Eli held his hand up to stop the torrent of words.

Trace closed his eyes for a few seconds and then started pacing, grabbing the knit beanie off his head and throwing it on the workbench. "Sorry."

"It's okay, man." Eli leaned forward. "What's up with you, lately?"

Trace glanced at his brother and then stopped walking. Instead, he stuffed his hands in his pockets and contemplated the ceiling, taking a deep breath to center himself.

"I'm tired, Eli."

"Tired of what? Aren't you off this week?" Eli narrowed his eyes at his brother, surprising Trace with the somber expression on his face. "Or are you tired in another way?"

At least I don't have to spell it out.

"Do you ever wonder what God has planned?" Trace waited a second while Eli caught up. "I mean, you dated Carrie long enough to meet her parents, which is not the norm for you. What made you think she might be the one?"

Eli drew in a deep breath, then puffed it out, fun, carefree Eli gone, and serious, grounded Eli in place.

"I prayed." He chuckled. "Boy, did I pray." He scoffed. "I

thought maybe if I decided to commit, God would bless it. I thought I loved her, but she was never quite sure. When I mentioned the *M* word ...”

“Marriage?”

His brother nodded. “When I brought it up just before Thanksgiving, she didn’t freak out, but I could tell it wasn’t happening for her the same way it was happening for me. She closed herself off, quit talking. I guess she was trying to figure stuff out, same as me.”

“Sorry you had to go through that.” Trace shook his head.

“Yeah, well, I think what happened was I got things out of order.” He scoffed. “Instead of me waiting on God to show me who He has for me, I thought I could decide and *then* get His blessing.”

“Patience?” Trace raked a hand across his face and over his beard, shaking his head the whole time. “What’s up with that, anyway?” He sent a half-smile his brother’s way, remembering Grandpa’s advice.

“Yeah, right?” Eli shrugged. “Anyway, I’m glad she had doubts, because, you know, I haven’t missed her like I was sure I would.”

Trace nodded. “So, what’s next?” He wanted so badly to hear whether or not Eli was interested in Hannah, because if he was, Trace may as well pack it in now.

“I talked to Nick and Del the other night—while we were waiting on you guys ...” Eli laughed, “... and they offered me a job if I’m interested.”

“And?”

Eli shrugged, then lifted his gaze to Trace’s. “I thought I might try it for a while. What do you think?”

Eli genuinely wanted to know his opinion.

“I wouldn’t be upset to have my brother around.” Trace twisted his lips in a slight grin.

"Glowing endorsement, huh?" Eli grinned. "I'll take it. Coming from you, it's high praise."

"Am I really so ... grouchy?"

Eli studied his twin. "No, but sometimes you're so economical with words that your ideas don't get across. Why do I have a feeling that's what's going on in that ornery head of yours?"

HANNAH LOOKED out her kitchen window toward the cabin. Trace's trailer was still there, and she tried to shift her eyes anywhere else. It was useless. She'd relived every conversation she'd had with Trace and concluded that she'd misunderstood every overture he'd made.

He'd helped her in so many ways, and then to compare her to his sister? A bucket of cold water over her head couldn't have surprised her more.

The sunshine outside did nothing to break the cloud cover in her heart. She went from sadness to disappointment to anger to despair, and she let God in on every emotion.

It was His fault, after all, that she was going through this. Wasn't it?

She took her time organizing her closet and the cabinets in her kitchen. Mom hadn't done too bad a job of placing things, but Hannah had some ideas of her own she wanted to try. Even if Trace turned out to be a dud, at least she had a house. Pride stirred in her chest. It was pretty if she said so herself.

And that's what she had to do. Take pride in her decision to buy her house. If she had to be alone, at least she'd have her own place. Nobody to stop her from decorating it any way she wanted, nobody to question the sanity of putting the dishes in one cabinet rather than what was expected ... and nobody to help her, encourage her, or lighten her mood when she felt like she was falling off a cliff.

Why me? Really? Why'd You pick me? Do You really think I can do this 'life' thing by myself? If that's what You want, I can do it, but right now, I'm a little perturbed and more than a little disappointed. It's not every little girl's dream to be alone. One thing's for sure, God—if You've got a man for me in this life, it's gonna have to be made as plain as day. No dilly-dallying.

She paused, wringing out her dishrag and hanging it neatly on the towel bar next to the sink.

I just told God I would tolerate "no dilly-dallying."

Pressing the heels of her palms on her eyes, she took a deep breath. She needed to get out of the house, even if just to get fresh air. Being around people didn't appeal to her right now. People were trouble. They might not mean to, but they hurt other's feelings and didn't live up to expectations. She grabbed her phone, and then laid it on the counter. Another way she could distance herself from the human race.

Gloves, scarf, and coat on, she went out and marched straight to the cabin. Sweeping it out again, her brain automatically went to Trace and how much she had enjoyed being here with him the day before.

Was it just yesterday? Wow.

A little flash of what could be. The fun of finding "buried treasure." Hanging out with Nick and Lisa. But then, when they were alone, everything fell apart.

Trace sees me as a friend.

Or even worse, compared her to his sister.

She puttered, riffling through the desk they'd uncovered.

The ladder was still in the corner where they'd left it, intending to bring stuff down from the attic. The entrance to the attic was a two-foot square hole in the ceiling. Grabbing the flashlight, she arranged the ladder and started up.

If I'm going to be independent, I can't wait for someone to help me. I can do this. It would be easier if I'd brought the lantern …

In the dusty recesses of the small space, there were boxes that had been there for decades. Nobody had thought to empty it. Stepping carefully on the loose boards serving as a floor, she eased to the far corner to check it out. She had to move a board here and there to get where she wanted to walk.

The trunk looked like the oldest item, and that was her goal. More treasures? She hoped it was enough to get her mind off of—she refused to think of Trace, so she just thought *things*.

Hoisting a board to get her directly to the container's latch, she bent over to avoid whacking her head on the rafters. She grazed one, so she paused, rubbing the spot on her head. There was no lock on the trunk as there had been on the box they'd found yesterday, so she opened it fairly easily. The creaking sound proved it had been a while since it had been used.

On top was a small, flat box. She tipped the lid to reveal tissue paper and then letters tied with ribbon. She put those aside to study later. Underneath was another box that held a man's felt dress hat—the kind she'd seen pictures of her great-grandfather wearing whenever he had on a suit. It was a nice one.

Unfortunately, moths had made their way into the trunk, so the topcoat was riddled with holes. Maybe the hat sated the moths enough that the white garment underneath had been left alone. The yellowed wedding gown had pearls sewn on the bodice. Was that hand-made lace covering the neckline and sleeves? There were fewer holes here. Maybe the dried bits of lavender she found between the layers had made a difference.

She didn't want to pull it out, lest it fall apart in her hands. She'd do that when she got the trunk down. Estimating the distance from the trunk to the opening, she wondered—would she be able to pull it to the opening and then lower it? Maybe.

Pushing the dress to one side, Hannah discovered small notebooks. More journals?

The cold was working its way through her coat and gloves, and the more Hannah thought about it, the more confident she was that she could get the trunk down on her own. The ceilings of the cabin were only seven feet high, so it wasn't like it would be dropped from a height that would destroy it. Lifting one end to test the weight, she made the decision. She could do this.

She'd have to get used to doing things on her own, wouldn't she?

The trunk was on the pathway boards, and she pulled on it. Nothing. One end wasn't too heavy, but the other end was stuck.

It had been there a long time and didn't want to budge. She shifted it, trying to work it loose from whatever had a hold on it. Finally, about the time she decided to give it up and get reinforcements sometime, it came free.

But it didn't just scoot across the boards as she'd planned. The force pushed the trunk forward and Hannah backward, knocking her head against the rafter she'd barely grazed earlier. Her arm flailed with nothing for her hand to grab onto. Unable to regain her balance, her leg slipped and her boot broke through the brittle bead-board ceiling. Her shoulder rammed against the ceiling joists, trapping her hand beneath her.

She didn't pass out, but when she tried to pull her foot back through the new hole in the ceiling, the pain in her leg and shoulder was so intense that her lunch almost came back to haunt her.

Not only was she injured, she was stuck. Stuck, with nobody around and no phone—for the second time in a week.

Except the last time she wasn't alone, and she wasn't hurt.

Compared to when she had Trace with her, and they were in a warm basement, she was in dire straits.

No phone, no people, and an injury that would keep her from climbing down a ladder. Unless someone specifically came looking for her, she was well and truly trapped.

Chapter 30

Trace moped around all day, trying to get his mind off Hannah and what might have been. He wasn't doing a very good job of it. He puttered around the wood shop, sorting hardware and putting tools back in place. Eli offered to help him. He appreciated his brother and knew he meant well, but Trace needed to think.

Because I'm not in my own head enough? If it weren't more than his masculinity could handle, he would have rolled his eyes.

That's my problem. Overthinking. Thinking I can control things if I try hard enough.

It was a beautiful day outside. Would have been perfect to finish the job clearing out Hannah's cabin, but he didn't dare. He wasn't sure he wanted to see her, anyway.

She'd made her feelings clear yesterday. She was ready for him to leave, and she didn't feel for him the same way he felt about her. Surely she knew he was attracted to her? She had to.

His phone buzzed with a text. Mandy?

Hey, cuz.

                                        Hey

Have you seen Hannah today?

                              Should I have?

In my opinion, yes, because you're a
cute couple. If she's there, go right
ahead and show her what I said. Maybe
it'll speed things along.

            She's not here. I think you're projecting.
            Just because you're in love doesn't
            mean everybody else is.

☹

                  Did you check with her mom?

Of course I did. She hasn't talked to her
today.

                                    Sister?

Yes. Nothing.

               I'm assuming you tried calling her.

Duh. She didn't answer calls or texts. I
sound very relaxed and carefree, but I'm
starting to get worried about her. I texted
her about five different bridesmaid
dresses and got no response. Nothing.
Nada. Zip.

              She's a big girl. Maybe she didn't like the
              dresses?

I know she's a big girl, and if she doesn't
like a dress, she knows she can tell me.
I'm a big girl, too, you know.

Three dots appeared then disappeared.

> Sorry, Clay called. (Heart emoji). He
> hasn't seen her around, either.

> Sorry I couldn't help.

Me too.

Trace frowned. *Lord, where is she?*

He pulled up his recents and found the last call he'd made to Hannah. Call her? He hesitated. What if she didn't want to hear another word from him?

Texts. He found the string they'd had going since right after Thanksgiving when they were assigned to carpool together. Maybe she didn't want to talk to anybody. Maybe she'd answer a text.

> Hannah?

He waited for the little dots to appear. Nothing. He checked, and there was the "sent" notification.

> You okay? Mandy's looking for you.

There. Maybe saying Mandy was worried would get her attention.

Still nothing.

He switched to the thread of texts with Mandy.

> Tried texting her. Nothing.

Told you.

Switching back over to the phone app, he pushed the button to call her. Several rings, and then straight to voicemail. "Hey, Hannah, just checking on you. Mandy's freaking out because you aren't answering her texts."

He waited a few seconds before going back to the conversation with Mandy.

> Tried calling, no answer, left a voicemail to call you.

UGH

Thanks for checking. I feel helpless sixty miles away. Bye

> Bye

He pocketed his phone, then pulled it out again. Was his ringer off? Did he have even the vibratesetting turned off?

No, everything was as it should be.

Where was she, and if he found her, what excuse would he make to explain his desire to drive over there and check on her?

He grabbed his coat and keys, muttering under his breath.

I don't need an excuse.

IN HITCHES, Hannah was able to pull herself up, inch by inch, until she leaned on her right side against the trunk. She tried to move her left arm, to no avail. The only way she could stand the pain was to hold her arm as tightly as possible with her good hand.

The cold seeped into her more quickly than before, and she grew drowsy and confused. Her leg had gone to sleep. She didn't think she'd injured it, but it was hard to tell. The tears that had been streaming down her face had dried, and she had no idea how long she'd been there, hanging from the rafters, so to speak. An hour? Maybe longer?

She stretched her neck, trying to work out the kinks in her back from the strange position she was in, stopping when the stabbing pain made her cry out in pain. One thing about it—she had time to pray.

It hurts, Lord. Sorry I couldn't get into Your Word, Lord, but, You see ...

Like God didn't know where she was and what a predicament she was in. After praying for a rescue and for her to stop hurting so badly she wanted to throw up, she started stewing on everything else, finally giving it to Him.

Father, there's not one thing I can do right now, for myself or any relationship I may or may not have. Forgive me for misunderstanding what You want for me. I like Trace, but it's up to You. From now on, I won't try to make things happen. That way I won't get disappointed and hurt. Give me wisdom, Lord ...

She may have slept a little, wedged in there. When she woke, she realized she'd dreamed about being inside a freezer.

Like those shows where the main character gets stuck in a flash freezer on a timer, and only the other main character can rescue them. Great. I have no other main character.

Just within reach, she winced as she pulled out the slim box of letters from the trunk. Untying the red ribbon on one stack, she trained her flashlight on the writing on the envelopes. Every other one was male and female handwriting. Beautiful, classic Copperplate writing like what she remembered seeing in her grandparents' memorabilia.

My dear Amy,

He called her Amy? How sweet.

How long will I have to wait until we can marry? I know it is only two months away, but two months is an eternity separated from you. I fear that if it takes too long, you will decide to forego the trouble.

It is good to have my brother here. It feels like home to have some of the home folks close by. It will never be home, though, until you come.

I have settled into a small cabin on a farm here in Kentucky. If we stay long enough, if my job allows, I will build us a house. I am learning about the community here and found the people to be welcoming. I found a church I hope you will like. Clementville is a new town, and I met the man who had the dream to build a town proper on the banks of the Ohio River. It is his daughter that my brother is courting. It seems to be serious. On his part, at least.

I apologize for the shortness of this letter, but I must get to sleep. Running a law practice on the one hand and looking for clues on the other, is almost more than one man can accomplish. I am in hope that once we are married, I will have finished my job here, and we might consider living here as residents and not intelligence-gatherers.

Too long until we next meet. I'm counting the days.

Yours, always,
Charles C. Woodward, Esq.

HANNAH CAREFULLY FOLDED the letter back in the exact creases she'd found it. *Nick and Rebecca need to have these.*

Her breath caught as she pulled out the next letter, so she stopped, eyes closed, until the pain subsided. This letter was written with a decidedly feminine hand:

My dearest Charles,

In the novels I read, the heroine who is parted from her lover is known to pine away with loneliness. I feel that if our wedding does not get here soon, I will succumb to the same fate.

My wedding dress is almost finished. Mother is sewing the pearls on the bodice now, and Grandmother is at work on the lace. I cannot wait for you to see it.

Sister is trying to convince me that we need to live in Tennessee after we marry. I told her that you were committed to your job and must see it to its finish. After that, we will decide where to begin our family. Now, my home is wherever you are, so Kentucky is home already. It isn't so far from the home folks that we cannot visit back and forth.

My calendar is filling up with bridal teas and brunches, and I worry I will not be able to fit into the dress my mother is so lovingly sewing. It is gratifying to know my friends and relatives care so for me.

Dearest, you need not fear the length of time before we wed.

I am yours, forever and always,
Amelia

How romantic. There were several more letters in the bundle she'd loosed, and another besides. She was tired, and tears were very near the surface.

It hurt to focus, and while her foot was numb, her shoulder, from her neck to the tips of her fingers, thrummed more deeply with pain.

She focused on the ceiling, hoping to find God there.

Lord, rescue me?

Chapter 31

Her truck was exactly where it was when Trace left the day before. That didn't bode well.

Trace went do the kitchen door and knocked, then held his phone up to find a cell signal. When he found it, he pushed the call button again. This time, standing next to the back door, he heard it. Probably on the counter just inside.

"Hannah?" He called out. What if she turned on the fireplace logs and didn't get it lit and she was overcome by carbon monoxide poisoning? What if she slipped in the shower and fell, cracking her head on the vanity? The one he made for her? What if she went out for a walk and came across wild animals or animals of the human kind, and they took her?

What if ...?

His mind was a flurry, and his heartbeat pounded in his ears. He considered calling her parents, but if Mandy had already called them, they were probably checking their resources too.

"Hannah!"

He stopped. It was quiet out here. Peaceful. He

understood why Hannah was drawn to the place, and after being in the house, he saw the vision she had for it. Even the cabin—

The cabin. Surely she didn't ...

He walked toward the cabin. The door stood open, and he dashed for it when he heard her voice calling. It was faint.

"Hannah?" Easing through the door, his vision had to adjust to the darker cabin. It was late afternoon, and the shadows grew long.

"Up here."

Trace jerked his head toward the sound and saw a single foot sticking through the ceiling, completely across the room from where the ladder stood, waiting, at the attic access.

His heart dropped to his stomach. "Oh, Hannah."

"Trace?" Was that a sniffle?

At least she can talk.

"It's me, sweetheart."

He closed his eyes and kicked himself mentally.

"How can I help you?"

She paused. "I can't pull my foot out, and I think my shoulder is hurt. I can't move my arm." Her voice was shaking.

"I'll get you out."

She didn't say anything, but he heard her crying. With relief? He hoped so.

"It'll be okay, Hannah. I promise. I'm going to my truck to get my flashlight, but I'll be right back."

He heard a loud sniffle, and then a weak chuckle. "I'm not goin' anywhere."

While he was outside, he sent Mandy a text.

> Call her parents. She's at her house,
> hurt. Getting her out now.

Three dots appeared. He didn't wait to see what Mandy

was typing, but he knew letting her folks know what was going on was a priority.

Should he call 911, or could he get her out himself?

When he got back inside to the ladder, he climbed it, and at the top shined his light over to where she sat in what had to be a very uncomfortable position. "I'm coming."

"Be careful. There are just boards to walk on, and this one slipped with me."

"I'll be there in just a minute." He carefully navigated the staggered planks until he got close enough to see her pale face, pinched with pain and cold. And maybe something else, but he wasn't concerned about that right now.

They'd deal with other things later.

"Let's see what's going on." The flashlight illuminated the site of the accident, showing not only her foot through the ceiling but some blood on her jeans where they'd ripped. "I think I need to call for help."

"Ugh." She closed her eyes and nodded.

"Hannah, look at me."

She opened her eyes, pain etched on her face.

"I don't want to run the risk of hurting you worse."

He fixed his attention on her eyes. Deeply. He wanted to hold her, cry with her and for her, but someone had to be the leader here, and right now, it was him. "I'm just relieved to find you."

Her eyes cut to his. "You've been looking for me?"

He grinned. "Mandy was, and when she couldn't raise you, she called me." A prick of sadness touched him. "She thought maybe you were with me."

Trace pulled out his phone and called Sherriff Clay directly, putting it on speaker. "Clay, I know I should have called 911, but I'm at Hannah's place, and she's had an accident."

"Need an ambulance?"

He glanced at Hannah's pale face. "Yes. I think she's hurt her arm or shoulder, maybe her ankle. She fell partially through the ceiling of her cabin."

"Ouch." Clay sympathized.

"Yeah."

"I'll have somebody out there ASAP."

Trace heard Clay notify dispatch.

"Is she alone?" Clay asked.

"No, I'm in the attic with her. Just got here. She's been out here for a while, so she's plenty cold." Trace was glad to see she was beginning to relax. A little.

"The ambulance should be there in about fifteen minutes."

"I'll be here."

"Good. Tell Hannah I'm sorry she's in a bind."

"She hears you." Trace held the phone closer to Hannah.

She squeaked out, "Thanks, Clay."

"Not a problem. You know, it's usually Reno women who fall through things," Clay said.

Trace knew Clay was trying to diffuse a stressful situation, but his first random thought was that Hannah would make a terrific Reno woman.

"Well, I guess I wanted to be one of the cool kids."

Trace shook his head as they ended the call.

"Mandy called Mom and Dad, didn't she?" The distress returned to her face. "They went with Heather and Clark and Vi to Nashville. I hope they're not rushing back."

"I sent Mandy a text to let them know you've been found." He pulled out his phone to see what his cousin had sent.

Chuckling, he stuffed it back into his pocket without answering.

> Now's your chance to be the hero, big
> boy. Don't mess it up. 😠

"What?"

"Just Mandy."

"Oh."

He caught Hannah sneaking glances his way.

"Why are you here, Trace?"

Okay, Lord, like Mandy said, this is my chance. Care to help me out, here?

He settled himself closer to her, in a more comfortable position.

"Because I care about you, Hannah."

Chapter 32

Hannah's heart froze, then started pounding. He cared about her? Then, memory rolled over her. Of course he did. Like a sister. Or a cousin. Or any other needy female who might land in his path.

She couldn't meet his eyes, as much as she wanted to, so she nodded, instead.

"Hannah ..."

Hazarding a look, she saw pleading in his gaze. Or was she imagining it? After all, she was feeling a little woozy from the pain and the cold. Maybe this was all a dream, and she'd wake up to find herself in her bed, or on the couch, dozing by the fire. She shifted a little, stopping short when her ribs raged at her, and a board stabbed into her thigh. "Ouch."

Nope, no dream. All too real.

"I'm so sorry, Hannah." He dropped his head for a moment when she didn't say anything, then turned back to her, his face coming closer to hers. "I don't know what happened yesterday. It was like ... like a switch flipped, and I wasn't aware there *was* a switch. You know what I mean?"

Could she trust him enough to tell him what she thought when he placed her in the same category as his sister? Could she handle the humiliation of knowing she was fonder of him than he was of her?

But his eyes. His eyes were so sad.

"Trace ..."

"I know I must have said or done something that ..." He gestured between the two of them. "... well, that changed things." He blew out a breath, the fog it created indicating how cold it was in there. "I've gone over everything I said, and I've decided I must be clueless."

He wasn't angry. No signs of annoyance at being stuck with her again. He said he cared, and she could tell he meant what he said. Her only question was, did she understand what he was saying?

"You're a man of few words, Trace."

"Mandy told me not to blow it this time." A glimmer of a smile crossed his lips as he held her gaze. "I don't want to."

Hannah shifted her head back to lean on the trunk, as she had when she dozed off. She took a deep breath and closed her eyes for a few seconds. When she opened them, he hadn't moved. "Remember when I was trying to thank you yesterday, and said you didn't have to do this?"

The furrow of his brow made her want to reach out and smooth it, but she didn't dare.

"Do you remember what you said?"

He shook his head. "Something about hoping there would be people around to help my sister if she were in need of assistance?"

She nodded slowly.

Ambulance sirens out on the highway grew closer. Whatever needed to be said would have to be said another time.

Trace hesitated. "I need to go down there and show them where you are." He reached for her hand. "This conversation isn't over. Not by a long shot." His expression was like granite.

Maybe she'd been wrong. Maybe as much as she was hurt by what he said, he was hurt by her actions after.

It was all so confusing.

TRACE CLIMBED down the ladder and met the EMTs with a gurney maneuvering around the trailer. "Sorry, I should have moved this."

"No problem." The woman, fifty-ish with curly dark hair, had a ready smile. "We've seen lots worse." She held out her hand. "I'm Michele. This is Doug."

"Trace Reno. Good to meet you."

"Hannah's got a nice place here." Michele nodded with approval.

"Wait until you see where she is. You may have set a new standard for difficulty." He shook his head, then followed them in, pointing to the booted foot and leg hanging out the ceiling.

Doug, the EMT, emitted a low whistle. "Another one for the book, eh, Michele?"

She stood, evaluating the situation, nodding. "Yep. That'll end up in my book." She turned to Trace. "Is she conscious?"

"Yes. I think she slept some before I found her, but she's been talking to me."

"Good. We've got some warm blankets to put over her once we get her down." She walked to where she knew Hannah was. "Hannah, sweetie, we're gonna get you down from there."

"Thank you. I'm sorry for making you come out here."

"Girl, that's what we're here for. People try to do silly

things like walk through a ceiling, and we get to come and figure out how to get them back down."

"I'm glad it's you, Michele."

Trace heard Hannah's sniff from where he stood.

He turned to both EMTs. "Do I need to go up there and help?"

"Wonder how fond she is of this ceiling?" Doug was pondering, asking Michele. "It might be easier to cut a hole in the ceiling than to carry her through the length of the attic."

Michele nodded, then looked up. "Hannah, how partial are you to this ceiling?"

The rough laugh made Trace's lips twitch. "Not very, considering I've already torn part of it out." She paused for a moment. "I may tear out the whole ceiling. The wood up here is nice."

The three down below grinned at one another.

"Good. I think we're going to cut a hole closer to you, get you out through there. That sound okay?"

"Whatever works. Just don't cut around me. I think I've fallen enough for one day."

"I agree." Michele laughed. She turned to Trace. "She's still got her sense of humor, which is a good sign. If you don't mind, I'll let you go up there and sit with her, and you can move whatever needs to be out of the way for us to cut our hole." She continued. "Doug, you follow him up and get the lay of the land. I'll get the Saws-all."

Trace went directly to the ladder and climbed it, heading back across the expanse to Hannah. Doug was right behind him.

"Hey, Hannah, sorry you're in a bind."

"Thanks, Doug." Hannah turned to Trace. "Doug and I went to school together."

"She got me through Physics lab." Doug grinned.

"You were doing fine."

"Not hardly, but thank you, anyway." Doug sized up the situation, finding a spot to check her out before they attempted to move her.

"What hurts?"

"Shoulder, arm, ribs ... maybe my ankle. Can't tell because my foot went to sleep."

When he began probing the tissue around her collarbone, she yelled.

Doug stopped. He had his answer. "I'm sorry I had to do that."

She closed her eyes.

Trace winced. Now would be a merciful time to pass out, but unfortunately, she didn't.

"Yep, collarbone is involved, so we'll have to be careful. Are you having any trouble breathing?"

Hannah took a deep breath and winced slightly. "Not really. It only hurts when I breathe."

"Probably looking at a bruised or cracked rib." He swathed her left arm and shoulder using a triangular bandage to hold it steady, then he inspected the ceiling boards between the joists close to Hannah but didn't present a danger of weakening the structure. "Who'd a thought you needed to be a carpenter to be an EMT?" He pulled a marker from his pocket and marked the spot, then went back to get the saw from Michele.

"You okay?" Trace touched her forearm tenderly.

She nodded, then shook her head. Tears swam to the surface after Doug's preliminary examination. "At least it'll be easier to get the trunk down." Twisting her lips, she looked a little sheepish. "I had this idea that I could drag the trunk to the access point, then lower it to the floor by myself. I guess I fooled me, didn't I?"

He smiled. She would find something positive or

something funny about any situation she found herself in. He hoped she was finding some positive things about his being here.

"I'll make sure the trunk gets down in one piece."

She scrambled a little, putting some letters back in a small box. "Here, put this box back in there. I do not want to lose these."

"What are they?"

"Love letters between Charles and Amelia Woodward."

TRACE WATCHED as they lowered Hannah from the attic the short distance down to the gurney. Her face was pale, her jaws clamped together, and her eyes closed. He climbed down the ladder and followed them out. Hannah's family and Clay drove up as they exited the cabin.

No more talking for the foreseeable future. But he would definitely get the trunk out of the attic for her.

Hannah's mom went straight to her daughter as they prepared to load her into the ambulance. Hannah raised her right hand to stave off a hug that would probably have been torturous.

"Oh, sweetie, I'm so sorry we were gone."

"You couldn't have done anything Trace didn't do. It was silly of me to go up there without my phone."

"Hey." Clay met Trace halfway and shook his hand. "Good thing you came out here."

Shrugging, Trace didn't want to be hailed as a hero. "I just happened to think she might be out there where we worked yesterday."

Clay nodded. "God's timing?"

It hadn't occurred to Trace, but yes, God's timing. It may

have been the one situation that gave him another chance to show her how much he cared for her, and hopefully, she might feel a fraction of what he did.

"Maybe. Everybody else was out of pocket, and I was at home. Worked out."

Michele walked back to where Trace and Clay were talking. "We're taking her on to Baptist Health in Paducah. The orthopedic doc will meet her there, and her shoulder looks pretty bad. Probably a few broken ribs too. They'll want to rule out spinal injuries. Foot and ankle seem okay, but that's for the ER docs to decide."

"You know those guys well, don't you?" Clay laughed, and Michele joined him.

"Uh, unfortunately." She turned to Trace. "My grandson fell off his bike. I was rushing to see about him. My body zigged and my foot zagged." She shrugged. "These things happen."

She turned to leave. "Oh, and the kid was perfectly fine."

"Of course he was." Clay grinned.

Michele climbed into the back of the ambulance with Hannah, closing the doors, and they were gone.

Mrs. Buckner waved at him, meeting him as they walked back to the house. "Trace, I don't know how to thank you for checking on Hannah." She wiped a tear from her cheek. "She's been so independent that we've hesitated to call and check on her too much, and then this happens."

When she stopped to blow her nose, Mr. Buckner approached and put his arm around his wife. "I have a feeling Hannah won't be leaving her phone in the house the next time she tries to take on a project alone." He shook his head. "That girl."

Trace smiled. "She's something, isn't she?"

Mrs. Buckner walked up and hugged him. "She is, and I'm so glad you were there for her."

Trace wanted to be there for her in every way a person needed another. It wasn't until he saw her in the predicament she was in that he knew what he felt was more than "love at first sight."

He'd told her he cared about her. Scoffing at himself as he got in his truck, he knew he didn't just *care* about her, he loved her.

Pushing the button to activate the hands-free phone app, he set a call to Grandma in motion.

"Hello?"

"Hey, Grandma, I'm leaving Hannah's house."

"You found her okay?"

He grinned and shook his head. "Not exactly okay, but I found her. She had a fall and they're taking her to Paducah to Baptist Health."

He heard her relaying the information to Grandpa and Eli. "Are you going?"

Hesitating, he considered his options. He wanted to go, to be there for her as she was treated, to find out how what he could do to help—but he had no real right to be privy to the details. Then he thought of the expression on her face when he first got up into the attic. Pure, unadulterated relief.

"Yes, I'm going." He raked his hand over his face as he turned left toward Marion and Paducah instead of right toward the Reno farm.

"Good. I'll get the prayer circle going." He heard a slight scuffle, and what sounded like Grandma holding her hand over the microphone of the cordless phone they still hung on to. "Grandpa wants to talk to you."

"Trace?"

"Yeah, Grandpa."

"Be patient, but don't give up. You hear me?"

He grinned as he drove into the magnificent sunset over Highway 60. "I do."

"That's all I wanted to say. Be careful, son."

"Yes, sir."

The connection was broken. Grandpa, much like Trace, didn't believe in long, drawn-out goodbyes, so he usually hung up without preamble.

Grandpa and Grandma had been eighteen when they decided they loved each other enough to dedicate the rest of their lives to one another. Here he was, ten years older, full of angst about whether Hannah was "the one," when he'd known pretty much since he laid eyes on her at Del's wedding that she would be important to him in some way.

For now, he'd go on that information and hope beyond hope that she felt a fraction for him that he did for her.

Chapter 33

The pain was intense, and Hannah may have passed out at least once on the way to Paducah. She wasn't sure. Everything was hazy. They'd given her a shot of something to ease her anxiety and pulled out the warm blankets.

The coverings were pure bliss as the heat worked its way through her, and as soon as one cooled, a new, warmer blanket was wrapped around her.

"You okay, Hannah?"

Michele had ridden with her, getting her to talk from time to time.

Hannah nodded, then winced with pain. Not a good idea.

Use your words, Hannah.

"Ankle feel okay?"

"Sore, but I can move it." She'd been testing it. When she went through the ceiling, her first thought was broken ankle, and she was relieved when she was able to move it up, down, and side to side.

"Good. At least you'll be mobile."

"How long did it take to recover when you messed up your ankle?" Hannah looked up at Michele as she took her blood pressure.

"Twelve weeks." Michele shook her head and laughed. "I don't recommend it."

"Wow."

"You may have some broken bones, but until you get an X-ray, as a precaution, we're treating it as if you have a back injury."

Scary. She'd never considered her back.

Michele smiled knowingly. "Yeah, at your age, the back is the last thing on your mind."

More misery came when it was time for her to leave the ambulance. The EMTs tried to be gentle, but the jostling between the vehicle and the Emergency Room made Hannah long for another shot of whatever it was they'd given her earlier.

The nurse in charge gave directions. "Put her in room ten."

She did a quick mental comparison to her hometown hospital. *Does Crittenden Hospital even have five ER rooms?*

"Name and date of birth, please ..." And it began. The questions and answers that she thought would never end.

Mom and Dad came in for a few minutes.

"Oh, Hannah." Mom had tears in her eyes.

"It'll be okay, Mom."

"You're the one hurt, and you're trying to comfort me?" Mom chuckled as she mopped her face with a disintegrating tissue.

"I'm just glad to be out of the cold."

"Trace is in the waiting room." Mom smiled sweetly and squeezed her right hand.

She didn't know what to say, and she was saved from

answering when finally—*finally* the door opened, and it was a doctor.

"Miss Buckner, I'm Doctor Crump from the Orthopedic Institute. How are you today?" He reached to shake her hand, then stopped. "It's your left shoulder, isn't it?"

"Thankfully." She shook his hand and hated to think what her smile looked like. Probably somewhere between exhausted and scary.

"We're getting you to X-ray as soon as the radiology techs get here, and they'll take pictures of your spine, shoulder, arm, hand, ribs, and ankle, just in case. Then they'll take you in for a CT scan while you're there." He probed her skull where she'd hit the rafter. She winced. "That's a pretty nasty bump." He flipped through the chart and shook his head. "It may take a bit to get all those done, and I'm sorry you're in so much pain. I'll prescribe pain meds for after the tests. Hopefully, it won't take too long."

When he left, the revolving door never stopped. Hannah was rolled in and out, then cleaned up and put in a hospital gown for at least an overnight stay.

Around midnight, she was finally installed in a room with the blessing of medication. She just wanted to sleep and wake up to find none of this had happened.

Today had been the longest day she could remember. What had she been thinking? Just this morning, she was drinking her coffee, and then, out of desperation for something to do, she decided to work on the cabin by herself. Alone. No backup.

Only one good thing came out of the whole situation—no, two: she found the trunk, and Trace was there.

That, she wanted to remember. The drowsiness intensified.

Drifting off, she was aware of his green eyes on hers in the dim light of the attic. Pain was lessening, and Trace's voice was breaking through the waves of sleep: *It'll be okay. I'm coming. I care about you.*

TRACE WOKE to sunshine streaming through the window next to his bed in Grandma's house. It had to be after eight a.m. A glance at the clock told him he was wrong. It was nearer to ten.

Raking his fingers through his hair, the first thing he did was pick up his phone and search for updates. When they finally called Hannah's parents to let them know she was being moved into a room, he'd given Hannah's mom his number, asking her to let him know if there was any change.

Exhaustion had set in as Trace drove home after midnight. He didn't see Hannah after they got her to the hospital, but he didn't want to leave until he knew she would be okay.

While nothing was life-threatening, a fractured clavicle, fractured and bruised ribs, scrapes, bruises, and a concussion weren't what he would consider *okay*. They'd done two more brain scans to check for a brain bleed, and there was no sign.

The smell of coffee and bacon drew him up and into the jeans and sweatshirt he'd worn yesterday. Pretty dirty after being in the attic, so he replaced the jeans with sweatpants. He wouldn't go to Grandma's kitchen with dirt and soot all over his clothes.

"There's sleeping beauty." Eli laughed. "I'm on my second cup, but we saved you some."

"Thanks. Hospital coffee isn't worth the paper cups they serve it in."

Grandma spoke up. "There's a coffee shop down by the gift shop. You don't see it coming in the ER entrance."

Trace nodded. *Good to know.*

"Kristi Buckner called about a half-hour ago." Grandma filled his plate with biscuits, eggs, and bacon.

"Thanks, Grandma. I gave her my number. Why didn't she call me?"

Grandma chuckled. "She hoped you were getting some sleep, and she had my number." She picked up the coffee pot. "More?"

"Please." Trace couldn't get breakfast down fast enough. He realized he never got supper the night before.

"I've got gravy if you want another biscuit with some?"

"Bring it." Grandma refilled his plate. He was torn between eating and getting information. Eating won, but there was no reason he couldn't listen and eat. Trace took another bite and started asking questions before he swallowed, choking a little. "Sorry."

"There's a reason you're not supposed to talk with your mouth full." Grandma patted his shoulder as she chuckled.

He held up a finger, asking them to wait, swallowed, and then spoke. "What did she say? Is Hannah all right?"

"She told me they gave her some medication that helped with the pain, so she slept some. They want to keep her one more night, then they'll send her home."

"That's scary, her living by herself." The very thought of her being out there, all alone, and recovering from an injury chilled him to his core.

Grandma's lips twitched, but all she said was, "I'm sure they'll figure it out."

Trace nodded, wiping his mouth with his napkin, then laying it on the table. "I'm gonna get a shower, then I'll go to the hospital."

"Whoa there, brother. Relax. You've got all day."

Trace shook his head. "Nope. I don't." He smiled at Eli, and for once in his life shot straight from the hip. "I told her I cared about her, and I want to show her just how much."

Surprise lit the features of Grandma and Eli.

"Grandpa will be proud of you, Trace," Grandma said.

"I'll be proud of what?" Grandpa came in the door from haying the calves in the barn, stopping to kiss his wife on the cheek. "Have you been takin' my name in vain, Mrs. Reno?"

"I have not."

"I'm heading upstairs to clean up." Trace gestured between the three of them. "You people talk amongst yourselves, and I'll be out of here in fifteen minutes."

As he jogged up the stairs two at a time, he heard Grandpa laugh. "'Bout time he took the bull by the horns."

And then Grandma's longsuffering sigh and return: "Does everything have to be related to cattle?"

STRAPPED into a sling designed to keep her left shoulder immobilized, Hannah frowned. How would she manage? Just getting into the car was a major ordeal between the shoulder and the ribs. The persistent headache didn't help, either. The doctors wouldn't release her unless she had someone with her the first few days, anyway, so she was going to stay with Mom and Dad in her old room.

Just when I thought I was on my own, I go and do something like this.

"Be careful," Trace told the nurse helping her get into the car. The nurse glared at him, then looked at Hannah and winked.

He'd been there every step of the way. When were they going to finish the conversation they'd started in the attic?

Wait. Did that really happen? The concussion made things

a little fuzzy, and it was difficult to determine what had happened and what was a figment of her over-active imagination.

Did he call me "sweetheart, or was that a dream too?

Hannah's dad had to go back to work, so Trace offered to drive Mom and get Hannah back to Clementville. When she was carefully ensconced in the front passenger seat, arm propped gently with travel pillows, Trace got in the driver's seat, and Mom sat in the back.

He turned and searched her face when she took a deep breath. "You okay?"

She turned tentatively toward him, mainly because the muscles in her neck had been pulled, as well as her collar bone fractured. "I just want to get home," she said. "I'll be fine."

His smile was warm but worry lurked in the dark smudges under his eyes and the slight furrow of his brow.

This was one of those times she was glad Trace was a man of few words because the scenery between Paducah and Clementville was so familiar she could sleep if her mind would shut down.

Leaning her head back, she closed her eyes. If she opened them in slits, it gave the appearance of slumber, but instead of sleeping, she observed Trace. Quiet, solid, dependable Trace.

He caught her observing him, and grinned. She'd relaxed and forgotten she was trying to be sneaky. She'd blame the concussion. What she couldn't blame it for was the heat rising from her neck all the way up to her cheeks.

"Do you think you'll feel like going to Del and Darcy's New Year's Eve party?"

She'd forgotten all about the party, but she wanted to go. Wanted to see the completed apartment and state-of-the-art safe room. Thinking about it made her grin, and her blush grew more intense.

"I don't know. Maybe?

"I can't believe you're even considering it, Hannah. You've got to take care of yourself." Mom was pretty emphatic.

"Oh, Mom ... I wouldn't have to stay the whole time. I'd just like to see the place finished. I haven't been up in the apartment since I rewired it last year." Hannah had almost forgotten her mother was in the car with them until she spoke up from the back seat. "I said maybe." She cut her eyes to Trace, who was trying to hide a grin.

Mom spoke up again. "I need to go over to your house and get some of your clothes and toiletries."

"Why can't we stop there now, and I can pick out my own stuff."

"You're not up to it, sweetheart." Mom was going into full-on mama-bear mode.

"I might not need to stay by myself for a few days ..." Hannah turned a little to catch Mom's eye. "... and I mean days, not weeks," she added, "But I think I'm able to walk into the house and point out what I will need."

She glanced over at the man next to her. "And besides, Trace is here to help carry stuff."

The loud sigh—like mother, like daughter, she supposed—from the backseat told Hannah Mom was relenting. "Your dad will be glad to not have to get out again after he gets home from work." Mom paused. "Trace, do you mind?"

"Absolutely not."

His words made Hannah smile, and not just a thank-you-for-being-nice smile. When he turned and sent her a secret wink, it fizzed through her like a soft drink that had been shaken and then opened. There went the heat hitting her cheeks again.

Yes, she was grateful to have a place to go while she was recovering, but oh, how she wanted to be alone with Trace. To finish the conversation that had been interrupted so many times.

In the meantime, she'd make sure she picked up just the right outfit for a New Year's Eve party, even if she had her arm in a sling.

Chapter 34

Getting to sleep was an exercise in futility. The events of the past week were dragging on Trace, and he'd fallen asleep watching TV with Grandma, Grandpa, and Eli.

He went upstairs to bed, only to find his eyes wide, staring at the ceiling, going over everything in his mind, always rounding back to Hannah.

Trace hoped to get the trunk out of the attic for her before she came back to her house. In the meantime, he'd climbed back up there and retrieved the box of letters.

Things were tense between Hannah and her mother, and he knew the tension came from a place of frustration on Hannah's part and mother-love on her mom's. For himself, Trace was happy to help in any way he could, trying really hard not to show the frustration he felt. The last thing he wanted to do was offend Mrs. Buckner—she kept telling him to call her Kristi—about anything. He'd stay out of disagreements between mother and daughter and would make himself available for anything they asked.

Was he making a mistake inserting himself into the

situation? He hoped Hannah would ask to be alone with him, but it was difficult with her at her parents' house.

He kept wondering how to get back to the conversation that kept being interrupted, replaying it over and over to remember what he said that flipped the switch in their communication. He'd been around women all his life. He had a mom, a sister, cousins …

Let's break this down logically. How would Samantha react to anything I said that day?

Then it hit him right upside the head, pulling him to a sitting position. He'd compared her to his sister.

His *sister.*

It ranked right up there with calling her a child.

Going over it, thinking about what he said, what she said, and the expressions on her face, he knew exactly when she shut him off. He tried so hard not to make her feel trapped and not to think he expected anything from her. As a result, Hannah thought he didn't *want* anything from her. Didn't want *her.* Nothing could be further from the truth.

He tried to make himself feel better by telling himself that maybe he was still afraid to commit to her lest she not be interested in committing to him.

Well, that might be so, but how will I know how she feels if I never tell her how I feel?

He wasn't a coward, was he? In this instance, he certainly felt like one. One of the most important decisions of his life, and he'd been afraid to take a leap of faith.

What time was it? He picked up his phone to check the time. 10:30. Not too late, but Hannah was recovering. Didn't she need more sleep?

He skimmed through the string of texts they'd shared, starting with the day they carpooled together. Scrolling through, he smiled in the darkness, seeing the difference in the before and after their experience in the safe room. After that, he found himself wanting to be near her more. To hear her voice, a little on the low and mellow side, but when she got tickled? Her laugh was epic. Loud, as if it surprised even her.

As he reached the day before her accident, his phone buzzed, and a message appeared.

Hannah:

Are you asleep?

> No, I fell asleep in front of the TV. Wide awake now.

Me too

> How are you feeling?

Like I don't care if I ever hear someone ask me how I'm feeling again, lol

> Okie-dokie, then

Ha!

> I helped Del unload supplies for the party tomorrow night.

Good stuff?

> Excellent stuff.

Can I ask you something? I feel so weird.

> You can ask me anything, and for anything, and you're not weird.

That's nice. :)

> What can I do for you?

Take an invalid to a party? I want to see
their place so bad, especially fixed up for
a party. And, if I have to spend New
Year's Eve with my parents, whom I love
and am grateful to, I will scream.

I'll bet your ribs would love that.

Exactly.

I would be honored to take you, but are
you up to it?

As long as my ride doesn't expect me to
ride it out until the ball drops, dance the
Watusi, or bob for apples, I think I can go
for a little while.

Pick you up at seven?

Yes.

It's a date.

Three dots appeared and disappeared.

We don't have to call it a date.

I'm okay with that.

Trace smiled into the darkness. She wasn't giving in completely, but it would give them a chance to talk, at least.

Please don't ask me to dance.

Now that you've reminded me about the
Watusi, I will definitely ask you to dance.
Lol Do I look like a guy who likes to
dance?

LOL Good, because I'm terrible at it
when I'm "whole." This would just be
pathetic.

> I'm pathetic no matter what. I had to take
> dance lessons for this wedding reception
> where they did this whole
> choreographed entrance thing, and it
> was awful. I would never force that on
> my friends.

Me, neither.

> Think you can sleep now?

Yawn. I think maybe I can. Thanks.

> For boring you to sleep?

No, silly. For being there.

> Always.

ALWAYS.

Hannah woke up the next morning and checked her phone. Her breath caught as she read Trace's last text. It was the word Charles Woodward used in his love letter to his then-fiancée, Amelia.

Yours, always and forever.

Did Trace mean it?

She didn't want to set herself up for a broken heart, but if she didn't get real with herself and with Trace, how would she know?

He'd brought the letters, giving her something to do. Mom enjoyed reading them too.

Amelia and Charles' letters leading up to their wedding

were sweet, and they did have a few disagreements along the way, which tickled Hannah. How does one argue with one's intended by mail?

Charles wanted a simple wedding, just wanted to be married, and Amelia's mother had other ideas. Amelia was doing her best to keep the peace. After a few letters, the conflict died down, and Amelia admitted to Charles that she, too, just wanted to be married already.

The next letter was Charles announcing he was coming home to get her. They would be married within the week.

It made Hannah shiver a little. It's nice to be rescued every once in a while, and she wondered how Amelia felt when she received that letter.

The second packet—tied with twine instead of ribbon—did not contain love letters. They were correspondence a few years later between Charles—carbons, no less—and Bureau of Investigation Chief Stanley Finch. She wondered if Chief Finch would have approved copying those letters? Charles was tasked with investigating rumors of smuggling operations along the Ohio River. When the Prohibition Act was signed, Charles Woodward was put in charge of three other agents, undercover locally.

The letters ended abruptly with a letter of condolence from Chief Finch to Amelia and their children.

So sad.

Hannah did an internet search with one hand and found nothing about Charles Woodward or any other criminal activity in the area. It was obvious that any records of the events were classified and had either been destroyed or redacted.

She'd love to get Trace's slant on it.

"Hannah? Are you up?"

Mom.

"I'm up, Mom. I'll be out in a few minutes."

"Let me know if you need any help." Her voice floated through her door.

"I will."

Hannah sighed. How long would she have to be away from her house?

Shrugging her right arm into her robe, she slowly rose to her feet. Better today.

Maybe the Watusi can happen after all ...

And then she took a few steps, vibrating her ribs and shoulder.

Nope. No Watusi for me tonight.

TRACE BRUSHED BACK HIS HAIR, still damp from the shower, and critiqued himself in the mirror.

Could be worse.

He felt for Hannah, having to get ready for a party with one arm. He was amazed at the lengths women went to for day-to-day living, much less for a special occasion.

Didn't matter with him. He thought she was beautiful, no matter what.

Stuffing his wallet in his back pocket, he went downstairs. Eli was already at the party. For once, Eli was the one going stag. If Trace wasn't on top of the world to be escorting Hannah, he would have more energy to be surprised at his brother not even trying to find a date.

"Grandma, thanks for letting me borrow the car. It'll be easier for Hannah to get in and out."

"Not a problem. I, for one, don't plan to celebrate anywhere but right here." Grandma sat next to Grandpa on the sofa. "Who knows, we might make it to midnight this time."

"Don't get your hopes up." Grandpa grinned as Grandma swatted his leg.

"Have a good time, Trace, and tell Hannah we said hello and Happy New Year."

"I'll do it. Thanks again." He jingled the keys in his hand and slipped out the door.

Hannah hadn't mentioned getting in and out of the truck. Knowing her, she would try, and there was no reason to.

When he knocked on the door, it opened almost immediately.

"Good evening, Mrs. Buckner—Kristi." Trace grinned when she gave him a sideways glance, reminding him of what she'd told him more than once.

"Come in, Trace. Hannah's almost ready." She led him through the foyer to the family room in the back. "Have a seat while I help her finish up." She shook her head. "I wish she hadn't agreed to go tonight."

"I know." Trace shook Mr. Buckner's hand and sat in the chair next to him. "I'll be careful with her."

Kristi twisted her lips in a grin, trying to remain stern, and utterly failing in her attempt. "I know you will. You've proven yourself."

"Thank you, ma'am."

Trace took in the evidence of a happy family. Photographs on the wall, a large family portrait hanging above the mantle, and random framed images in various locations. It reminded him of Grandma's house.

"Hannah tells me you start a new job in a few days," Mr. Buckner queried, pulling Trace from searching for young pictures of Hannah in the photographs.

He nodded. "GE in Madisonville."

"Good outfit."

"I've heard good things."

Mr. Buckner nodded. Could it be that he was as quiet as Trace?

When Hannah and Kristi entered the room a few minutes later, Trace noted first the hesitation on her face. Was she regretting her claim that she could make it without any problem? He stood, and when their eyes met, though, her smile grew before he got a word out.

"You're beautiful, Hannah."

"I would curtsy, but my balance is a little off these days." She chuckled warmly.

"No curtsy necessary." He reached out for her right hand and squeezed it gently, and she took his, returning what felt like a hug. Everything in the room faded away for a few seconds.

"Here's your phone, Hannah." Kristi broke the spell, holding out her cell.

"Oh ..." She frowned, a little confused. "I hadn't thought. I can't carry a purse." She looked down at the sling on her arm. "Do you think it would fit in here?"

Trace smiled. "I can keep it in my pocket if you don't have one." He took in her outfit, a gauzy, loose-fitting top with just enough sparkle to make it festive, paired with a pair of silky, wide-legged pants. He wasn't sure what those were called, but they reminded him of pictures he'd seen of his grandparents in the 1970s, back in the day. He knew one thing—her top brought out the sparkles in her eyes.

Her sideways glance made his lips twitch.

"I don't have your passcode, so there's no way I can read your texts," he teased.

"I have nothing to hide ..."

He held a hand up. "I understand—I'm the same way about people seeing my phone."

When she handed it to him it opened as it registered her face, and her text application came up for all to see.

"Grumpy?"

Hannah reached out and snatched it from him, her face reddening immediately. "I was going to change that ..."

The combination of humor and attraction was something he'd never experienced, and he wanted to feel it again. How he would like to pull her into his arms right then and there. But he wouldn't. Not yet.

"You can call me Grumpy anytime."

Her lips parted as if she wanted to say something, but instead, her face bloomed with a saucy yet tender smile. "Might take you up on that."

She handed him the phone, and he placed it in his shirt pocket and patted it. "Safe and secure, and handy any time you want it."

"It's a pain using it right now. It's slow with only one thumb available." She shrugged.

"You seemed to be doing okay with it last night," Trace said before he thought, which was totally unlike him. He didn't realize until he saw her eyes widen and shift to her mother.

Great work, Trace.

"Aaaa-nyway," Hannah said, changing the subject, "I think it's time we go, don't you?"

Her pleading eyes made him want to laugh. He was used to hiding his feelings, so beyond a twitch of a brow, he was pretty sure his expression remained bland. When her eyes widened, he had a tough time controlling his smile.

"Your chariot awaits." He held out his left arm for her to take.

When they got to the car, she let out a breath of relief. "You have no idea how much I was dreading climbing into a pickup."

"I had a sneaking suspicion." Trace winked at her. It might have been his imagination, in the dim glow of the Christmas lights still hanging from the gables of the house, but did her face redden? Maybe a little?

Chapter 35

Hannah wriggled into the luxurious heated seats in Trace's grandparents' car. When he got in the driver's side, her heart fluttered when he smiled. Still embarrassed about his seeing her phone screen, she was a little off-kilter at his response.

"Are you in okay? Do you need help with your seatbelt?" Her independent streak said she should resent his thinking she couldn't take care of herself, but his care only made her fall even further. She pulled the strap from the right and handed it to him as he pulled it carefully around her and into the buckle. "Thanks."

"No problem." He paused when she released a long breath. "Are you comfortable? We can still back out."

"No, I'm ready to get out of the house." She chuckled. "I love my parents, but it's nice to feel like a grownup for a few hours."

When they arrived at the Clementville Café, the place was lit up, and cars were parked all along Main Street. The jangle of the sleigh bells on the door was cheery, and while the café had been decorated beautifully for Christmas, now it was purely magical. Everything except what was gold and silver had been removed and more added. The white icicle lights around the dining room perimeter and along the opening to the kitchen transported them into a winter wonderland.

Del and Darcy greeted them.

"Hannah! I can't believe you made it!" Darcy gave Hannah a careful hug and looked back and forth between her and Trace, raising her eyes in question.

"Wouldn't miss it for the world." Hannah silently begged Darcy with wide eyes, projecting to her the idea of not making a big deal out of it.

But it was a big deal.

Hannah was pretty sure her life would be different after tonight. If it wasn't, then the signals she'd been receiving and trying to send had all been in vain.

Trace took her hand and led her through the crowd to a booth on the edge of the room where Mandy, Clay, Caryn, and Ben were sitting. "Are these seats taken?"

"Yes," Mandy said pertly, "by the two of you." She smiled up at Hannah. "Here, sit by me."

"How are you feeling, Hannah?" Caryn frowned at her with concern. "You've been through it the last week, haven't you?"

Ben laughed. "First you get stuck in the basement with this guy," he pointed to Trace, "and then, you have to be rescued by the same."

"Coincidence?" Mandy was all over this. "I think not."

Hannah held up her hands. "It's been an exciting few weeks. I also moved, if you recall."

"When's the housewarming party?" Mandy sat up straight. The girl did love a good party.

"Maybe when I can go back and live there?"

Mandy scrunched her nose. "Sorry." She twisted her lips,

thinking. "I'm thinking we may just have to throw a party for you."

"That would be lovely. Give me a couple of weeks, okay?" Hannah winked at her friend.

"Gotcha."

"Where are Lisa and Nick?" Their absence was hard to miss considering how exited Lisa had been about the party.

Del ambled up to their table. "Lisa wasn't feeling well, and Nick decided she was going to have to take better care of herself." He checked out the occupants of the table. "Is this the cousin-slash-employee table?" Del tilted his head, considering Ben, Caryn, and Hannah. "I'm not sure what to call you guys."

"Honorary cousins?" Mandy bumped shoulders with Caryn.

"Cousin-adjacent?" Caryn quipped.

"Works for me," Del said, smiling easily. "Darcy is taking tours of the apartment, and I'm taking tours of the basement if y'all are interested."

Hannah turned to Trace, excited, then answered Del. "That's the whole reason I came tonight, Del."

"Are you up to the stairs?" The slight frown on Trace's face did something to her insides.

She put her good hand on her hip. "Of course I am. It's not like I'm climbing a ladder."

Trace tilted his head in deference. "Then tours we shall do. Apartment or basement first?"

"Apartment. I came in and did the last wiring before the countertops and fireplace were completed."

"Then Darcy is your girl." Del waved at Darcy and pointed down to the group at their table. She nodded and gestured for them to come over. "Y'all are first up, then. I'll take you downstairs when you're ready. I think more people are interested in the upstairs than the downstairs."

"I don't know. The basement and caves have seen a lot of action," Clay said, then swallowed a yelp. Had Mandy kicked him under the table? "What I meant to say was, there's a lot of history down there."

Mandy shook her head and leaned her face into her palm.

Hannah glanced over at Trace. What was he thinking? She felt herself flush furiously when his eyes met hers, his slow smile growing.

"Okie-dokie, then." Del's left eyebrow lifted.

Hannah took Trace's hand and let him lead her across the makeshift dance floor, having a little difficulty facing him without coming apart.

She'd think about the ramifications of the basement later.

WHEN TRACE CAUGHT a glimpse of himself in the reflection in the plate-glass window above their table his eyebrows raised. He wasn't one of those people who practiced smiling in the mirror. That was the most inane thing ever.

Tonight, his senses were on overdrive. Any time he glanced at Hannah, he noticed a glow—his imagination, maybe. That wasn't all. His hearing perked up when it registered her voice, and it didn't matter where they were, when he was with her, he noticed the smell of her shampoo as soon as she entered the room. Lavender.

Except for him, the scent of lavender didn't have the usual calming effect. It excited him.

Totally unlike him. He would roll his eyes at anyone putting those feelings into words, but tonight, the guy in the reflection could pass for happy.

And the reason for these utterly confusing experiences? It was the lady on whose back his hand rested as he supported her up the stairs to the apartment above the café. Every chance he got, he reached for her, anticipating a *zing* of electricity.

Paying little attention to Darcy's tour, he was fascinated just watching Hannah's expressions as she studied the improvements made in the apartment. Having not seen it before, it didn't mean as much to him. It was a nice apartment.

His attention was caught when they got to the main bathroom and closet. This was part of the inspiration for Hannah's bathroom. He took note of the closet area. In Hannah's house, if the tiny third bedroom was sacrificed, a good-sized walk-in closet could be built and the bedroom made larger.

When Hannah caught his glance, eyes glowing, he imagined the wheels of inspiration turning in her head. She was getting ideas too. Since when had he paid attention to design? He smiled and nodded, and her eyes widened.

A longing in his soul grew for Hannah, so deep that he couldn't pinpoint where it came from.

God, if this isn't what love feels like, I'm not sure I can handle the real thing.

Now his mind was filled with her, and the last thing he wanted to do was scare her off. He was scared enough himself.

Tour done, Trace monitored Hannah closely as she maneuvered the stairs going back down. Del stood at the door leading to the basement.

"Just finished another tour of the basement. Y'all ready?"

Trace checked Hannah. "Do you feel up to it, or do you want to rest a few minutes?"

Was the flush on her cheeks from overdoing it, or did it have anything to do with the idea that the basement had registered a change in their relationship?

"Oh, I'm ready now, if you are?"

He shrugged at Del. "The lady says go for it."

"Good deal. You guys in?" Del queried the rest of their little group.

"We're in," Mandy spoke, as usual, for the group.

"Then watch your step, use the handrail, and keep hands, feet, and belongings close to you at all times." Del chuckled. "Sorry. Projecting my inner historic landmark tour guide."

"It's pretty historic." Darcy joined them, slipping her hand in her husband's.

"You guys go on ahead of me." Hannah sighed. "I'm slow, so I'll catch up."

Trace hung back and spoke to Hannah. "Hey, I promised your mom I'd take care of you."

The smirk on her face was endearing, as was her dry sense of humor.

When they got to the bottom of the stairs, Caryn and Ben were coming out of the safe room, Mandy and Clay taking their turn through the small space.

Caryn's eyes were wide. "I can't believe you two were trapped down there for hours."

Hannah snorted a little. "Good times." She glanced up at Trace, the infinitesimal lift of her brow almost undoing him, and the blush on her cheeks finished the job.

"And in the dark too. How did you handle that?" Caryn was still watching Hannah with concern.

So, Hannah's closest friends were aware of her fear of the dark.

"I wasn't alone." This time, when Hannah looked his way, she didn't try to hide her appreciation. He placed his hand gently on her upper back.

"Glad I was there."

Mandy and Clay came out, Del and Darcy behind them.

"I think you know the way?" Darcy grinned, gesturing to the open door.

Trace hadn't thought about the two of them being alone down here until he heard the rest of the group heading back up the stairs.

"I CAN'T BELIEVE how much different it looks down here." Hannah appreciated the finished product. There was a small sofa and a box of toys as well as a built-in shelf holding bottled water and non-perishable snacks. The lamp illuminated the room softly. "Wish that had been here when we were stuck down here."

She chuckled, then turned to catch Trace staring at her. Unable to look away, she said, "Trace?"

He glanced away momentarily, almost so quickly she questioned if he had. When he stepped closer to her, warmth spread through her.

"Hannah—" Trace began and then seemed to be searching for words.

"That's me," she said, her heart feeling like it was being squeezed and expanded at the same time.

He took her small hand and held it between his two larger ones, slowly tugging her closer. "Hannah, I—"

She squeezed his hand that held hers, and he looked into her eyes. Was he silently pleading for encouragement?

"I seem to remember a conversation we started up in the attic of my little cabin ..."

Nodding, he cleared his throat. "I seem to remember mentioning that I care about you."

"I recall that." She held his gaze with hers. No way she was going to make this easy.

Facing her, he reached toward her, tucking some loose hair behind her ear. Mom had done a great job fixing her hair, but, as usual in cold, dry weather, it had a mind of its own. The feel of his fingers at her ear made her shiver.

"Are you cold?"

Hannah was always surprised when Trace—a conspicuously quiet man—instinctively noticed little things about her.

Her voice didn't work, so she shook her head, tilting her head to the side.

His hand was still there, tentative, waiting for a signal from her?

Nodding again, she saw his eyes brighten as, without a word, he lowered his head to hers. As soon as his lips touched hers, a spark—maybe not stronger, but infinitely more delicious—than any electrical shock she'd experienced— shook her, and she kissed him back.

There was nothing she could think of beyond his lips touching hers, deepening, exploring. His hand on her lower back gently drew her toward him. He was mindful of her injuries, so careful not to hurt her.

It was frustrating not to be able to wrap her left arm around his neck and draw him closer, but it didn't matter. At that moment, she wasn't even sure where she was, except in in Trace's arms. The conversation seemed pretty unnecessary now.

When he lifted his head, staring at her with pure disbelief, all he said was, "Wow."

She smiled, trying to pull herself closer with her right arm. "'Wow' is right."

"Hannah, I ..."

She heard the clatter of footsteps on the stairway leading from the main level to the basement. "Can we talk later?"

"No way." He took her hand and led her to the loveseat. "Wait here," he said. "Don't move."

She knew her face was red, but she didn't care. "I'm not going anywhere."

Nodding, he pointed toward the door. "They fixed the lock."

"Um-hum," she said and then laughed when he pushed the door into the *closed* position and secured the lock.

"Trace Reno, have you trapped us in this basement again?"

He sat next to her, carefully pulling her into his arms, nuzzling her neck before his lips claimed hers once more. "Nope, I've just trapped *you*."

"And *this* is why you can't rent my cabin."

Laughing out loud, he had the most tender expression she'd ever seen. "Busted."

There was a knock at the door, and the doorknob shaken. "Anybody in there?" Del.

Hannah was embarrassed, but not so much that she was willing to leave the circle of Trace's arms. It surprised her, then, when he lifted his head, winked at her, then turned away, shouting, "Occupied."

She heard Del's laugh, then Darcy's voice saying, "Leave them alone, Del."

Then Del's voice, after he cleared his throat. "Take your time."

Epilogue

Six weeks later

Hannah spread the blanket on the floor in front of the rock fireplace in her cabin.

While she was recovering, Trace took the time to start a new job and finish cleaning up the cabin, which included cleaning the chimney and getting it up to speed to burn wood. He wouldn't let her see it until it was done, and, if he did say so himself, the results weren't too shabby. He'd hauled off the old sofa that was in the cabin, replacing it with an old sofa of Hannah's parents' that had seen better days. Kristi donated it to the cause, so by the time Hannah saw the finished space, there was a comfortable place to sit and enjoy the crackling fire.

It was obvious that Hannah preferred the floor.

The easel he'd made for her sat next to the window, a half-finished piece propped on it and her paint supplies spread out on the antique desk next to it. She might not be able to work her regular job with only one good arm, but she had used the time to rekindle her love for painting.

Trace brought the skewers, s'mores ingredients, plates in a picnic basket slung over his arm, and carried two large mugs of Hannah's famous—to him, anyway—hot cocoa.

Carefully, he handed Hannah hers, then waited until she set it down before he gave her his.

"Trace." She glared at him from beneath her lashes. "It's been six weeks, I think I can handle two cups of cocoa."

"Nope. Put that one down, then I'll hand you the other. The doctor said nothing heavier than a coffee cup. Have you seen the size of these mugs?"

"That's just for my bad arm, not both of them." She huffed, but did as he said, then reached out for the second cup, putting it in a safe place while Trace got comfortable, leaning against the couch on the floor next to her and spread out what was in the basket.

"Let me take care of you, okay?" He leaned over to kiss her, fully intending a sweet peck, but as soon as their lips touched, he was scooting closer and pulling her into his arms with her a quite willing participant. Between kisses, he pulled back and stared into her eyes., unable to break their connection. "How's the shoulder?"

"Hmm?" She nodded and reached up to take over the kiss.

Once she had weaned herself off the sling a few weeks earlier, Trace discovered the delight of not having a sling between them. He was pretty sure Hannah noticed it too.

"I love you, Hannah." He rubbed her nose with his while Hannah's eyes were closed, running her fingers through the hair at the nape of his neck.

"I love you, Trace."

"Happy Valentine's Day." He kissed her fiercely, with her returning it kiss-for-kiss.

"Oh, Trace." Her voice was breathy as she rested her cheek against his chest, and it made him smile.

"When can we get married?"

She leaned back, eyebrows arched incredulously and laughed out loud. "Um, when I get a ring, big boy."

"Oh, man." He shook his head, snapping his fingers. "I knew there was something else I was supposed to do."

She pulled away and grabbed her hot chocolate, then leaned back on him, shaking her head. As soon as she took a sip, she looked into her mug, her nose wrinkled. "Ugh. I need a spoon. All the chocolate has gone to the bottom."

"That, I can take care of. Check the bottom of the basket."

He watched her closely as she pulled the basket closer and tipped it to get a better look inside. She froze.

"What? Did I forget the spoons?"

She turned slowly, pulling a spoon out and dropping it in her cup, then reaching back in. Wide eyed, she held up a small velvet box. "What's this?"

He clamped his lips together nervously. What if the last six weeks were a fluke? What if she came to regret saying, "I love you?"

"It's not a spoon."

"I see that."

"Here, let me see." He took the box from her shaking hand and opened it, holding it up, out of her sight-line, pretending to study it closely. "Huh."

"What?" Her curiosity was getting the best of her, he could tell.

"Looks like I might get my Valentine's Wish after all."

"Trace, there is no 'Valentine's Wish.'"

"Oh, but there is." He pulled her closer, until she sat on his lap, her arm around his neck as they got comfortable. It struck him often that they'd found a comfort level between them quickly, even working around an injury. As she recuperated, they'd been able to include her ability to raise her left arm just enough to place it around his neck.

Desire was a great form of physical therapy. He highly recommended it.

Trace turned the opened box her direction, reveling in the expression of astonishment on her face. "Hannah, you said we could get married when you got a ring." Laughter bubbled up in him.

A very un-Trace thing, he knew.

"Will this one do?"

The way they were situated, their height difference was obliterated. She sat, eye to eye, and he saw the tears as they formed. She nodded.

"So, can we get married now?"

"Now? No." She grinned. "But soon?" Tapping her chin, she pretended to think about it.

"Well?"

"Trace Reno, are you trying to rope me into the Reno clan?"

"I sure am."

She twisted her lips in a rueful smile. "It was when I fell through the ceiling, wasn't it?"

Trace nodded. "I knew, then, that you were definitely Reno material." He jerked as she goosed him in the side, smiling when her laughter teased his senses.

"In that case," she paused, examining the ring, her lips twitching, "I will marry you as soon as possible."

His relief was palpable as he hugged her to himself. "It can't be soon enough for me." He pulled back suddenly, giving her a side-eye. "You said as soon 'as possible.' Does this mean you need a year to plan a wedding?"

"How about we put the ring on my finger, and then we'll talk."

He was unconvinced. He'd been around weddings all his

life with his mom's business and then with his cousins. When he thought he'd never find "the one," he thought a year was a reasonable amount of time to be methodical and well-prepared. Now, however, a year sounded like ten in solitary confinement.

It was hard to pull the ring out with one hand, but he managed it. When she held her weaker left hand out toward him, he pushed it gently in place. The pride that filled him was something he'd never known was possible. He pulled her hand to his lips, then threaded his fingers through her silky tresses and kissed her to seal the bargain.

As he explored the crook between her neck and shoulder, Hannah shuddered, then spoke. "Honestly, Trace, if you had the vacation time, I think I could put a wedding together in a few weeks ..."

His plan was working. Trace stopped and broke in quickly, lest she change her mind. He trapped her in his gaze. "I talked to my supervisor and he said he'll put me down for two weeks whenever I ask, as long as he can cover my shifts."

Her eyes tendered at his rush of words, desire pouring out of him as he countered the main opposition to a quick wedding.

"Do you realize we've only been dating six weeks?" She stroked his bearded cheek. "What will people think?"

"They'll think, 'Now that's a smart couple of kids. They knew what they wanted, and it wasn't a fancy wedding. It was a marriage. Did you know Grandma and Grandpa only dated six weeks before he was drafted and went to Vietnam?"

Her eyes widened. "How old were they?"

"Eighteen." He considered her solemnly. "And I'm twenty-eight. Compared to them, I'm dilly-dallying."

Hannah smiled, her eyes drawing him in. Those expressive

eyes. Did she know how much she said without using any words?

Their gaze held. Trace shook his head in wonder, his voice husky. "I don't want just a wedding, I want a marriage. I want forever. Do you believe me?"

"I do, Trace." She said, her lips quivering.

Kissing her trembling lips, one thought ran through his mind.

She tastes like forever.

THE END

Acknowledgments

Christmas books are fun! I loved writing Trace and Hannah's story, and as usual, there is a lot of "me" in the story, whether it be Grandma Reno's smirk (my grandmother did the same thing), Grandpa Reno's name, Eddie Clarence Reno, named after my great-grandfather, Eddie Clarence Rudd, or Hannah's aggravation over her mom putting her things away in her kitchen – I think this has happened in every generation of women in my family, lol!

In the last three years, our family has suffered a lot of loss, including both my parents and my father-in-law, and many times, I draw from good memories of them when I'm writing. It makes me feel closer to them. We've also done a lot of renovating, so the Renos will always be near and dear to my heart! I wish I could hire them!

So many people support me and my writing. At Scrivenings Press, Linda Fulkerson always has more faith in me than I have in myself. Amy Anguish, part of my writing sisterhood, made this book better with her content edits.

The other two members of my writing sisterhood, Heather Greer and Erin Howard, along with Amy, are my go-to people for running ideas by them and for listening when I complain that the words aren't coming. I hope I do the same for them.

My husband is a great cook, loves to clean the kitchen (thank you, Lord!), and helps me to protect my writing time as much as possible. He talks me down when I think there's no way I can finish a project. Thank you for loving me so much more than I deserve.

I have an amazing support system in my church and community, and I love living in the small town of Marion, Kentucky. I have dear friends who love me, who pray for me, and who, like Aaron and Hur holding up Moses' arms when they were in battle against the Amalekites, hold me up until I can stand on my own. Thank you, Lord, that I'm never really on my own. My discipleship group and praise team are that support. Pam, Britt, Mary Lou, Teresa, Brenda, Terri, Kristi, to name a few.

My prayer is that you will take courage in the fact that the LORD will fight for you, and in this Christmas season, that He will show you the joy that only He can give.

Blessings,
Regina Rudd Merrick
Ps. 37:4

About the Author

Regina Rudd Merrick started her journey as a life-long lover of reading in first grade, and eventually parlayed that love of literature into a degree in library science, with stints as both elementary and middle school librarians, and later as a public library director.

After finding the enjoyable world of reading and writing "fan-fiction"—original stories based on characters from familiar stories, television shows, and movies—she realized that for some reason God had given her the ability to weave a story, whether it be in this online community or with her own original characters. Her first novel, *Carolina Dream*, book one of the Southern Breeze Series, was the winner of a publishing contest with Mantle Rock Publishing, LLC (later purchased by Scrivenings Press), and her writing career was born.

Now the author of seven novels and a contributor to four novella collections, Regina writes about people like all of us who sometimes struggle with their faith and trusting God.

Regina's first historical fiction novel, released in 2023, was *Window of Peace*, book 2 of a multi-author series entitled the Stained Glass Legacy.

Adding to the RenoVations Inc. series is book 2, *Twelve Days of Mandy Reno*, a short Christmas novel, *Rebuilding Joy*, book 3, and *Christmas, Rewired*, book 4.

Carolina Connections, Book 4 in the Southern Breeze Series, is a compilation of two previously published novellas, recently added to the series with Scrivenings Press.

In addition to writing, Regina has recently added the title of "editor" to her resume.

Regina loves chocolate, the beach, playing keyboard and vocals in her church's praise band, historical homes, watching other people renovate on HGTV, and Hallmark movies. She and her husband of forty-plus years are empty nesters in rural western Kentucky and are the proud parents of two grown-up daughters and a son-in-law.

More from the RenoVations Inc. Series

Heart Restoration

RenoVations Inc.—Book One

For interior designer Lisa Reno things go from bad to worse when her contractor-brother falls off a ladder and breaks his leg. Now she has to deal with the past coming back to haunt her, an old house with a corpse in the creepy cellar, and her best friend trying her best to fix her up with any man that moves.

Nick Woodward is willing to do his old college roommate a favor–especially since it involves renovating his own inheritance. The last thing he wants is to get involved with anyone. When he lost his wife and unborn child so suddenly, he had made the decision to keep God and everyone else at arm's length. So far, so good.

Ah, the difference a trip to a dingy basement makes.

Get your copy here:

https://scrivenings.link/heartrestoration

12 Days of Mandy Reno

RenoVations Inc.—Book Two

Law student Amanda Reno is stuck in her tiny hometown in Kentucky to complete her studies virtually and work part-time at the Clementville Café. Her parents are stuck in Brazil, leaving Mandy to celebrate Christmas without them.

Young Sheriff Clay Lacey takes matters into his own hands, devising a plan to take Mandy's mind off her crushed expectations. She is no longer his classmate's tagalong kid sister, but a young woman he is increasingly attracted to.

How will Mandy react when she finds out Clay is the one working to make sure she has a memorable Christmas? Will she be pleased? Or will she cringe as she thanks the man who may be falling in love with her?

Get your copy here:

https://scrivenings.link/12daysofmandyreno

Rebuilding Joy

RenoVations Inc.—Book Three

Single mom Darcy Emerson Sloan has enough to do raising twins and running a restaurant. She's doing fine on her own and doesn't need the complications of a man in her life. But when her café turns into a crime scene, putting her and her children in danger, she begins to take interest in the handsome young FBI agent that comes on the scene.

Contractor Del Reno is as even-keeled as they come, but even he has his limits. And Darcy Sloan has pushed him too far. Every time he tries to help, it backfires. But now that Darcy and her kids are in trouble, he has no choice but to come to her aid and to protect her. She's just going to have to deal with it. Secret tunnels, organized crime, adorable children, and a wedding.

Just another day in Clementville.

(Previously published as Rebuilding Joy by Bellville Street Books.)

Get your copy here:

https://scrivenings.link/rebuildingjoy

Carolina Dream

A Southern Breeze Series: Book One

Sarah Crawford wants more from life than to attend the wedding of her ex-fiancée. An unexpected inheritance in South Carolina comes at the perfect time, just as Sarah is willing to use any excuse to get out of town. When she meets potential business partner Jared Benton and discovers that a house is part of the inheritance, she is sure that God has been preparing her for this time through a recurring dream.

But will a dream about an antebellum mansion, many rooms to be explored, and a man with dark brown eyes give her the confidence to take a leap of faith, leaving friends, family, and her job behind?

https://scrivenings.link/carolinadream

Carolina Mercy

A Southern Breeze Series: Book Two

She's always gotten everything she's wanted. He thinks he has to give up everything. Her best friend's wedding is foremost on Lucy Dixon's radar. Her biggest concern is once again meeting Tom Livingston, who has ignored her since an idyllic date on the boardwalk of Myrtle Beach the previous summer. At least, it is her biggest concern until tragedy strikes. Where is her loving, merciful God, now?

When Tom Livingston meets Lucy, the attraction is instant. Soon after, his mother is diagnosed with an untreatable illness, and his personal life is pushed aside. His work with the sheriff's department, his family—they are more important. He knows about the love of God, but circumstances make him feel as if God's mercy is for everyone else, not him. Can a wedding and a hurricane—blessing and tragedy—bring them together?

https://scrivenings.link/carolinamercy

Carolina Grace

A Southern Breeze Series: Book Three

First-year Special Education teacher Charly Livingston demonstrates God's love on the outside but is resentful that God allowed back-to-back tragedies in her family.

Rance Butler is a top-notch medical intern. He's on his way to the top, and when he meets Charly, he knows things will only get better. When he discovers family secrets and a dying father he never knew, his easy, carefree life seems to disintegrate.

Even in the idyllic ocean breezes and South Carolina sunshine, contentment turns to bitterness and confusion except for God's amazing grace.

https://scrivenings.link/carolinagrace

Carolina Connections

A Southern Breeze Series: Book Four

Enjoy two novellas connected to Regina Rudd Merrick's A Southern Breeze series in one convenient volume. Both of these stories were included in multi-author collections: "Pawleys Aisle" (Coastal Promises) and "Mr. Sandman" (Candy Cane Wishes and Saltwater Dreams). Now you can complete your collection of A Southern Breeze stories with this novella duo, Carolina Connections.

Pawleys Aisle—Leaving a lucrative position in the banking world for the creative world of weddings, Chelsea Prince finds the perfect venue, Pawleys Island Chapel, next door to the perfect walled garden. Her elderly neighbor and partner-in-planning have an agreement, but when the unexpected happens, she has to deal with the cranky grandson who wants to be left alone to write the next great American novel. Since Chelsea has sworn off men, it shouldn't be a problem to ignore him and go on her way hosting weddings in the chapel. But when Marc McCallum offers up a compromise, she wonders if maybe there is one man out there who can be trusted.

Mr. Sandman—Events manager Taylor Fordham's happily-ever-after was snatched from her, and she's saying no to romance and Christmas. When she meets two new friends—the cute new chef at

Pilot Oaks and a contributor on a sci-fi fan fiction website who enjoys debate—her resolve begins to waver. Just when she thinks she can loosen her grip on thoughts of love, a crisis pulls her back. There's no way she's going to risk her heart again.

https://scrivenings.link/carolinaconnections

Other titles by Regina Rudd Merrick

Window of Peace

Stained-glass Legacy—Book Two

Michael Connor "MC" Dunne led a charmed life. He had a plan—finish veterinary school, get married, and take over the local animal clinic. Enter the Vietnam War.

MC returns home, injured, to Park Haven, Tennessee, and soon learns there's a new vet in town, hired when the local veterinarian suffered a heart attack. So much for his plan.

Violent flashbacks and nightmares pull MC away from his faith and turn him into a hermit. His safe place is the family farm, working on the old cabin and restoring the chapel his great-uncle built in the early 1900s, with the family's heirloom stained-glass window.

Nancy Jean Baker struggles to prove herself as a competent veterinarian to the small-town skeptics of Park Haven. Fighting her own demons from a traumatic past, she's driven to succeed.

But when war veteran MC Dunne returns home, wounded and wary, Nancy discovers she's standing between him and his dream.

Can they help each other overcome their hurts and horrors? Or is their hope of happiness doomed when the past threatens to ruin their future?

Get your copy here:

https://scrivenings.link/windowofpeace

https://scrivenings.link/candycanewishes

Stay up-to-date on your favorite books and authors with our free e-newsletters.

ScriveningsPress.com

www.ingramcontent.com/pod-product-compliance
Lightning Source LLC
Chambersburg PA
CBHW060620100726

47907CB00006B/1700